ALWAYS

TOGETHER

FOREVER

Samuel C. Knighton

Other Books by Samuel Knighton:

Will the Real Paul Please Stand Up

White Roses

Soft Red Hills of Alabama

Compendium

Always Together Forever

Samuel Knighton

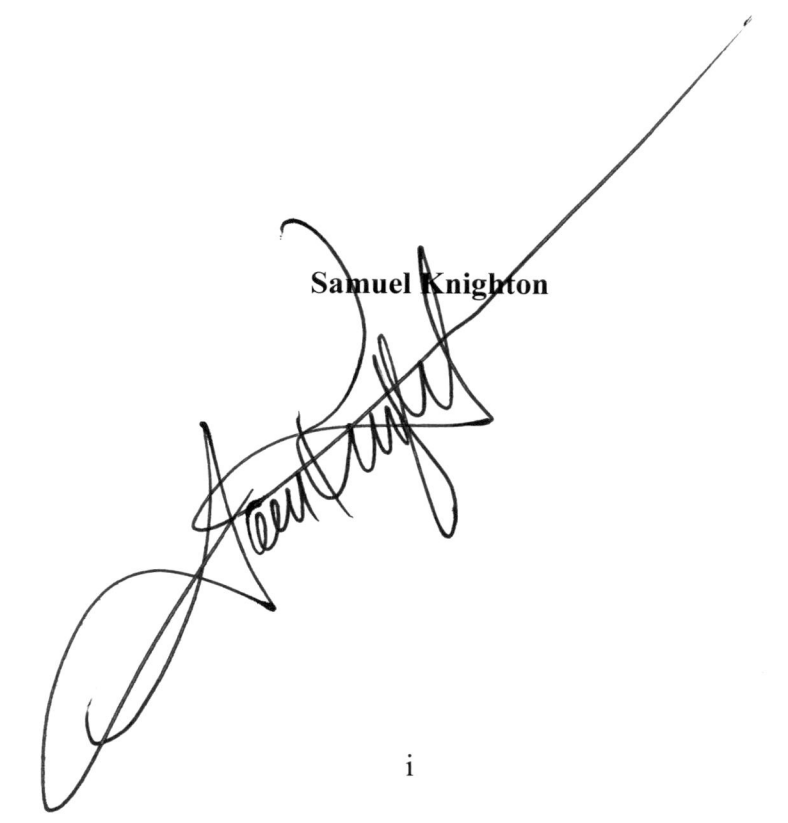

Copyright © 2008 by Samuel C. Knighton

All rights reserved. No part of this book may be reproduced in any form, except for the inclusion of brief quotations in review, without permission in writing from the author/publisher.

ISBN   978-1-60458-395-3

Printed by Fundcraft Publishing Company, InstantPublisher Division,
 PO Box 985, Collierville, TN

Manufactured in the United States of America

DISCLAIMER

The story presented here is completely fiction and only lives in the mind of the author. Any reference to any person living or dead, any place, or event is not intentional and is absolutely coincidental.

DEDICATION

This story is dedicated to two very special individuals that loved life, loved each other, and touched many hearts along their life-pathway.

May they both rest in eternal love that they felt for each other, forever.

FORWARD

Martin Luther King delivered his "I had a dream" speech on the Lincoln Memorial in Washington, D.C. on August 28, 1963. President Kennedy was assassinated on November 22, 1963 making Lyndon Johnson president.

The country was rapidly changing. The war in Viet Nam was escalating and people were protesting against it.

The Civil Rights Act of 1964 was signed into law on July 2, 1964. But, integration had taken place in many areas of Wisconsin long before 1964. Oakwood Heights High School was one of them and had been very progressing in integrating blacks, whites, and Native Americans, Still, some types of discrimination was very much alive and well. It wasn't discrimination against race so much, but rather, discrimination against handicapped kids.

It's hard to imagine such bias existed so few years ago, but it was commonplace.

It's been said that the 1960s were simpler times. It was a time before cell phones, iPods, home computers, microwaves, the Internet, and many other conveniences that we now assume were always there. Simpler? Maybe in technology, but certainly not in discrimination.

It was in the fall of 1965 and Ryan Wakefield was a senior in Oakwood Heights High School. He was a top student and a good football player. But, Ryan was much more than that. He was a terrific person to be around. He was humble, yet very friendly. Wherever Ryan was, lots of kids gathered around him.

Morgan Carter also went to Oakwood Heights High School. She was a sophomore, beautiful, and very bright. She, too, was very friendly and had a captivating smile. Kids were naturally drawn to her. Morgan was physically handicapped, but only slightly. Yet, a few kids and even some adults discriminated heavily against her. Somehow, she always seemed to have risen above it. She saw the bright side of everything, including life at its worst.

CHAPTER ONE
Playing the Game

"Morgan," Miss Anderson commanded from the front of the classroom. "Please tell us what the President had to say on the evening news last night."

Miss Anderson was not quite thirty, very slender, and had blonde hair which she kept perfectly styled. She was a former cheerleader all during her high school and college years. She was feared by most of her students, except anyone on the cheerleading squad, and Ryan. He was a "straight A" student and one of her favorites.

Morgan's face turned a bright shade of red and, after a long hesitation, she tried desperately to get the words to come out the way she heard them in her mind.

The class consisted of seventeen students ranging from sophomore to senior with a grade-point standing high enough to be accepted into this accelerated class. Morgan was a very bright sophomore.

"Pppresssident Johnson," Morgan struggled, "urged ... Congress ... to pass ... the bill ..," The harder Morgan tried, the more frustrated she got and her hands and arms started to make odd jerky movements.

"I'm sure Congress had plenty of time to debate the issue from all sides while we're waiting for you to tell us about it," Miss Anderson interrupted.

The class snickered, especially the four cheerleaders that sat across from and behind each other. They mimicked Morgan's uncontrollable arm and hand jerks.

Ryan hated that kind of thing. He had certainly seen kids being kids and teasing each other unmercifully, and on occasion, he had been guilty of it himself. But, this was the first time he'd ever seen an adult ridiculing a student, and a teacher at that.

Ryan's mind came in quick focus when he heard Miss Anderson say, "Ryan, could you pick up on our question while Miss Carter tries to get her brain into gear."

More snickering.

"Yes, Miss Anderson," he heard himself say without much thought.

"President Johnson stressed the importance of passing the Energy Bill and said that every day that goes by while the Congress debates it, will cost the American taxpayers millions."

"Perfect, Ryan," Miss Anderson glowed and smiled at Ryan. "Very precisely done."

Vicky Hendricks looked at Ryan warmly with a huge smile. She was the head cheerleader and sat in the front seat of the first row. She and Ryan had dated some and she considered them a couple.

Ryan wasn't the primary jock in school. That was Tom the quarterback of the football team, but Ryan was probably second in the jock ranking. He was tall, slender, and very handsome. He had rusty colored hair that was always just a little untamed and dark brown eyes. Virtually every girl at Oakwood Heights High School considered Ryan one of the few ultimate catches. Ryan played wide-receiver on the football team and was often the hero of the game when he scored the winning touchdown.

"Now, everyone look at the front page of yesterday's newspaper and read the second article there called, 'Corporations reap record profits.' Oh, Ryan. Will you pass back the test papers from last week's quiz while the rest of the class works on the article?"

"Oh, Ryan," Misty, one of the cheerleaders rolled her eyes and moaned, mimicking Miss Anderson, which caused two of the other cheerleaders to laugh out loud.

But, Vicky wasn't laughing. She was staring right at Ryan with a warm smile.

Ryan stood, came up to Miss Anderson's desk, and picked up the test papers. He walked nonchalantly up and down the rows shuffling through the tests until he found the right one and handed it to its author. He picked up Vicky's test and noticed that she got an "A." All the other cheerleaders received similar marks. Ryan continued on with his work. He gave his friend, Edward, his test.

"Wow," Edward exclaimed. "C+. That's even better than just passing."

Edward was a pretty big guy. He played offensive lineman, tipping the scale at over 190 pounds. School wasn't hard for Edward, but he didn't like to study and somehow just managed to get by.

When Ryan reached Morgan's desk, she didn't look up at all. He handed her test to her and saw that she had scored a "C," but didn't think much about it.

Last, he took his paper back to his desk and sat down. He'd received a perfect score. Not only was Ryan a very good football player, but he was a top student as well.

The bell rang and the room exploded as Miss Anderson tried in vain to shout out tomorrow's assignment.

Lunch was next for Ryan and Edward. They were joined by Brian as they stood in the cafeteria line.

Brian was huge by comparison to most boys in school, even larger in height and weight than Edward.

"Man, I'm starved," Brian said as he settled in line following Ryan. "I thought my last class would never end and my stomach, it growled so loud, even Mr. Lausch had to laugh right out loud."

Ryan got a fruit salad, hotdog, brownie, and milk. Edward frowned when he saw Ryan put the dishes on his tray. He ordered four hotdogs, two large cookies and three containers of milk. Brian ordered the same as Edward, but added a hamburger and potato chips to his tray.

"Hey, Ryan," Edward exclaimed as they found a table and sat down. "You're going to shrivel up and blow away eating stuff like that."

Brian nodded agreement as he ate his first hotdog in two huge bites.

"Gotta keep thin so I can outrun lumbering giants like you guys," Ryan smiled as he finished eating his salad.

"You gonna eat that brownie?" Brian asked as he noticed that Ryan was just picking at it.

"Naw. Here, you can have it."

"Look over there," Edward pointed. "That's Sherry. She's in my math class.

"Boy, she's really stacked," Brian noted as he devoured the brownie in a single gulp.

"Hey, you'd better be careful what you say about her."

Brian looked at Ryan and they both looked at Edward.

Suddenly, both Brian and Ryan burst out into laughter.

"Edward's got a girlfriend," Brian teased.

"Have you ever even talked to her?" Ryan asked as he watched Edward look at Sherry like a little puppy dog worshipping his master.

"Almost did, once. She bumped into me when we were all leaving class last Tuesday."

"Almost did," Brian grinned. "How can you 'almost' talk to someone? Either you talk or you don't."

"Well," Edward stammered. "She was walking out the doorway when she suddenly turned around to talk to one of her friends. Guess she didn't see me and crashed right into me."

"That's still not talking to her, you dumb buffoon."

"Did too. I said, 'cuse me."

Brian and Ryan burst into laughter followed by Edward. He knew it was all good lighthearted fun and enjoyed the bantering.

The conversation then turned to Friday night's game.

"Sure hope you guys are strong enough to keep those goons from Melville High from nailing me Friday. I'm really depending on both of you."

"Aw, don't worry about a thing, little Ryan," Brian said. "The bigger they are, the harder we take 'em down."

"We're not talking about the bottom team here. Melville hasn't lost a game all season."

Talk and banter went on for a little while longer. Lunch was over and each went off to their next class.

The next day was Thursday which was pretty much a repeat of the day before and the day before that. Then, came Friday. Wonderful Friday. It was usually a pretty easy day, all except Miss Anderson's class who always had a quiz on Friday. And, then the all important game on Friday night followed by the dance after the game.

Miss Anderson's class went about the same as always. She began by picking on Morgan, which always caused the four cheerleaders to laugh and mimic her. That was followed by asking Ryan to rescue the class, and then by the dreaded Friday test.

The test was easy and Ryan was pretty sure he knew all the answers, but rechecked his work just to make sure. Finally, Miss Anderson asked him to pick up the papers and the class was dismissed.

"Good luck tonight in the game," Vicky twittered and smiled warmly as she waited for Ryan to pass by her. "We'll all be cheering for you."

"Thanks," Ryan said as he looked over and smiled back at the four very petite, bubbly cheerleaders.

"Don't forget about the dance afterward," Vicky gloated especially for the benefit of her friends. "We sure wouldn't want to miss that, would we?"

Ryan didn't acknowledge Vicky's last remarks. Even though they had dated some, there was something about her that Ryan didn't trust. Oh, she was certainly cute enough. Virtually every guy in school would have done about anything to date her. But, Ryan decided not to think about that anymore right now and concentrated the game.

Fortunately, tonight's contest was a home game so at least the team didn't have to be crammed into school busses. The coach had ordered a meeting before the game, as usual. The assistant coaches told everyone that it was to discuss the plays, just to make sure everyone knew exactly what was going on.

"Now Melville has a great team," the coach began. "They're rated best in the conference, but that doesn't mean they can't be beat."

Coach Reddmen was probably in his late fifties. He was tall and big. He'd played football during his years at Nebraska and won lots of awards. He was drafted by the Colts and played two seasons before being forced out by a severe knee injury. He still had a noticeable limp. He was gruff and forceful. He acted like an army drill sergeant most of the time, but was fair and the whole team respected him.

The room grew silent and everyone leaned forward to listen closer.

"You guys on the defensive line have to be the toughest you've ever played tonight. You offensive linemen have got to protect the quarterback at all cost. I mean it. Cover him like glue. I'll send in the plays from the sidelines. Now, you make darned sure and keep watch, so you don't miss any play I want you to execute, Tom."

The coach went over each routine in their play book and held the attention of everyone right up to game time.

Just as the coach had predicted, Melville was tough, but so was Oakwood Heights. During the first half, the Oakwood Heights defense took a terrific pounding, but held Melville scoreless. It was zero to zero at the half. During the third quarter, the quarterback, Tom, threw a short pass to Ryan and he sprinted into the end-zone for a touchdown. The extra point was good, which made the score Oakwood Heights 7, Melville 0. Ryan frequently received passes and carried the ball often. He was hit hard and sometimes had to just lay on the ground for a few seconds to shake off the blows his body had received.

All through the fourth quarter the Oakwood Heights defense played their hardest to keep the massive Melville offensive attack at bay. When the clock showed three minutes to play, the Melville team had moved the ball to the Oakwood Heights' ten yard line on their second down. On third down, they scored. But, somehow, on the attempt to kick the extra point after the touchdown, either Melville rushed the play, or it was through a superhuman effort that allowed the Oakwood Heights players to block the kick.

The game ended in a great upset with the final score of 7 to 6. The Oakwood Heights crowd exploded into pandemonium. The players doused the coach with the big jug of Gatorade and all congratulated each other on their truly unbelievable win.

When the players were walking back towards their locker room, Vicky suddenly appeared with a huge smile and grabbed Ryan's arm.

"Terrific game, Ryan," she screamed to be heard above all the chatter. "You were wonderful."

"Not me. It was a total team effort."

"Don't be modest, Ryan. You were the one that scored the touchdown," Vicky yelled as she put her head on his shoulder.

"It was our defense that allowed us to win, Vicky," Ryan yelled, but Vicky wasn't listening as she continued to openly show affection to Ryan until they reached the locker room door.

"Don't forget about the dance tonight," Vicky cooed smugly, loud enough for all the players to hear. She wanted everyone to know that the coolest girl in school was going out with the hero of tonight's game.

"Can't Vicky," Ryan said and the pandemonium instantly quieted to silence. It was almost like everyone was shocked and wanted to hear Vicky's reaction.

"And why not?" Vicky's smile and voice instantly turned ice cold.

"I took some really hard hits at the game, tonight. I'm just going to take a shower and lay in the hot tub for a while."

Without saying another word, Vicky turned and walked away.

Everyone around Ryan agreed with his decision. They all hurt too, but, most just planned on going home.

When Ryan undressed he noticed lots of purple bruises forming all over his body. The hot tub felt good and seemed to ease some of the aches and pains.

"Tough game," Brian said as he eased his tired hulk into the hot tub. Ryan nodded.

Just then, Edward appeared, leaped up, and jumped into the hot water making a huge splash.

"Hey, man. Leave some of the water for us," Brian joked.

"Sorry. Boy, Ryan, I'll bet you really ticked Vicky off when you told her you weren't going to the dance with her tonight."

Ryan just shrugged his shoulders and sank lower into the water to let the turbulence work on his sore shoulder.

It was about ten o'clock when Ryan came in through the front door.

"Hi, son," Ryan's father, Benjamin, said as he looked over from watching TV. "How was the game?

"We won by one point."

"So, you guys beat Melville, eh? Guess that was a real surprise."

"Kind of, but we sure worked hard at it. The coach had us practice extra hard and we had meetings all week to plan our strategy.

"Weren't you and Vicky going to the dance tonight, Ryan?" Ryan's mother, Katherine, asked as she looked up over her reading glasses and put down the book she had been reading.

"Guess Vicky was. I got a little bruised up during the game tonight and wanted to get into the hot tub for a while. Some of the others did too."

Ryan wanted to minimize how badly his body felt because he didn't want his mother to worry about it. She was completely against him playing football as she considered it a "barbarian" sport, just as bad as boxing.

"See, Benjamin? I told you this football was dangerous. And, what about poor Vicky. I'll bet she was heartbroken, wasn't she Ryan?"

Ryan just shrugged his shoulders and started for the stairs. He told them that he had better get to bed as he had to be up early for work in the morning.

Ryan worked Saturdays at the Phillips Lumber Company, along with three other guys from his class. They started at seven o'clock in the morning unloading lumber from railroad cars and stacking it into the proper racks. They worked until the cars were empty and all the lumber had been put away. It was hard work, but Ryan didn't mind. Besides, it paid $3.50 per hour and always lasted at least ten hours, plus Mr. Phillips always bought them all pizza for lunch.

"Now, Katherine. Don't fret," Benjamin said as he waved goodnight to Ryan. "The boy wasn't injured. He's just bruised a little. Football's a contact sport. People do get bumped and bruised sometimes."

Benjamin went back to watching television, but his mind brought up memories of some of the games he was in during his high school and college years playing football. He had been fairly good, too, but he lacked the raw talent he saw in his son. Benjamin smiled, but then became engrossed in the show.

"Girls don't like it much when you break a date, Ryan," his mother scolded him slightly. "That Vicky seems like such a nice girl, too."

Ryan went up to his room, threw off his clothes, set the alarm, and was just about to get into bed when he noticed his image in the dresser mirror. He was almost purple from head to foot and felt every bruise, too. He eased into bed and was asleep in a few minutes.

Saturday morning came early, but Ryan was up, showered, and out the door by 6:30. He drove by Edward's house and picked him up.

The weather was cool and there was lots of work to do. Ryan loved it all. He liked the smell of the freshly cut lumber. He enjoyed the heavy lifting. He did his share of bantering with his fellow workers. There were two parts that Ryan loved best; lots of free pizza and of course, his pay at the end of the day.

Work had been fun, but Ryan was glad it was over. He peeled off his clothes and jumped into the shower.

"Phone's for you, Ryan," his little sister Stacey, screamed at the bathroom door.

Stacey was ten years old, had blonde hair the color of straw, and beautiful blue eyes.

"Who is it?" Ryan shouted as he grabbed a towel and opened the shower door.

Ryan quickly dried off. He wrapped the towel around himself, ran downstairs, and picked up the phone.

"Hello?"

"Well, hello yourself, Ryan," Vicky's syrupy voice twittered into Ryan's ear.

"Hi, Vicky."

"It's Saturday night, you know."

Ryan knew what day it was, but didn't respond.

"Where are you taking me tonight?"

Ryan had completely forgotten that each Saturday evening over the last few weeks, he had picked up Vicky, and they went to see a movie or out to eat.

"Sorry, Vicky. Can't tonight," Ryan said as his mind flew into a fog as he tried desperately to think up a reasonable excuse.

"And, just why not?" Vicky's voice instantly changed from a sweet cooing sound into a sharp, steely snarl.

Ryan suddenly noticed Stacey playing with her Barbie dolls at the dining room table.

"Have to watch my little sister tonight," Ryan fibbed a little, but it instantly caught Stacey's attention.

There was a long pause and then Vicky said, "That's strike two, Ryan Wakefield. You know what happens after strike three?"

"You're out?" Ryan responded as Stacey rushed over, bringing all the Barbies she could carry.

Stacey loved it when her big brother paid attention to her. She hadn't heard that he was going to baby-sit tonight, but whatever the reason was, she was all for it.

"That's right. Strike three and you're history. Dropped like a box of rocks. Get the picture, Ryan?" Vicky virtually shouted and hung up.

"Can we have a tea party, Ryan?" Stacey asked excitedly.

Ryan stood and thought a minute.

"Sure, Stacey. I'll get dressed and do a quick run down to the gas station and get some Oreos and orange pop. We'll have a great tea party right after supper. How will that be?"

Stacey was delighted and had a hard time holding back her enthusiasm all during supper.

"Aren't you and Vicky going out, tonight?" Ryan's mother asked as she passed a plate of rolls.

"He's having a tea party with me and Roly-Poly," Stacey said happily.

Roly-Poly was the family's honey colored lab who just happened to love Stacey's tea parties.

Ryan's father cast a quick eye, first on Ryan and then on his wife to see if he could read what was going on behind the words being said.

"I'm a little tired from working at the lumberyard and just thought I would rather stay home tonight and go to bed early."

"Anything wrong between you two?" Ryan's mother continued her investigation.

"We're not a 'two,' Mom. We've just dated a few times. That's all."

"And, Ryan wants to eat Oreos and drink orange pop at our tea party," Stacey said as she spooned in her last bite of potatoes.

"I've always thought you two looked so cute together," Ryan's mother continued her probe and waited for his response.

"Cute? Mom, that's because you don't really know her."

"She's always been very polite and kind when you've brought her over here."

"Yah. Well, that's just for show. Come on, Stacey. Let's get our tea party set up."

Ryan's father didn't say anything, but listened carefully because he knew his wife. She would interrogate him extensively to see if she had missed anything. Benjamin had noticed that something seemed a little wrong the last time Ryan brought Vicky over. There was something about her that said she was trying too hard to be nice.

The tea party was a great success. Stacey loved anytime her big brother paid any attention to her and she enjoyed every minute. Roly-Poly loved tea parties too, and was always invited. Sometimes, he was a minor problem because his manners were not the greatest. When the cookies didn't come quickly enough, he tended to drool and watched intently each bite everyone ate. He drank his orange pop from a saucer, but had learned over time to let it sit a little while first, and let some of the fizz wear off before he lapped it up.

Monday brought the start of another week at school and all the rest of Ryan's routine. Vicky was especially cold to him, which he was beginning to feel was a bonus rather than having the effect Vicky wanted.

Miss Anderson followed her regular routine, too. She picked on Morgan, kidded with the four cheerleaders, and had Ryan pass back last Friday's test papers. Ryan again noted that the four cheerleaders got "As" along with him, Edward got a "C+" which he was very grateful for, and Morgan got another "C."

For the next three weeks, Ryan's routine continued as usual. The only change was that he saw less of Vicky. They went to one dance after the Friday night football game and to a movie one Saturday night.

It was a Tuesday and Ryan had an appointment with his counselor to work out the final details for the state university where he had been awarded an academic scholarship for the next year.

While Ryan waited, he glanced at the bulletin board. Not with much interest, but more for something to do to pass the time.

TUTOR URGENTLY NEEDED
Sophomore student needs immediate tutoring in a class called Modern Problems. Flexible hours can be arranged to work around your schedule. Telephone:

| 3 | 3 | 3 | 3 | 3 | 3 |
| 2 | 2 | 2 | 2 | 2 | 2 |
4	4	4	4	4	4
2	2	2	2	2	2
9	9	9	9	9	9
4	4	4	4	4	4
3	3	3	3	3	3

Ryan could always use more money, so with little more thought than that, tore off one of the phone numbers and stuffed it into his wallet just as the door opened and his counselor invited him in.

All during the rest of the week Vicky was back to her old self and had seemed to have put her anger behind her. She really wanted to make sure that they were going to the dance together Friday night after the game.

"Now, don't get hurt tonight," Vicky said softly as she leaned up against the locker door as Ryan got a book out for his next class. "I heard that Misty will be going with Tom."

Misty was an arch-enemy of Vicky's and Tom was the quarterback of the football team and the top "jock" of the school. The only problem was, Tom wasn't a very good dancer and that's where Vicky really shined. Especially when Ryan was her partner.

Oakwood Heights lost the game to the last place team in their conference. Not only did they get beat, but the score was a humiliating 17 to 0.

Vicky was in her glory at the dance afterward. She and Ryan danced every dance. She was filled with sweet, but very cutting remarks to Misty whenever they were close enough for her to hear. But, Misty was not about to be outdone, and gave them right back. All the bickering back and forth truly bewildered Ryan. All he could think about was going home.

Saturday was a fairly easy day at the lumberyard and Ryan was home by four o'clock. He went upstairs and took a shower. As he was dressing, his attention was suddenly drawn to the little scrap of paper he had laid on the dresser a few days ago. It was the one that had the phone number for the person needing a tutor.

Ryan finished dressing and went back downstairs. He picked up the phone and dialed the number on the little paper.

"Hello," a young boy said.

"Hi. I'm calling about your advertisement in the counselor's office at school. You know, about needing a tutor."

Ryan heard the phone hit the floor followed by a young kid yelling, "Mom. It's for you."

"Hello?" a mature woman's voice said.

Ryan explained who he was and why he was calling.

"Well, Ryan. You might be just perfect for what we need. When can we meet you?"

"I suppose I could drive over right now. That is, if you aren't too busy, and all."

"No. We're not busy right now. That would be wonderful. Let me give you our address. It's 1292 Prince Court Close."

Ryan wrote the address on the little pad his mother always kept by the phone.

"Are you sure you can find us, Ryan?"

"Yup. I think I know about where it is. Doesn't Prince Court run off the road into the Oakwood Heights Country Club?"

Ryan had golfed there with his father quite a few times, and remembered seeing the street sign, or rather the huge stone walls that surrounded the entrance with the large sign for the very exclusive subdivision.

"We're about a half mile from the entrance. Look for a cul-de-sac on the left. Our house is light brick with three pillars in front."

CHAPTER TWO
The Tutor

Ryan had no trouble finding the right street and quickly located 1292 Prince Court Close. The driveway was a "U" shape with a huge flower garden in the center. The house was massive compared to the one he lived in. He parked his car, got out, and rang the doorbell.

"Hello," a young boy said and turned and screamed, "Mom!"

Ryan stood there facing the open front door for a few seconds, and then saw a woman with reddish-brown hair wearing a tan colored skirt and a dark brown blouse striding towards him.

"Come in. You must be Ryan. I'm Mrs. Carter. Welcome."

Ryan stepped into the foyer that seemed to be about the size of the living room at home.

Just then, a girl Ryan thought he recognized from school came in from another room.

"Wow!" she exclaimed and quickly came over to where her mother and Ryan were standing. "I know you. You're Ryan Wakefield. I'm Karen."

"Do you two know each other?" Mrs. Carter asked as she turned to face her daughter.

"Well, we both go to the same school. He's a senior and I'm just a junior."

Ryan didn't say anything, but smiled slightly. He remembered her now. She was the one that was always standing by her locker and said hello to Edward and him when they were going down the hall to lunch everyday.

"Come in and sit down, Ryan," Mrs. Carter said motioning towards the massive living room. "Karen, please go get your sister."

"Boy, is she ever going to be surprised," Karen said more to herself as she sped away through an large archway.

Mrs. Carter talked with Ryan about school, the classes he had, and more specifically about the class called "Modern Problems."

"For some reason, this class has become a real problem for our daughter."

"Here she is, Mom," Karen announced as she and a slightly shorter girl came into the room.

Ryan recognized Morgan immediately.

"Hello, Morgan," Ryan said and smiled warmly.

"H…h.eeee..ll..o," Morgan stammered and immediately looked down to break eye-contact.

"Do you two know each other?" Mrs. Carter quickly asked.

"We're in the same class together. You know, the one you were looking for a tutor."

Morgan's face turned scarlet red as she stood silently by her older sister.

Mrs. Carter continued to talk to Ryan about the class and how he might be able to help Morgan bring her grade up.

"Ryan. You sound perfect. When can you start, and how often can you come here?"

Ryan thought a few seconds.

"I work at the lumberyard each Saturday, and I have football on Friday nights," Ryan said as he tried to work out something that might look like a schedule.

"He's the hero of the team," Karen interjected and smiled warmly at Ryan.

"Not me. I'm just one of the team," Ryan said modestly, which caused him to be a little nervous. "I could come over after practice the other nights, though. How about Monday through Thursday for an hour each night? I could get here right after supper. How would seven o'clock be?"

"Sounds perfect, Ryan. What do you think, Morgan?"

Morgan shook her head that it would be fine, but still didn't say anything.

The two girls were then excused as Mrs. Carter wanted to talk a little more with Ryan.

"Maybe I should start flunking one of my classes," Karen said slyly as she and her sister left the room. "He's a real hunk, Morgan. You're a real lucky duck, you know."

"Now, Ryan. We'll pay you $10 per hour, and if it works out that

Morgan is improving, I think you can plan on tutoring her for the rest of the semester."

Ryan was startled and shocked. Ten dollars an hour for four hours work per week was forty bucks. That was more than he earned working all day on Saturdays at the lumberyard. It took all his will power to not explode with excitement.

Mrs. Carter explained that Morgan was born with cerebral palsy. She, fortunately, was not disabled too much. It was often hard for her to talk and her left foot dragged a little, but otherwise she was as normal as any girl her age. She was also quite gifted academically and had carried a very high grade-point average. That is, until the class called 'Modern Problems.'

Ryan was elated. He couldn't wait to tell his family that he had just landed a job that paid ten dollars an hour.

The next day, just as he promised, Ryan arrived to begin his new job as tutor. Mrs. Carter showed him into their library which really astounded him. He had heard about houses that had dens and that some even had lots of bookshelves, but he had never seen or ever heard of, for that matter, a house so big that it had its own library.

"Now, Ryan. Talk openly to Morgan about whatever you think will help her, including her disabilities. We really need your help here."

Mrs. Carter quietly left the room, but made sure the door was left open.

Ryan started out talking about the class and what he thought was important for Morgan to know.

"I….think…..the…..work….is," Morgan struggled, "not…..hard."

"What we have to do is second-guess Miss Anderson. Let's watch the evening news on TV and write something about each of the stories."

Morgan led him out of the library and into the family room. Ryan was astounded, especially at the size of the television screen. He had never seen the news that size before in his life.

After watching for about a half-hour they went back to the library and each wrote about the stories they had just seen.

"I think this could be one you might get asked about, Morgan," Ryan said as he pointed to the notes on one of the stories they had watched. "It sounds like something Miss Anderson would think is important."

Morgan shook her head in agreement.

"Now, Morgan. Let's write a short sentence that tells about it and you practice saying it."

Morgan struggled as she tried to get the words out. Her understanding of the story was good and her grammar was terrific, but for some reason, Ryan noticed, some words really hung her up when she tried to say them.

"Hey, let's try changing this word of 'vessels' to 'ships.'"

Morgan tried again, but found that pronouncing the new word was as difficult as the old one.

"How about 'boats,' Ryan suggested.

It worked. Morgan could say the new word just fine. They then looked over each word carefully and exchanged words that were hard for her to pronounce to something that came easily for her.

Mrs. Carter peeked in and had to smile as she watched the two working together.

Ryan just happened to notice, asked her to come in, and listen to Morgan tell about a news story they had watched on television.

Morgan said her sentence with a little hesitation now and then, but not much, which caused her mother to smile.

"Let's hope it's something Miss Anderson might ask," Ryan smiled as he got ready to leave.

Class the next day was a disappointment. Miss Anderson, as usual, picked on Morgan right away, but asked about a different story. Morgan struggled and was rebuffed which made the four cheerleaders laugh and tease.

When Ryan came to her house after school, he told Morgan not to be discouraged. Tonight, they would pick out two stories and be better prepared.

It worked. The next day, when Miss Anderson asked Morgan a question, it was one of the stories she and Ryan had practiced. This time, instead of stumbling, she knew exactly what she wanted to say, with words she could pronounce easily.

Miss Anderson was suddenly shocked and didn't know what to say. Instead of making fun of Morgan, which always caused the four girls in front of the class to laugh, she didn't say anything and just moved on.

When Ryan arrived at the Carter's house that evening, Morgan met him at the door.

"Give me a high five," Ryan shouted and held up his hand which was met with vigor by Morgan's hand.

A few weeks went by. Ryan and Morgan continued their work and refinement. Morgan could do the class work easily, but it was Ryan's persistent help and practice that seemed to really help the most. They became very good at predicting what question Miss Anderson might spring on Morgan and practiced the answer ahead of time.

Three more weeks passed and Miss Anderson was a little baffled at the improvement in Morgan's speech and reaction to her teasing. It no longer elicited the same reaction from the cheerleader-four either.

"Today," Miss Anderson said as she adjusted her glasses, glided out from behind her desk, and stood in front of Vicky. "Today, you are to pick a partner and together, over the next two weeks, select an appropriate current newsworthy topic. You will write a five page paper and make an oral presentation two weeks from today. You can divide up the work however you see fit. Just remember, the grade you receive will be a single grade for both partners, and, will count as fifty percent of your overall grade."

Moans went up. Edward groaned as he thought that he might have to actually do some work for a change, and he tried to avoid that at all costs.

"Let's start right here for picking partners with this row."

Misty picked Jo Ellen, the fourth cheerleader in the pack.

The picking went down the row until it was now Ryan's turn.

"Ryan?" Miss Anderson smiled. "Who's your partner going to be?"

Vicky smiled and winked at Ryan.

Ryan thought a moment, smiled, and said, "Morgan."

The class grew silent for a few seconds and then everyone heard Vicky exclaim, "You picked the dummy. Damn you, Ryan Wakefield. You picked the retard."

Morgan couldn't believe she was actually picked quickly by anyone. All her life, in any activity where kids had to pick others to be on their team, she was always picked by default and was often the last person standing. But, this time she was actually picked right away. And, it was by none other than Ryan. Morgan heard Vicky's remark, but completely disregarded it because she had been picked after all.

After partners had been selected and recorded in Miss Anderson's lesson-planner, she passed out the instruction sheets. The bell rang and the class was dismissed.

Vicky was waiting in the hallway for Ryan and attacked him when he and Edward walked by.

"Ryan, you stupid pig," Vicky screamed. "That's strike three, you weasel." She and her three friends turned up their noses and stomped away.

Ryan looked at Edward and suddenly they both exploded into laughter.

After school Morgan burst in the front door and shouted, "Picked me! Picked me!"

Her mother, Lillian, came running in to see what all the commotion was.

"What's all the excitement?"

"He…..picked….me, Mom!"

"Who picked you, and for what?"

"Ryan."

"Ryan picked you, Morgan? What for?"

"Part..ner. I am….part..ner."

"Yes? You and Ryan are partners. But, what for?"

"Class ppp..roject….Ryan…and..me." Morgan said and was almost beside herself with excitement.

Karen got home from school and came into the living room.

"Boy, did you ever cause a stir today, Morgan. It's all over school that Ryan picked you and dumped that stupid ol' Vicky. She's so mad she's screaming all over saying that it's over between her and Ryan."

That evening when Ryan came to do his regular tutoring session he suddenly became aware that something was different. Mrs. Carter, Karen, and Morgan all seemed to be keeping a secret and only smiled at him when he happened to make eye-contact.

Football season was over and the Oakwood Heights team wasn't even close to playing in the championship, but their record was not that bad either. They had won more than half of their games. Now with the season over, Ryan could increase his tutoring to five nights, which meant more money, and Ryan liked that very much.

He and Morgan had no trouble selecting a topic for their project and then, spent hours doing research. They decided that Morgan would write the paper, as her grammar was impeccable. For the oral presentation, she would introduce Ryan who would then present the program. The two spent hours working and practicing.

It was Wednesday evening and Morgan was struggling to get the few words she had to say to come out to her satisfaction.

"Hello, darlin'," Harlan, Morgan's father, said as he came in the living room and put his arms around his wife, Lillian.

"You're home early," she said and hugged her husband back. She loved the feeling of his strong arms around her and the masculine scent of his clothes.

Harlan was tall, almost six feet four inches. He had graying hair which made him look very distinguished. He worked out every day at a health club and his body looked trim and lean. He was wearing a dark blue, tailor-made suit with a flower covered necktie. Harlan always dressed conservatively, with just a little flair. Especially, when he was scheduled to be in court. He was a lawyer and quite successful.

"Come here," Lillian said as she led her husband towards the library. "I want to you watch Morgan practice with Ryan."

"He's the tutor you've been telling me about?"

"Yes. You can't believe how she's improved."

The two adults stood in the doorway and watched as Morgan struggled and Ryan coached, pushed, and even scolded a little to get perfection.

Suddenly, Morgan noticed her mother and father standing in the doorway.

"Hello," she said and jumped up. "Daddy….this is…Ryan."

Harlan immediately walked into the room, held out his hand, and shook Ryan's hand.

"I've been hearing lots of good things about you, young man. My wife tells me you and Morgan are a team for some kind of school project."

"Sit...down, ...Daddy," Morgan interrupted, "and watch us."

Harlan and Lillian sat down and Morgan and Ryan did their whole program for them and, it was flawless.

When it was over, Harlan jumped up and applauded. He rushed over and hugged Morgan, which caused her face to turn red with embarrassment. She was, after all, sixteen. While it was alright for her parents to hug her with just her family around, it certainly was not a thing she wanted her father to do with another classmate there. Especially, when the classmate was a boy.

Finally, it was Friday and the kids all filed into Miss Anderson's classroom. Vicky did her best to completely ignore Ryan, but to infuriate her further, he seemed to have completely missed the point.

"Let's begin," Miss Anderson said as she seated herself in a chair behind the rear most seat. "Edward. You and your partner may begin."

Edward and his partner, Jean, stammered and struggled to get through their program, but finally made it.

"Thank you, Edward and Jean. You may be seated. Vicky. You and Patti are next."

The two girls quickly moved to the front of the classroom and gave a quick, spirited talk as to why it was important for a school and its students to have a cheerleader squad followed by an actual cheer routine.

"Thank you very much, girls. That was a very rousing and convincing program."

Ryan and Morgan were called on next. They moved to the front of the classroom while Vicky imitated Morgan as she dragged her foot under her desk which caused the other three girls to giggle.

Morgan started the program.

"Ryan and .. I ... decided to study ... the problem ... of the medically uninsured."

Ryan then made the rest of the presentation along with charts and graphs he and Morgan had made.

The whole class was drawn into Ryan's talk. When it was over, three hands flew up. Jean wanted to know why Medicaid didn't cover at least the kids who needed it. William asked why those families without insurance couldn't just go out and buy it.

"If this is such a problem," Vicky asked sweetly not wanting to be left out, "why don't the politicians just get involved?"

Ryan answered each question quickly and precisely.

"Well, Ryan. That was very well done," Miss Anderson said completely ignoring that Morgan had anything to do with their program.

The presentations went on until everyone had given their programs.

"Don't forget everyone. Finals are one week from today."

The bell rang and the room emptied as all the kids rushed out into the hall.

That evening, Ryan drove over to Morgan's house at his usual time.

Morgan had already told her mother and sister how well Miss Anderson thought their program went by the time they welcomed Ryan inside.

After a few minutes, Ryan went over and asked Morgan's mother if it would be alright if he took the three kids out to the Burger Emporium to celebrate. Lillian looked over at her daughter and noticed her eyes pleading for her permission.

"I'm sure it will be alright, Ryan. Let's ask the kids."

Morgan was ecstatic. Karen was impressed and glad to be going out where she might possibly be seen with one of the best jocks in school, and a senior at that. Charlie was just glad to be going anywhere.

They all ran out to Ryan's car and for just a split second, Karen thought about getting into the front seat. After all, she was the oldest. But, when she saw Morgan trying to hurry along towards the car, she just held the door open for her, and then she got in the back seat with Charlie.

They all had a terrific time. They ate burgers of every variety, fries, and chocolate shakes until they could hold no more. They kidded each other and laughed, especially at Charlie who thought he had died and gone to heaven not having his parents along to make him be careful.

That same evening, Miss Anderson got things ready so she could read and grade the class-project papers. Her house was small, but very tastefully decorated and comfortable. She made herself a cup of mint tea and laid out two little scones that were filled with a delightful mixture of chocolate and whipped cream. She settled into her big chair, took a sip of tea and began to read.

Miss Anderson smiled to herself as she read each paper. She had always predicted the final grade for each student early on in the semester, and she was always right. The final grade was an average of the class project and final exam. The weekly exams were just busy work, but of course, she never let the students in on that little secret. She smiled smugly to herself.

The first two papers where not written very well and tended to ramble on and never got to the real subject. After referring to her notes that she made during the oral presentation, she graded each paper accordingly.

She read Vicky's and Patti's paper and smiled to herself as she remembered their cute little skit that was an actual common cheer with different words. She wrote "A" on their paper.

The next paper was Ryan Wakefield's and Morgan Carter's paper. Miss Anderson frowned as she carefully began to read. Quickly, she realized that the paper was very well thought out and extremely well written. It didn't quite seem to have Ryan's voice in it, however. There was no doubt that the work was considerably better than any of the other papers. In fact, it was probably the best she had read in a long time.

She laid the paper down and her frown grew deeper. She took off her reading glasses, took a sip of tea, and pondered her dilemma

She had planned all along to give Ryan an "A" for his class grade, but if she graded this work with such a high grade, that would mean that Morgan's grade would have to come up. Especially, if anyone should question it. Miss Anderson had planned to give Morgan a "C" for her overall grade.

Why did they let that retard into my class anyway, Miss Anderson thought to herself and continued to decide what to do. *She should have been put into a special education class somewhere. Away from all the normal kids, anyway.*

Finally, she couldn't think of any other alternative than to just mark a big red "A" on Ryan's and Morgan's paper. She couldn't do anything less for Ryan.

The next week flew by. Ryan went to Morgan's house every night so they could study together. They worked on some of her other subjects, too, but it was easy to see that Morgan was very bright and needed little help.

When Friday arrived the final exams began. Ryan's first two classes were a breeze. He finished them in less than half the time allotted and still was able to not only double-check his work, but even go over some of it for the third time.

Jeanette Dobbins was in charge of Miss Anderson's class. Miss Anderson had called in sick. Mrs. Dobbins was a staunch, very strict, old teacher. Ryan estimated in his mind that she must be approaching a hundred years old. She wore her hair pulled back so tightly into a bun that it seemed to make her eyes squint. She allowed no nonsense in any of her classes.

The final was quite easy and straight forward. When the class was dismissed Ryan walked with Edward towards the cafeteria.

"What'd you think of the test, Ryan?"

"Not too bad. How about you. How do you think you did?"

"Actually, I think I knew most of the answers. At least I'm hoping I did. I actually studied for this test a little. Well, maybe, just a little."

Ryan kidded Edward that he never studied for anything.

That evening Ryan drew up all his courage and dialed the Carter house.

"Hello," Charlie answered.

"Is your mother there?"

Ryan heard the receiver hit the floor followed by a loud scream, "Mom."

"Hello?"

"Hi, Mrs. Carter. This is Ryan."

"Well, hello Ryan."

"I was wondering if I could talk to you and your husband."

"Certainly. About what?"

"Oh, just stuff. Would it be possible to meet you two somewhere? You know, not at your house."

"This sounds very secretive, Ryan. Harlan just got home. Can you hold on a minute and I'll go discuss it with him?"

Lillian found Harlan in the family room sitting in his huge recliner looking through a stack of magazines.

"Harlan," Lillian said as she approached him. "Ryan is on the phone and acting a little strange."

"Strange? How is he acting strange?"

"He's being quite secretive and wants to meet you and me somewhere. And, not at our house."

All sorts of thoughts whizzed through Harlan's mind. He put the magazines on the floor and stood up.

"I'll bet he's found out something about that teacher that Morgan was having so much trouble with. Maybe that's it."

"Or, maybe he's knows some sort of trouble Morgan is in," Lillian said as her face showed some serious worry lines.

"Only one way to find out," Harlan said. "Let's go meet him."

"Where would you like to meet us, Ryan?" Lillian said into the telephone.

"Whatever would be convenient for you."

Lillian thought a few seconds as she tried to think of someplace that would be appropriate.

"What about the restaurant at the golf course?" Harlan whispered.

Lillian agreed and asked Ryan if that would be alright.

It was agreed that they would meet at the restaurant in about fifteen minutes.

It took no time for Harlan and Lillian to get to the golf course clubhouse. It was just down the street from their house. Harlan parked their BMW and they walked inside. The hostess showed them to a booth where they could have a little privacy, but Harlan could clearly see the lobby so he could motion to Ryan when he got there. They ordered coffee and sat and speculated as to what was on Ryan's mind.

"I'll bet it has something to do with that Miss Anderson," Harlan said as he emptied a packet of sugar into his cup, and then took a spoon and stirred.

"Well, I know that both Ryan and Morgan didn't seem to care for her, for some reason."

Just then, Harlan noticed Ryan running across the parking lot towards the restaurant. He sprinted through the lobby and up to the hostess' desk. Harlan waved to him and Ryan hurried right to their table.

"Sorry I'm late," Ryan said. "I had to help my little sister with her school project for a few more minutes than I thought it would take."

Ryan sat down and ordered a Pepsi.

"Now what's all this secrecy, Ryan?" Lillian asked. The suspense was really killing her. If someone was bothering Morgan, she was ready to rise to the occasion, as she always had, to defend her daughter.

Ryan sweated. But, the room wasn't too warm at all. In fact, it was rather on the cool side. He struggled to find the right words. He liked both Mr. and Mrs. Carter, but, after all, they were adults and, he was a little intimidated by Mr. Carter. He had every right to be, too, because he was one of the most powerful attorneys anywhere around.

"Come on, Ryan," Harlan said calmly. "Just spit it out. We'll sort through the pieces once you have them all out on the table.

"Well, alright," Ryan said softly almost to the point to where Harlan was not sure he said anything at all.

"It's alright, Ryan. We're your friends, aren't we?" Lillian said and reached out and held Ryan's hand.

"You both know me. I guess you probably think I'm a crazy person or something. But, I'm not really. I'm a pretty good student and have a part-time job at the lumber yard."

"We don't question who you are at all, Ryan. To us, you are a terrific young man," Lillian said, still holding Ryan's sweating hand.

Finally, Ryan mustered up all his courage and let it out. "I would like to ask your permission to date your daughter."

"Karen?" Lillian smiled and let go of Ryan's hand. "I think she would be delighted."

CHAPTER THREE
It's a Date

"Not, Karen, Mrs. Carter. Morgan."

The silence was stifling. Mrs. Carter wrung her hands, but didn't say anything. Mr. Carter held his coffee cup as if he was desperately warming his hands, but stared off into space.

Finally, Mrs. Carter found her voice.

"Ryan. Morgan has disabilities."

Mr. Carter didn't say anything, but continued to gaze at some far-off object.

"Yes, Mrs. Carter. I know," Ryan said relieved for an opening to discuss the situation. "Her disabilities don't interfere in the least. She's smart and funny. We've studied together a lot and have really gotten to know each other."

"But, Ryan. Morgan can't do lots of things you probably enjoy. She has a hard time just walking sometimes."

"Sure she has some problems, but don't we all?" Ryan pleaded.

"What would you plan to do? I mean where would you take Morgan?" Mrs. Carter said still very skeptical.

"I thought maybe a movie. There's a new one playing that Morgan told me she wanted to see when it came out."

"I don't think it would work, Ryan," Mrs. Carter said firmly and looked at her husband for support. "Harlan? What do you think?"

It took a few seconds for Harlan to rein in his thoughts, but then reached for his wife's hand and held it.

"I think we should let Morgan decide."

Again, there was silence. But, not as long this time.

Harlan called to the waiter to bring a telephone to their table. "Call her and see what she has to say."

Gladly, Ryan dialed in the number and waited while he heard each ring.

On the fifth ring, he heard, "Hello?"

"Hi, Charlie. Is Morgan there?"

Ryan heard the phone hit the floor and Charlie yell, "Morgan. The phone's for you."

"Hello?"

"Hi, Morgan."

Ryan quickly asked her if she would like to go see a movie. He didn't mention that he was sitting with her parents at a restaurant while he was talking to her.

"Yes."

"That's terrific. How about if I pick you up in a half-hour?"

Ryan smiled at her acceptance and hung up. Mrs. Carter didn't believe what they had just let happen.

"Ryan," Harlan said. "I think Lillian and I had better get home first, before you arrive. That way it won't look suspicious. Now, when does the movie start?"

Ryan told him that he had looked at the newspaper and saw that it was playing at the Palace. It started at seven o'clock and the movie was a little over two hours long.

As they walked out to their cars, Lillian held onto Harlan's arm for support. He was her rock and right now, she needed to lean on him.

"Mom! Mom! Guess … what? Ryan … is coming … to … take me … to the … show."

Karen came down stairs to see what all the excitement was about and when she found out, she couldn't believe it.

"Ryan is taking you out?" Karen teased. "On a real date?"

"A real … date, Karen," Morgan said smiling at her sister. "Me. Going … out … on … a … real date."

"Can I come, too?" Charlie whined not wanting to be left out.

"Not this time, son," Harlan saved the day. "I'm going to need your help making popcorn in a little while."

Within a few minutes, Ryan arrived. Everyone was polite, but as soon as he made eye contact, they would look away, smiling.

Morgan picked up a sweater she left on the sofa and they were off to the movies.

"I can't believe our little girl is growing up," Lillian said mostly to herself, but loud enough so Harlan could hear.

"That's what kids do, Lillian. Like it or not, that's what they do. They grow up. But, let's not get too depressed over it. After all, they're not moving to England. They're just going to a movie."

"Wonder if a boy will ever ask me out?" Karen whined a little. "I am a year older than Morgan."

Ryan bought a large tub of popcorn for them to share and a Coke for each of them. They found their way into the theater and were just a little early, so the lights were still on which made finding seats pretty easy. The movie started and they settled down to watch.

When it was over Ryan helped Morgan get up from her seat. Whenever she sat in one place for too long, it made her left foot not want to follow her brain's orders.

"How'd you like the movie?" Ryan asked as he started the motor in his car.

"Even better than I thought it was going to be."

Ryan helped Morgan out of his car and slowly walked her to the front door.

"Thanks for going with me tonight, Morgan. I had a terrific time."

Morgan smiled and opened the door.

"There're home," Lillian whispered to Harlan. "Thank God."

"They only went to a movie, Lillian. Not the moon."

Ryan said goodnight to Morgan at the door and left. She came into the family room where her parents were sitting on the couch, supposedly watching television.

"Did you have a nice time, Morgan?" Lillian asked, trying to be nonchalant.

"Wonderful, Mom. The … movie .. was … bet..ttter …. than …. I … expected."

Morgan went upstairs to tell Karen about her first date, and then got ready for bed.

"Suppose we might just as well call it a night, too," Harlan said as he got up, picked up the huge popcorn bowl, and took it into the kitchen.

Harlan got into bed and picked up the remote. The television came on and he started to flick through the channels.

Lillian got ready for bed, but just sat on the side pretending to have a nail that needed attention. Finally, she stood up.

"I'll be right back, Harlan. I'm just going in and check on Morgan."

"You mean search for any juicy details, don't you?" Harlan asked as he clicked to another channel.

Lillian was already out the door and didn't pay any attention to his last remark. She tapped softly on Morgan's door and stepped into her bedroom.

"Hi, Morgan. I just wanted to make sure everything is alright."

"Sure, Mom," Morgan said as she sat up in her bed. "Is something wrong?"

"Oh, no. Just curious about how it was to be alone with Ryan. You realize that he is a boy, don't you."

"Are … you … kidding, Mom? He's … just … about … the best boy in … school."

"But, he is a boy, after all."

"Sure … he's … a boy. Do … you think … I'm … that stupid, … or something?"

"He didn't …… you know, try anything?"

"Try … anything? What … do you … mean, Mom?"

"Like maybe kissing you 'goodnight' at the door?" Lillian fished a little.

"No …, Mom. Remember? It … was … Ryan."

"I know, Morgan. But, he is a boy, after all and you're a girl."

"I … know … that."

"Well. Remember our little talk last summer? About what boys want to do?"

Morgan covered up her head with her blanket.

"Ryan … would … never … do … anything … like that, Mom. He's too …nice."

Lillian kissed her daughter's forehead and told her goodnight.

She came back into the master bedroom and saw Harlan propped up on his pillow watching some late-night movie.

"Well? Did the dating police find out anything?"

"Oh, Harlan," Lillian sighed as she got into bed and pulled up the covers. "Our little girl has had her first date."

"Yes," Harlan said as he clicked the remote to shut off the TV. "And, she's survived it just fine. But, the jury is still out on the parents, though."

"Hold me, Harlan," Lillian said as she turned on her side. She felt his body snuggle up to her back and his arm go around her. "I need your strength and security right now."

Harlan smiled to himself. He loved to be his wife's knight in shining armor. He also smiled to himself about Morgan, with all her problems, having her first date, tonight. And, not with just anyone, either. It was with a young man that he really was beginning to like, even though he completely realized they were just kids and this would only be a passing thing.

Morgan's first date soon became history and things got back to normal. There was school and lots of homework. Ryan came over quite often and he and Morgan went out for burgers, the movies, or just for a drive.

It was early Sunday morning and Ryan's father, Benjamin had gotten up a little early, got the paper in from the porch, and made a pot of coffee when Katherine came downstairs and into the kitchen.

"Good morning, dear," Benjamin said not looking up from the paper. "Coffee's hot."

Katherine had just poured herself a cup of coffee when Ryan came bounding down the stairs.

"You're up awful early for a Sunday," his mother said reaching for one of the Sunday advertisements.

"I'm going over to pick up Morgan and take her to church," Ryan responded quietly as he picked up a piece of toast.

"You seem to be seeing a lot of that young lady, Ryan. Don't you think it's about time you brought her over here so your father and I can meet her?"

When Ryan got to Morgan's house, he found that she was waiting for him outside by the huge flower garden. He noticed Charlie running around and then saw Karen was standing guard making sure he didn't get too dirty before they left for church.

"Why don't they ride with us, Morgan?" Ryan said.

Morgan thought it would be fine for them to come along and told Charlie to run inside and tell her parents that they were all going to ride with Ryan.

After church the four piled back into Ryan's car and he drove out of the parking lot. When he turned right instead of going straight, which was the way back to Morgan's house, she looked up at him curiously?

"This ain't the way," Charlie said with a tone of authority.

"I know," Ryan said looking at him in the rearview mirror. "I thought it might be fun for you guys to come over and meet my parents."

Morgan shook her head that it was okay, but inside she was worried.

"You got any kids?" Charlie asked.

"Not me, Charlie. But I've got a little sister that's pretty cool."

"But, she's a girl, ain't she?"

"Girls can be fun, if you give them a chance."

There was a little pause.

"Girls stink," Charlie said firmly which caused everyone to break out into laughter. Even him.

Ryan drove into the driveway and stopped. Stacey came running out of the front door waving to Ryan.

"Hi, Ryan."

"Everyone? This is my sister, Stacey. Stacey, this is Morgan, Karen, and Charlie."

Charlie immediately looked away.

"Hi Charlie. You wanna come and see my dog? His name is Roly-Poly."

Charlie had always wanted a dog, but his parents would never give in. They told him that he would never take care of it and they were a lot of work. He, of course, didn't believe any of it. Anyone that had a dog had to be pretty cool. Even if it was a girl.

They all went inside and were introduced to Ryan's parents. Katherine told them that she had a ham in the oven that was just about done and asked them all to stay for lunch. Stacey and Charlie sped out the back door to play with the dog in the fenced-in backyard.

Lunch was fun and filled with lots of conversation. Charlie and Stacey had to sit at the kitchen table, which was just fine with them.

Finally, it was time to go.

"So glad to have met you, dear," Ryan's mother said to Morgan and hugged her. "We've sure heard lots about you."

Morgan liked to be hugged, but Mrs. Wakefield was almost a complete stranger. Still, she really liked her. She hugged her back a little and noticed an ever so slight hint of light perfume when she was close to her. She liked Benjamin, too. He was friendly and told really funny stories about Ryan when he was little, which seemed to embarrass Ryan.

"Maybe you can come to my house sometime and play, Stacey," Charlie said as he got into the back seat of Ryan's car. "I don't have nothing near as fun as your dog to play with, but we could go swimming in our pool."

"Wow! Mom? Did you hear that? Charlie's got a real pool!"

"Maybe you could bring your dog along, too," Charlie pushed on hoping she would as he leaned out the window.

"Can't, Charlie. He's got to always stay home."

"How come?"

"He pees too much."

"That's okay."

"Yah. But, he's not very particular what he pees on."

They all laughed. Ryan started the motor and backed out of the driveway.

"Bye. Bye, Charlie," Stacey yelled as she ran down the sidewalk after Ryan's car.

"See, Charlie?" Ryan smiled. "Girls aren't so bad."

Charlie was still suspicious. After all, he did have two sisters that weren't always that great. But, on the other hand, Stacey had a dog. And that made her a step above his sisters in his book.

More days turned into weeks and winter came in full force. Ryan loved to ski, but didn't because he knew it would be beyond Morgan's capability. They did take a sleigh ride once. It took both Ryan and the driver to get Morgan into the sleigh. When it was over, it took both of them to get her out. Still, they both had a terrific time.

February was finally behind them and March came in with a roar. On a Thursday, the wind blew, the temperature dropped, and it snowed for two days straight. The roads were almost impassable so Ryan had to walk to school. It wasn't really too far, but it was still over fourteen blocks from his house. Lots of kids were absent the first day, but even more on the second. Morgan's dad brought both her and Karen to school.

The next day was Saturday and Ryan and his coworkers shoveled snow at the lumber yard most of the day just to clear the way to the railroad car that had been left to unload. Mr. Phillips asked the boys if they could come back on Sunday and unload the car because it was scheduled to be picked up on Monday by the railroad. He said that he would pay double time and all of the boys jumped at the chance.

Ryan was pretty tired when he got home from working Sunday. It took more than ten hours to unload the train car and put the lumber away in the proper bins.

"You look exhausted, Ryan," his mother said as she came over to look him over better when he came through the kitchen door. "Why don't you take a nice hot shower while I get supper on the table?"

It didn't take much coaxing. Ryan was cold and ached all over. He tried to let the hot water steam away his body aches and almost went to sleep leaning against the shower stall wall.

Tuesday night, Ryan took Morgan to see an art exhibit at the new gallery on the downtown square. She especially loved the artists that painted in the surreal style and liked their use of bold strokes and bright colors.

Afterward, they stopped for burgers at a little restaurant. They went inside, sat down, and talked for a long time while they ate.

When Ryan dropped Morgan off at her front door he could tell that she was really upset, but for the life of him, couldn't understand why.

Morgan opened the door and slammed it behind her leaving Ryan standing alone on the front porch. Bewildered, he turned, got into his car, and drove home.

"What's wrong Morgan?" her mother yelled when she noticed her daughter and heard the little honking sounds she made when she was crying. "Morgan. Morgan, what's wrong?" Lillian said jumping up and running towards her.

CHAPTER FOUR
The Invitation

"Morgan?" Lillian said softly as she tapped on the bedroom door. "Are you alright?"

Lillian didn't wait for a response, quietly opened the door, and stepped in. She saw Morgan laying on her side in the fetal position tightly holding her favorite teddy bear. Lillian went over and sat on the bed beside her sobbing daughter. She reached out and put her hand on Morgan's shoulder.

"Are you okay?"

Morgan shook her head that she was.

"Did Ryan try something he shouldn't have?"

Morgan shook her head violently, "no."

"Come on, honey," Lillian said softly and pulled her crying daughter up into her arms. "What is it?"

"Prom," Morgan sobbed and cried harder making little honking sounds.

"Prom? Oh, honey, I guess I should have known. Did Ryan invite Vicky to the prom?"

Again, Morgan shook her head, "no."

Lillian was puzzled. If Ryan didn't invite Vicky, then who did he ask?

"Did he ask someone else?"

Morgan shook her head, "yes."

Lillian hugged her daughter and remembered some of her bitter disappointments back in high school. Her boyfriend had kept her guessing for weeks as to whether or not he was even going to her high school prom and it turned out that he had asked her best friend, and they had kept it a secret.

"Do you know who it was, Morgan?"

Morgan shook her head, "yes."

"Who was it?"

There was a long pause, and then Morgan's soft voice somehow managed to say, "me."

"You?"

Morgan's crying began again and Lillian held her close, just like she did when she was a little girl.

"He asked you, honey?"

Again, Morgan shook her head, "yes."

"Then, everything is alright?"

Morgan shook her head violently, "no."

"Tell me what the problem is, then."

Another long pause.

"Can't ... dance," Morgan sobbed.

Just then, Harlan peaked his head into Morgan's bedroom.

"Everything okay?" he asked.

"Ryan invited Morgan to the senior prom."

"That's a bad thing?"

"I'll tell you later, Harlan."

Harlan softly backed away and closed the door. He never really understood the fine workings of the female mind and probably never would. He wondered why Morgan was crying if Ryan invited her to the prom. Maybe it was tears of happiness. That had to be it.

Lillian stood up and told her distraught daughter that she would be right back. She quickly went out of the bedroom and down the stairs, many two at a time. Her ire was up and her temper rose by the second. She went over to the little table, grabbed the phone, and dialed in some numbers.

"What's going on, Lillian?"

"Disgrace our daughter, will he. Well, I'm going to show Mr. Toonice what it's like to tangle with the she-lion of the clan."

"Hello," a woman's voice said.

"Hello," Lillian said trying to control the anger in her voice. "This is Mrs. Carter. Morgan's mother. Is Ryan home?"

"No. I'm afraid he's not here. I thought he and Morgan were going to an art show tonight. Do you want me to have him call when he gets home?"

"The very second," Lillian snapped and hung up.

"What's going on, Lillian?" Harlan asked as he got up from his recliner and came towards his pacing wife. "I thought that Ryan wanting to take Morgan to the prom would be a good thing."

"If she wasn't disabled, it probably would be," Lillian snapped, turned, and walked back towards the dining room. "Where is that boy. It certainly doesn't take more than ten minutes to drive from our house to his."

Harlan finally caught up to his near exploding wife and put his arms around her.

"Maybe he had to stop and get gas or something. We don't even know, for sure, where he lives. I've heard the kids talk about going over there with Ryan and it seems like it's over near The Cloisters Mall. That's quite a distance from here."

Lillian wasn't convinced at all and pushed Harlan away. She continued to pace like a caged lioness.

Suddenly, the silent, icy atmosphere was broken by the ringing of the phone. Things were so tense that the noise startled Harlan. Lillian ran and grabbed the phone to answer it.

"Hello? Ryan is that you?"

"Yes. Hi, Mrs. Carter. Mom told me that you wanted me to call just as soon as I came in the door."

"Don't 'Hi, Mrs. Carter' me, like nothing is wrong, young man. You may have fooled Morgan with your smooth talk and filling us with how smart … ."

Before Lillian could continue, Harlan gently, but firmly took the phone away from his wife.

"Hello, Ryan. This is Morgan's father."

"Hello, sir. Wow. What did I do to upset your wife so much?"

"She's upset because Morgan is upset and is just trying to protect her."

"Protect her from me?" Ryan's voice rose to an almost female octave. "What did I do?"

"You invited Morgan to your prom."

"That's all? I thought she would like to go. It's a real honor for a sophomore to go to the senior prom, I've been told."

"It's not that, Ryan. Proms are mainly for dancing and with Morgan's disability, well of course, you must know it's just beyond her capability.

She doesn't want to be humiliated."

"Humiliated? That's the last thing I would ever have happen to her. Would it be alright if I came over? I'd like to talk to you, if that's okay."

"Well. I guess so. I'll try to calm Mrs. Carter a little before you get here."

"I'll be there as fast as I can."

Now Lillian was really fuming. She was sharpening her wits and her claws for a face-to-face confrontation, and she was ready.

"Make a fool of our daughter in front of her friends. Ha!"

Harlan did his best to smooth things over a little and tried to take the edge off Lillian's temper. He knew it could rise in a flash, but would soon lose it's edge, so he hoped that Ryan would take a little while to get there. He even got her to sit on the couch and watch television with him.

The doorbell rang and Lillian almost leaped to the ceiling.

"Now, stay calm, I'll go let him in."

Lillian couldn't wait to confront Ryan, but Harlan held her at bay.

"Come on in, Ryan."

"Can Morgan come down? I'd like her to hear this, too?"

"You think I'll subject our daughter ... ," Lillian shouted before Harlan could get in between her and Ryan.

"Now, Lillian," Harlan said trying to act like a peace-maker. "Let's not convict him immediately. At least, not until he's had an opportunity to say what's on his mind."

"That's the trouble with you, Harlan," Lillian retorted. "You can't get that lawyer image out of your mind, can you? This isn't some trial, Harlan. This is about our daughter."

With much soothing and a calm voice Harlan managed to get control of a rapidly exploding situation. He was even able to convince Lillian to bring Morgan down and hear Ryan out.

"This better be good, Ryan," Harlan said softly as they both waited for Lillian to return with Morgan. "For both of us."

Morgan was dead set against going downstairs to hear Ryan's explanation. She was too embarrassed. But, somehow through gentle persuasion, Lillian managed to get her up and into the bathroom. She washed Morgan's face and loving thoughts ran through her mind as she remembered taking care of Morgan when she was a little girl.

While Ryan waited with Harlan in the huge family room neither noticed the television was still on. Harlan, without thinking at all, picked up the remote and clicked it off while he told Ryan what he knew about the situation.

Meanwhile, Morgan felt a little better, but her stomach was still in turmoil. She wanted to just turn around and run away, but of course, she couldn't.

"Hi, Morgan," Ryan said as he immediately came towards her only to be blocked by Lillian.

Morgan peeked at Ryan and instantly looked away when his eyes met hers.

"I'm sorry I upset you, Morgan," Ryan said still trying to maneuver around so he could make eye-contact. "I thought it would really be fun to go to the prom. We don't have to dance. It's just supposed to be a really great time."

"Ryan. You know perfectly well that Morgan can't do all the things other kids can. And, we've heard that you're quite a good dancer. So, what should she do when other girls ask you to dance? Just sit on the sideline, like a bump on a log?"

"But, Morgan," Ryan was pleading now. "I know how … ."

"Know how to make a fool of her?" Lillian snarled and moved closer.

"I'm … sorry I … can't … go," Morgan's small voice spoke up.

"Sure you can," Ryan suddenly said with authority. "I know how we can make it work."

"There you go again. Giving her false hopes."

"Not false hopes, Mrs. Carter. I'm pretty sure we can make it work."

Morgan somehow found a little of her spirit and came out from behind the protection of her mother's skirt.

"How, … Ryan?"

"Like this," Ryan said as he grabbed Morgan's hand and pulled her into the center of the room. "Mr. Carter, do you have any slow music you could put on the record player?"

"Well, I've had just about … ," Lillian was interrupted.

"Now, Lillian. Let's see what the boy has in mind," Harlan mumbled as he thumbed through his huge collection of records.

Within a few minutes he found what he was looking for and put the record on. The music filled the room.

Ryan approached Morgan. He put his right hand on the back of her waist and his left hand held hers.

"Put your left foot on top of my right shoe," Ryan commanded. "My little sister and I dance like this all the time."

At first, Morgan had a hard time keeping her foot on Ryan's. She was sure she was going to hurt him. But, somehow, it didn't seem to. It wasn't long and she found that she didn't really need to keep it there all the time. Only when it needed to change direction. By the third song, they were actually doing the waltz fairly well.

"I'll be damned," Harlan said and noticed his wife wasn't paying any attention to him at all. Tears were streaming down her face.

"Hey. What's going on?" Karen asked as she come into the living room. "Morgan's dancing?"

"Shhhh. Come in and watch."

When the song was over Karen rushed up to congratulate Morgan on her new-found dancing talent, and to bring some news from school.

"I just got back from the school newspaper meeting and, guess what? Vicky is the prom queen and Tom, our quarterback, is the king. There's a real pair. They both hate each other."

Some of the success Morgan was feeling from dancing with Ryan started to fade as she remembered Vicky's sharp tongue. Most of all, Morgan felt inferior, especially because Vicky was Ryan's old girlfriend and she wasn't too sure just how old a girlfriend she was either.

Ryan told Morgan that he would come to her house every night after school so they could practice, which helped relieve some of her tension, but certainly not all of it.

Lillian pulled Ryan aside and said, "Ryan, I'm really sorry for being so mean to you. I was only trying to protect Morgan. I hope you can forgive me."

Ryan smiled widely and told her not to even think about it. It was all past history.

Finally, Ryan left and the girls went upstairs to their bedroom. Harlan was in bed clicking the remote from one channel to the next when Lillian came to bed. Harlan shut off the TV and turned off the light.

"Hold me, Harlan," Lillian said weakly. "I'm exhausted."

Her hero turned over on his side and pulled her close.

"I apologized to Ryan, Harlan. I sure hope he knows how sorry I am for the stupid way I acted."

"I'm sure he does. I don't think he even thought about it. I think the only thing on his mind was getting the opportunity to teach our daughter to dance."

"I thought you told me that boys always had more on their mind than what they show," Lillian teased and snuggled down.

"Maybe not Ryan," Harlan said, but smiled a little as he knew what he said probably wasn't true.

They both lay silent for a while.

"Lillian? I've been thinking."

CHAPTER FIVE
The Gown

"About what?"

"Well. Our little girl has had her first date and now she's been invited to the school's biggest social event of the year."

"Yes?"

"I guess we can't call her our little girl anymore, can we?"

"No. Guess not," Lillian said with lots of tiredness showing in her voice. She was really exhausted because of the stress of the evening.

Suddenly, Harlan sat straight up in bed.

"What's wrong, Harlan? Are you alright?"

"Do you know," Harlan said completely ignoring Lillian's question about his health, "that dress shop or bridal store across from the entrance to the mall?"

"I don't know that I've noticed it."

"My secretary, Shirley, told me that it's the most exclusive woman's store around and that people come from all over just to look at some of their dresses. She said it's owned by some famous designer."

"Hmmm. Suppose so."

"I want you to take Morgan there and get her a dress. I don't care what it costs. We can certainly afford it. Well, maybe this once, anyway. If she has crossed all the hurdles that have been put in her way, we can surely do that for her. If Cinderella is going to the ball, I want her in a dress that will drop the jaws of all that are there. Including this Vicky, or whatever her name is. I don't care if she is the prom queen or not. There'll be no question as to who the real queen is."

Lillian didn't say anything, but had a huge smile. Harlan was truly a terrific guy and would go to any extreme for his family. And, this was one she would work on as hard as she could.

The next afternoon Lillian was parked outside the high school when Morgan and Karen came out. They got in and she drove off towards the mall.

"There it is, Mom," Karen said as she pointed to a very exclusive looking shop on the left.

The sign said, "Fashions by Ferrolli." The appearance said, "money."

When Lillian opened the huge door they stepped into a beautifully decorated room. The carpet was a lush heavenly blue. The walls were a darker blue accented by what appeared to be lighted stained-glass windows. Soft music played some familiar classical piece. The whole atmosphere was almost like being in church and everyone spoke in soft, hushed tones. But what surprised Lillian the most was that there was no inventory of dresses like she expected to see.

They stood gaping. No one said much of anything. Interestingly enough, there didn't seem to be anyone there to wait on them.

Suddenly, out of nowhere, a voice said with a hint of snobbish sarcasm, "Good afternoon. May I be of service?"

The voice came from an elegantly dressed, middle-age woman who was quite tall and had light brown hair that looked so perfect it appeared that she had just come from a beauty salon. Her tan colored suit fit perfectly and was most certainly tailor-made.

Lillian stepped forward, but totally ignored anything the elegant figure said. She was quite used to dealing with people that portrayed self-importance and an appearance of "upper-class."

Finally, Lillian spoke with an icy edge to her voice.

"Yes, possibly you might be of service."

The lady was instantly aware that her charade of authority wasn't going to carry much weight and she tried to be much more friendly, still in a reserved sort of way.

"Is it a wedding? Of course you realize that the bride will have set the style and color of the dresses. Would you have her name?"

Internally, Lillian was becoming a little irritated with this person, but her long time training allowed her to appear very calm and reserved.

"I do realize, that if we were here to be in a wedding, the bride would have decided on the style and color of the dresses. Our case is not a wedding, however. We are here to look at some possible choices for my daughter to wear to the senior prom."

"We are not called upon very often to provide such dresses, but I can bring out a few for you to see," the woman said and walked away towards an open door at the back of the room.

"You're ... not ... very nice," Morgan said as she and Karen tried their best to be serious, but couldn't and burst into laughter.

After a few minutes, the woman returned with three gowns. The first one she held up was yellow and looked almost like something a clown might wear. The second one was pink and probably would have been fine, if the wearer was ten. The third was a deep magenta and a little more stylish than the other two, but still not very acceptable.

"Does madam find any of these three a possibility?"

Silence. Lillian looked at Morgan and could tell instantly by the negative shaking motion of Morgan's head that she didn't want any of them. More silence. Finally, Lillian turned and faced her adversary.

"Madam," she said firmly with a note of command in her voice. "I was led to believe that your organization provided some of the finest dresses and gowns in the area. It appears that I was certainly misled. What we have been shown would not even be appropriate for a dinner at the homeless shelter. Now, if you have nothing further to show us, I must say that you have certainly wasted our time."

Morgan and Karen stood in awe. They had never heard their mother act like an army commander before. But, who was in real shock was the sales woman. She was really taken aback. She stood for a few seconds trying desperately to think of something to say.

"I'm very sorry to have been so rude," the woman's attitude had instantly changed. "But you see, we hardly ever get anyone in that is looking for a gown for a prom. Oh, occasionally a mother will bring her daughter in to see what the latest in fashion might be. Some even try something on. But, when they find out the price, they quickly retreat and run to Penny's or Sears."

Lillian softened and smiled, but stood, which was also the signal to the two girls that it was time to leave.

"Please don't go. Mr. Ferrolli happens to be here today rather than at one of our other stores. Let me see if he's available."

The woman quickly walked to one of end of the plush room and picked up the phone. She talked in low, hushed tones.

"Mr. Ferrolli will be right in. I'm certain he will be able to help you far beyond what I am able to do. May I get you come tea perhaps? Hot chocolate for the young ladies?"

Lillian and her brood sat back down and waited for a few minutes. In no time, the woman returned carrying a silver tray with a beautifully decorated tea pot along with an extremely dainty, hand-painted china cup. There was a similar pot, although larger, that was filled with hot chocolate accompanied with two more china cups. There was also a cobalt-blue dish with three scones. Within seconds the woman set the little table for a late afternoon tea that was truly delightful.

"Mmmmm," Karen said. "Morgan, try one of these. They're wonderful."

The woman poured a little tea for herself and told them that her name was Sylvia and that she was primarily a wedding planner for Mr. Ferrolli. She had worked for him for over 15 years and that he was not only one of the leading fashion designers, but a kind and considerate man as well. Sylvia's personality had changed in just a matter of a few minutes, from one of aloofness to a warm, friendly, and even funny manner as she related some of the humorous things that had happed to her over her career.

Suddenly, a tall, slender man came into the room and rapidly walked toward the little tea party. He appeared to be in his late forties. His hair was black with gray streaks and quite wavy. He was dressed in an Italian tailor-made suit with the jacket left unbuttoned.

"Good afternoon, ladies," the man said with a slight Italian accent. "My name is Ferrolli. Frank. Has Sylvia taken good care of you? I'm sorry for the wait, but I was on the telephone and just couldn't shake loose."

"Mr. Ferrolli," Sylvia said as she set her cup on the little table. "This is Mrs. Carter and her two daughters. Mrs. Carter is interested in a gown for her daughter, Morgan."

"I see. And, just what's the occasion, young lady?" Frank Ferrolli asked, even though Sylvia had already told him on the phone.

"Prom," Morgan managed to say.

"What a wonderful time. Being a teenager in high school. Don't you agree, Sylvia?"

Sylvia smiled slight agreement, but her mind whirred back to when she was in school. Both of her parents were from old wealthy families and she had attended boarding schools her whole young life. She went to an ivy-league college and graduated with honors. But, she still remembered back to her terrible disappointment of not being asked to the senior prom in high school. Even though she hadn't thought about it in years, the wound seemed almost as fresh today as it was back more years than she wanted to recognize.

Frank Ferrolli was a highly talented fashion designer and nationally respected. But, first and foremost, he was a "people person." He loved talking with people and especially women. The more affluent, the better.

"Mrs. Carter?" Frank turned and faced Lillian. "Do you have anything specific in mind for your daughter?"

"Not really. I was hoping you might have a few gowns for us to look at, but I'm afraid the three we were shown were totally inappropriate."

"Ah, yes. I certainly understand. I'm sure Sylvia has explained our little dilemma with some people that visit us that are probably better suited to some of the chain stores rather than our offerings."

"I understand. But, that still doesn't help our situation. What can you show us? Do you have a catalogue or pictures we could look at?"

Frank was a master salesman and showman. He hesitated for a few seconds. He pointed his two fingers under his chin and appeared to be in deep concentration.

"Young lady, may I call you Morgan?"

Morgan was completely taken by surprise. She looked up at the older man and when their eyes made contact, she somehow found her voice and meekly said, "Yes."

"Oh my, Miss Morgan, you certainly are a beautiful young woman," Frank said as he reached out his right hand and grasped her hand lifting her to her feet. "Please come with me and stand here in the center of the room under these lights."

Four ceiling spots flooded light down on Morgan. Frank moved around her, looking at her from every angle. It all made Morgan very nervous.

"Sylvia? Could you please step into my studio and bring me my sketch pad?"

Within a matter of seconds, Sylvia brought a large pad of paper along with a charcoal pencil. Frank made some quick strokes on the pad followed by more short movements of the pencil. He walked around Morgan and made some more marks on the pad.

"Do you have a favorite color in mind for your dress, Morgan?"

"Gggreen ... or ... blue."

Frank continued to refine his drawing and constantly made small talk with Morgan. Within a few minutes, he had her completely at ease.

"There. Now, ladies. Please follow me into my design studio so I can refine this a little more before I show it to you. Oh, yes. Sylvia, dear, would you be so kind as to go into our fabric samples and bring out swatches of this fabric in these two colors."

Frank wrote the name and color numbers on a corner of another sheet from his sketch pad, tore it off, and handed it to Sylvia.

Frank led the way followed by Lillian, Morgan, and Karen. Morgan gasped when they entered the studio. One wall was completely glass windows facing a beautiful courtyard of flowers. There were four easels with various designs of what looked like wedding dresses. In the center was a cart that was about the size of a grocery store shopping cart, but with rows and rows of colored markers in many racks that were sorted into primary colors. Frank ushered his three prospective customers to some large leather chairs located near the desk along one wall.

"Now," he said as he virtually danced across the room, threw one of the sketchpads on the floor from the easel closest to the huge wall of windows and replaced it with the pad he was carrying. "Let me just grab a few markers here and add a little color."

Frank made a few last touches with one of the markers and pronounced his work ready for viewing.

"This is just a suggestion, I must remind you. But, here is how I see Miss Morgan here, going to the prom."

At first, the three women were speechless. Finally, Karen found her voice.

"It looks just like Cinderella, Morgan! That gown would make you look just like a princess."

"May I take the liberty of correcting you, young miss? Not make her look like a princess, but she would be one, don't you see."

"Ppp …rince … ess.." Morgan managed to mumble. She was absolutely astonished at the drawing. It was beyond anything she had ever dreamed, and the face even resembled her.

Lillian was still trying to take in the drawing. The face had some resemblance to her daughter, but it was plain to see that it intentionally had not been completed. The cleavage plunged from the high points of the extraordinarily high collar terminating into a center point of a wide belt forming a very narrow elongated V. It certainly was daring and suggestive, but in a way it really didn't show anything. It was an incredible design. She wondered what her husband would think. But, he did say that he wanted Morgan to look like the queen of the ball, and she was quite sure this design would certainly "one-up" any gown the actual prom queen might have found at any of the mall stores.

"Don't you think it is a mite too daring?" Lillian asked in her more motherly voice. "I'm quite sure my husband will have a heart attack if he sees his daughter in this."

"Ah, yes, Mrs. Carter. I understand. But, your daughter is so beautiful, especially with her long cascading blonde hair and her mysterious eyes which you see will all add to the illusion we are trying to make."

Sylvia returned from the material store room carrying two small bundles of cloth. She handed them to Frank.

"Here's what I think might work out just right." Frank handed the green material to Morgan. The material was electric green and flashed in the light as it moved in her hand. The fabric was so light it almost felt like she was holding a newly woven spider web. Morgan loved the color and the feel which Frank detected immediately.

"This is the same exact material in blue," Frank said and handed the blue sample to Morgan. "What color tuxedo will your escort be wearing?"

Morgan thought for a few seconds. "Tan," she said so softly it was almost like a whisper. She was still lost in the mysticism of the magic material she held in her hands.

"Tan. Hmmm. Do you perhaps know where he is renting it from?"

"The ... mall."

"Oh yes. Dannon's Formal Wear. Yes, I know Mark very well over there. Sylvia? Will you call Mark and ask if we can borrow one of his tan jackets for a little while? Then, send Margaret over to pick it up. Here's my car keys." Frank tossed his key ring to her.

Sylvia was astounded, but never underestimated what he might do. Especially when he was on the scent of money.

"Here's my idea, ladies," Frank said as he walked around Morgan again. "I want the tux jacket so I can get the exact color to make the wide belt and also, make his cummerbund out of the same material as your gown. We want you two fit for any high-fashion ball, even if it were held in the White House itself."

Morgan certainly didn't see herself as standing out at anything, but the thought of maybe, just for once, not having people look at her funny wondering what was wrong with her, would be wonderful. Especially if it might possibly, even if just a little, compare to what Vicky and her group might be wearing.

"I still don't know. What do you girls think?" Mrs. Carter sighed.

"You've got to do it, Mom," Karen rushed over to her mother. "Morgan will be the absolute talk of school with that gown. Nobody, and I mean nobody will have anything close to it."

Lillian was still unconvinced. Unconvinced and a little afraid what the price tag might be. She wondered what her husband would say. But, after all, he did tell her to spend whatever it took. What really made the decision for her was when she happened to glance over at her daughter still holding and feeling the material samples. Morgan looked up and her pleading eyes closed the deal.

"Well, Mr. Ferrolli, I can see the merit of your design. If we decide on it, is there enough time to get it done?"

"Certainly, Mrs. Carter. I can assure you, we will not disappoint you in any way."

"I guess you have convinced us, then," Lillian said, but before the last few words came out of her mouth, the two girls jumped up and down screaming with joy.

"Perfect," Frank smiled broadly. "We will do our very best. Our organization has four of the very best seamstresses anywhere. Now, let me take some final measurements here."

Frank hovered around Morgan with his cloth tape-measure calling out the results of each one which Sylvia wrote on an order-pad.

Morgan thought the whole thing was funny and even tickled on occasion. It made her laugh right out loud.

Frank smiled warmly and continued right on with his work.

"We'll need a fitting well before the final day just to make sure that everything is perfect. How will next Wednesday work for you, Mrs. Carter? Say, late afternoon?"

"Yes. That should be just fine. I can pick the girls up right after school, just like today, and be here by four o'clock. Will that be alright?"

It was all agreed. Lillian herded her brood back to her car and they drove home. All the way, Morgan and Karen talked constantly.

"Now remember, you two. Don't breathe a word about this dress to anyone. It's to be a complete surprise."

"Not … even … Ryan?"

"Not even Ryan, Morgan. Don't let this slip out to anyone."

"How about Daddy," Karen asked as she leaned as far forward as her seatbelt would let her as if she was trying to make sure her mother heard the question.

"Not even him. Not for right now, at least."

Lillian drove into the driveway and noticed her husband's BMW was already in the garage.

"Hi ladies," Harlan called out from the opened refrigerator. "Thought I might starve so I decided to make a little snack to hold me over until my girls got home."

"It's only a little after six, Harlan. Fix yourself a glass of wine and one for me while you're at it. I'll have dinner ready in a little while."

"How'd your trip to the dress store go?" Harlan asked Morgan, but all she and Karen would do was grin. "What's the big suspense?"

All through dinner Harlan couldn't determine what the big deal was. What was so secret that they couldn't even hint of what went on. All they would do is look at each other and grin, which then turned into outright laughter.

When Lillian got the dishes into the dishwasher, locked the doors, and turned off the lights, she went upstairs to get ready for bed. Harlan was already in bed, clicking the remote up the channels and then down, which always drove Lillian crazy.

"Okay, dear. Tell me how it really went," Harlan said and put the remote on the nightstand.

"It went fine, Harlan. Morgan was treated very nicely. No, let me say that she was treated more like a queen."

Harlan smiled. So often people treated their daughter like she was some kind of freak.

"The fitting is late in the afternoon on Wednesday. Just to make sure everything fits just right."

"Wednesday afternoon. I'll tell Shirley to not schedule any late appointments. That way, maybe I can meet you all. Then, we can all go out for dinner afterward."

"That would be wonderful, dear. Morgan is dying to tell you about her gown anyway and that way, you would get to see her in it."

"It must be something pretty special with all this secrecy."

"Not special, dear. It's outright spectacular. Good night."

Lillian kissed Harlan, got into bed, and pulled up the cover. Sleep didn't come easily. She stared at the ceiling for a long time while her mind went over each detail of the afternoon.

The days went by slowly. Morgan wanted desperately to tell Ryan her secret, but somehow managed to keep it to herself. Her father was even more difficult. He kidded, probed, and even tried to trick both girls into telling about their experience at the dress shop, as he called it.

Wednesday finally arrived. The whole school day dragged for both Karen and Morgan. Their classmates asked repeatedly what was wrong as to why they were so quiet and reserved. Little did they know that it was all about keeping a huge secret.

Lillian was waiting in the school parking lot when Morgan and Karen came out.

"Hi girls. Let's get going. Your father said he was going to meet us there."

"Dad's going to meet us?" Karen asked as she buckled her seatbelt.

"Thought … it was … secret," Morgan said as she buckled up, too.

"Your father needs to see what we are buying. After all, he is paying for it. We've sure had our fun keeping our little secret from him, but let's all hope he will approve of it."

When Lillian pulled into the parking lot, Harlan was already there waiting.

"Well, it's my three lovely ladies," he smiled and escorted them all into the salon.

Frank bounded into the room followed by Sylvia.

"Ah, you must be the father of truly one of the most beautiful women in all of the world," Frank said as he rushed over to shake Harlan's hand.

Harlan smiled openly. He loved all three and knew beauty ran in Lillian's family and both Morgan and Karen must have inherited the "beautiful" gene.

"Morgan, now come with Sylvia and me so we can see how our little creation fits."

"Little creation?" Harlan questioned as he pretended to be a little miffed. After all, he was pretty sure whatever it was they made for Morgan, it was going to carry a much higher than "little" price-tag.

The main lights slowly lowered until it was almost dark in the room. Three shadowy figures appeared in the doorway and looked as though the center person was being guided by the two on either side. Suddenly the room exploded in a bright white light cascading down from the ceiling high above.

"Great God," Harlan exclaimed as he struggled to bring the vision he saw into focus.

Lillian gasped and put her hand up to her mouth.

Karen broke the spell and yelled, "Go, Morgan!"

The gown was even more spectacular by far, than Frank's drawing. So was the open, plunging neckline.

Tears were now streaming down Harlan's cheeks. Lillian reached up and hugged her husband, Her tears were flowing, too.

"Looks like our little girl has grown up," Harlan somehow managed to say.

Frank rushed around Morgan testing each fit, length, and seam.

"Need to tighten up a little here," he said to Sylvia who made notes on her little steno pad. "I want the length let out just a tad, too. I've made chalk marks for Miriam, so she'll know what alterations to make. We should have everything ready so you can pick the gown up Friday afternoon."

Harlan, Lillian, and Karen rushed over to get a closer look.

After the commotion settled down a little Frank walked over to Sylvia to make sure that she recorded all the adjustments for the seamstress. Harlan, Lillian, and Karen had moved slightly away towards the little table along the wall where the three women had enjoyed refreshments the day they had ordered the gown. The house lights came up to better illuminate the room, but the overhead spots still shone brightly down on Morgan.

At first, she just stared at her image in the huge wall size mirror. Was that really her? She was shocked to see the face floating above this magic gown really was her own.

Suddenly, Lillian noticed the tears on her daughter's face and rushed to her.

"Morgan, are you all right?"

"Oh ... Mom," she sobbed with a few little soft honking sounds she made when she was upset. "It's ... so ... beautiful."

Harlan immediately came to the rescue.

"It's not the gown that is so beautiful, my dear Morgan," he said softly. "It's because you are so beautiful, you make the dress radiate like an angel."

Lillian hugged her sobbing daughter until the wave of Morgan's emotion was under control. She loved her husband all the more for being able to say just the right thing, at the right time.

Sylvia came over and told Morgan she would help her change.

"Do you have a suggestion for jewelry?" Lillian asked Frank as she moved away from Morgan towards the side of the room where he was standing. "I've sort of thought maybe just a simple strand of pearls might be nice."

"Pearls?" Frank said thoughtfully as he put the fingers of his right hand up to his lips. "Yes, pearls might be nice, but I think what we need here is something that will complement the color of the gown. Maybe something green. An emerald perhaps, if you have one. Yes, that's it. An emerald on a long gold chain, I think."

Lillian's mind raced through the contents of her jewelry box. She didn't remember any emeralds, but wasn't sure. Her husband had usually given her jewelry for her birthday and their anniversary over the years and she had accumulated quite a collection.

Harlan came over and interrupted.

"Maybe you can help Morgan get changed," he said softly to Lillian. "I want to talk with Frank for a little while, anyway."

Lillian turned and walked towards the salon where the dressing room was, but her mind was still sorting through her collection of fine jewelry.

"Let's go into my studio," Frank said as he led the way.

"I overheard what you said to my wife about Morgan needing a necklace."

"I think something along the line of a small emerald would accent the cleavage perfectly."

"I've bought lots of jewelry for my wife over the years, but don't have much expertise. Could you describe exactly what you think would work?"

"Certainly. Here, let me write it down," Frank said as he wrote a description of his vision on a small piece of paper.

"Also, Mr. Ferrolli, I would like to pay for the dress tonight. That way all my wife has to worry about is picking it up Friday afternoon."

Frank quickly prepared the bill. Harlan was a little surprised at the total price. It was pricey, no doubt about that, but considerably lower than he expected. He handed Frank his credit card.

By the time Frank and Harlan came back out into the main room Morgan had changed back into her regular clothes. Lillian and Sylvia were standing near the door, talking.

"Well, ladies," Harlan announced. "All this dress stuff has made me hungry. How about if we all go out for dinner? Morgan, you pick the restaurant."

Morgan thought for a few seconds and then said, "I think ... Karen ... should pick."

Instead of Karen deciding on one of the really fine restaurants that Harlan liked to go to, she decided on one of the town's teen hangout pizza joints.

They stopped at home and picked up Charlie. Then they all dined in high style at the Pizza Buffet accompanied with pitchers of soft drinks. All except Harlan. He decided that it was a festive occasion and ordered a beer.

Finally, they were home and the excitement had calmed down. The girls had gone to bed and Harlan was in bed clicking the remote when Lillian came to bed. She slipped in beside her husband and snuggled up close. Harlan clicked the television off.

"I was talking to Sylvia tonight while we waited for you and Mr. Ferrolli. She and he are married."

"I didn't know that. I thought she was just someone that worked there."

"So did I, at first. Didn't you notice that huge rock on her finger?"

"Come on, Lillian," Harlan said and put his arm around her. She snuggled in easily. "You know I never see things like that."

"Anyway. Sylvia told me that her husband had always done quite spectacular work and won many awards and citations for it. But, she said the he virtually worked night and day on this gown for Morgan."

"It certainly shows. I've never seen anything like it."

"She also told me how lucky we were."

"Oh? How so?"

"She and her husband also have a child with cerebral palsy. They have a son. He's four years older than Morgan, but much more disabled. They finally had to put him into a shelter-care facility because he needed far more help than they could provide at home."

The next few days were a whirlwind of activity which was fortunate because it kept Morgan's mind off of the prom. She had extreme emotions about it. On the one hand, she felt privileged that she was going with Ryan. She loved her dress and hoped desperately that she wouldn't stand out. But, on the other hand, she was terrified. What if she couldn't dance after all? What if she did something really stupid, like falling down? What if someone asked her a question and she couldn't find the right words to answer them? The "what ifs" flew through her head so fast that they made her dizzy.

The irony of everything was that time waited for no one and continued to march on. Friday came. Morgan went to school and her mother picked her up when it was finally over. They went and picked up her gown. Things were falling into place.

Morgan picked at her supper. Her biggest surprise was when Ryan showed up saying he wanted to practice dancing a little more, which gave her a little more confidence.

When Lillian finally fell into bed she noticed that Harlan was still up. This was more than a little unusual. He was always in bed first running the remote up and down the channels on their TV.

"You okay?" Lillian called out towards their bathroom.

Harlan came out dressed in his red striped pajamas and was holding something in his hand.

"Remember when we were at the dress shop Wednesday night?"

CHAPTER SIX
The Prom

"I asked Mr. Ferrolli to write down what he thought would be just the right kind of jewelry. Then, I called Brian Chandler. Remember him? He owns the Diamond Development at the mall and I play golf with him pretty often. Well, I went to see him Thursday at lunch and told him what I wanted. I picked it up right after work today."

Harlan opened the long jewelry store box and handed it to Lillian.

She picked up the long fiery gold chain and let it pour through her fingers as it sparkled even in the dim light of their bedroom. Then she fondled the emerald that was surrounded with diamonds. Lillian turned on the light on her night stand to get a better look.

"Oh, Harlan. It's beyond breathless," she whispered. "It's absolutely exquisite."

Harlan smiled with the satisfaction that his wife approved and came to bed.

Saturday morning opened with a whirlwind of things to do. Everyone was rushing around with their own list of things to accomplish. Even Morgan was caught up in the rush, which was a godsend because she felt nervous and jittery whenever she thought about the prom.

In the afternoon, they all went to the most upscale hair salon in town to get their hair done, and to keep Morgan busy. Lillian took the cosmetologist, Ellen, aside who was to do Morgan's hair and told her she wanted something really elegant. Ellen reassured her that she knew Morgan and would do her very best. She also said that she would have Mrs. Bestler, the owner, help her if she needed it.

Lillian's hair was finished first, and then Karen's.

"Ladies. May I present, Miss Morgan," Ellen announced with great fanfare.

Morgan shyly came out into the waiting room with all eyes on her.

"Fabulous!" Karen screamed and jumped up to hug her sister.

Lillian's eyes filled with tears when she saw how glamorous and sophisticated her daughter looked. But, most of all, Lillian felt pangs for seeing Morgan grow from a young high school girl into a beautiful young woman.

The afternoon was filled with all sorts of things to do helping Morgan get ready. Finally, at a little after seven, she was bathed, coiffed, dressed, and standing in front of the huge mirror in her parent's bedroom.

Harlan came in and exclaimed how terrific she looked. He walked around behind her and reached his hand up to her shoulders. Something, almost alive with fire and sparkle seemed to virtually slide down Morgan's cleavage. The diamond-cut of the long gold necklace created a brilliant, sparkling pathway that led to the emerald surrounded with diamonds that literally burned with fire to the eye.

Tears welled up in Morgan's eyes.

"Don't cry, dear," Lillian said as she quickly rushed up to her daughter and dabbed her eyes with a tissue.

Harlan put his arms around his daughter and said, "I love you, Morgan. We all do."

It was ten after seven when the doorbell rang.

"I'll get it," Charlie yelled.

"Hi, Charlie," Ryan said as he smiled down at Morgan's little brother.

"What kind of clothes do you have on?"

"It's called a tux, Charlie. Morgan and I are going to the prom tonight."

"Oh. What's a prom?"

"It's a big deal where everyone gets really dressed up. There's a band and we all dance."

"Don't sound like nothin' I'm ever doin'."

"Don't be too sure. Things change when you get to high school."

"Not me. I ain't never going to nothin' like that unless there'll be dogs."

"No dogs allowed," Ryan laughed.

"Hello, Ryan," Harlan said as he came down the stairs. "Morgan said she'll be right down."

Ryan stepped inside and talked to Morgan's father for a few minutes. Then, Morgan appeared on the stairway. Ryan's mouth dropped open.

"Morgan? Is that really you?"

"Yup … Ryan… it's … me," she said and came down the stairs.

Ryan fumbled around trying to say something, but he was still in shock. Morgan looked like a movie star. He had never ever been this close to anyone so beautiful.

"Oh. I brought you some flowers," he somehow managed to find voice enough to get the words out.

Ryan opened the box and pulled out the orchid corsage. He placed it up on Morgan's shoulder, but couldn't see how in the world he was ever going to pin it on her.

"Here, Ryan," Lillian came to the rescue. "I think your corsage is supposed to be worn on the wrist."

Ryan's face turned beet-red.

"Don't be embarrassed," Lillian laughed. "One time, Morgan's father completely forgot to get me a corsage when we were going out in high society. We ended up stopping at a grocery store and buying some cut flowers. I made the corsage on the way."

"I … think … they are … bebeeautiful," Morgan smiled at Ryan, but immediately looked away.

"Picture time," Lillian announced and herded Ryan and Morgan into the family room. "Take lots, Harlan. I want to make sure we get some good ones."

"We had probably better go, Morgan," Ryan said as he took Morgan's hand. "The limo is waiting outside."

"Who's … riding … with us?"

"Edward and Brian with their dates. Well, Edward has a date. Her name is Sherry Gittleberg. I think she's in some of your sister's classes. Brian couldn't get a date and Edward and I think he was too chicken to ask anyone. But, he asked his cousin, Lauren, that lives about 50 miles from here. Brian said that way nobody will know who she is."

Morgan laughed. "I like … Edward … and Brian, … too."

Harlan and Lillian walked them to the door.

"What's the schedule for tonight, Ryan?" Harlan asked as he opened the huge front door.

"The prom starts at seven-thirty and is over at ten. We have dinner reservations at the Shelby Estate at the country club. Morgan should be home around midnight or a little after."

"Not going to any party after that?" Harlan asked. "Always was a pretty common thing to do after prom."

"My friends and I are not much into that kind of thing, Mr. Carter."

Secretly, Lillian was very relieved. She remembered her senior prom and she stayed out all night and half of the next day. Her parents were worried sick and she was glad she didn't have to add that to her worry list.

"Shelby Estate's pretty pricy, Ryan," Harlan smiled. He and Lillian had eaten dinner there on a few occasions and he remembered that he thought it was extremely overpriced.

"As long as Morgan doesn't mind eating a hamburger we should be alright. I cashed my check from the lumberyard this afternoon, so I should have enough."

Ryan was sweating a little. Edward took $42 out of his savings account and Brian's father gave him two $20 bills. Ryan's check was for $46. Ryan, Edward, and Brian had talked it over before they picked up Sherry. If they pooled all the money together, they had $128 in all. Dinner sure couldn't cost more than that. After all, that was $32 each.

"Oh, Ryan," Harlan said suddenly. "I forgot something. Come into the library for a few seconds."

Suddenly, Morgan looked worried. Was her dad going to give Ryan a real talking to? Was he going to scare him? She sure hoped not.

When they were both inside the dim room that was illuminated only by one small lamp on the reading table, Harlan closed the door.

"Here, Ryan. Take this and call it a loan. I've been to the Shelby a few times and I know it's pretty expensive. I don't want any of you to run short. Oh, yes. And let's not eat hamburgers. I doubt if they even have them, anyway."

Harlan pushed something into Ryan's hand.

Dumbfounded, Ryan opened his hand and noticed a $100 and a $50 bill.

"Mr. Carter, I can't take this."

"Sure you can, Ryan. With the six of you, I don't want any of you to be embarrassed. Just add it to the pool of money you have. What you don't use, just give back. Whatever you need, call it a loan and when you get the money, you can pay me back, then."

"Mr. Carter, I don't know what to say."

"Don't say anything, Ryan. Just take it. And, don't feed my daughter a hamburger. Not at such a fine restaurant, anyway."

Harlan put his hand on Ryan's shoulder and walked with him back to the front door.

They said goodbye and Harlan and Lillian waved to them as they walked to the limo.

"Hey. I didn't know the prom queen was riding with us," Edward teased as Ryan helped Morgan get into the limo.

"I'm ... not the ...queen, ... Edward. I'm Morgan."

"Wow, Morgan. I didn't recognize you."

Morgan was introduced to Sherry and Brian's cousin, Lauren.

"That's about the most beautiful gown I've ever seen, Morgan," Lauren said as she leaned out from the seat to get a better look.

Sherry immediately agreed. While the girls raved over Morgan's dress the boys found dress-talk pretty boring and talked generally about sports, cars, and teachers.

The limo sat in line in front of the school gymnasium for quite a while waiting for their turn to unload. Finally, it stopped right in front of the door. Brian moved up and opened the door. He was huge and was pretty tired of being cramped up inside the limo, even though it was very spacious. He held out his hand and helped Lauren step out. Edward was next and he fumbled trying to help Sherry out, but instead pretty much got in the way. They both lost their balance and fell in a heap with arms, legs, petticoats, and tux parts flying everywhere. It struck everyone funny and they all laughed hysterically. Edward finally got himself situated and stood up. He rushed to help Sherry get set upright. While all the commotion was going on, Ryan stepped out of the limo and held his hand out for Morgan.

The three couples walked into the highly decorated gym. Beautiful streamers of gold and green hung everywhere. Tables had been set up on the opposite side of the gym so couples could sit, talk, and watch. The tablecloths and centerpieces were also green and gold. It was as if it had all been planned perfectly to complement the color of Morgan's gown. The stage was set up with tables with elaborate decorations for the king, queen, and their court.

As they walked across the gym floor toward the tables, Brian and Lauren were first, Edward and Sherry next, followed by Ryan and Morgan. Morgan suddenly became aware that people stopped talking and stared when they walked past. Especially, the girls.

"Ryan," Morgan whispered. "Am ... I ... unzipped ... anywhere?"

Ryan nonchalantly scanned around her.

"I don't think so. Why?"

"Because everyone is staring."

Sherry overheard and said, "They're all astounded at your gorgeous gown, Morgan. They're all green with envy."

They found a round table that was just right for the six of them. The girls sat down while the three boys headed for the refreshment tables.

"Look at those tiny sandwiches!" Brian exclaimed. "What's up with that? I could eat a whole dish of them without even trying."

"Shut up, Brian," Edward teased back. "This ain't no buffet. This here is a high society thing. You're only supposed to take one. Two at the most. My dad gave me the 'heads-up' before I left home so I wouldn't make a total fool of myself."

Brian was still doubtful, but did moderate some. Still, each boy ended up filling their plates. They justified it by saying it was for both themselves and their dates.

Morgan noticed that Vicky was flitting around the whole gathering smiling, teasing, and talking to everyone and dragging Tom around with her almost like an afterthought. She was dressed in a very pretty, light blue gown.

Edward and Brian returned to the table with their arms loaded with plates for everyone while Ryan came behind them with glasses of punch.

"Good evening, Ryan," a soft, almost too-friendly voice said from behind him. "I sure hope you'll save some dances with me tonight. Tom isn't much of a dancer, you know."

Ryan spun around and was face to face with Vicky. She smiled sweetly, but didn't allow any time for him to respond. Instead she went right on greeting each one at the table.

"Well, well. Good evening Edward, and this must be your date," Vicky reached out her gloved hand towards Sherry. "Where do you go to school, dear?"

"I'm a senior right here," Sherry said not being shy or intimidated in the least.

Vicky smiled as if she never heard Sherry's remark at all and moved around behind Brian.

"Brian. Right?" she said almost too sweetly and patted him on his huge shoulders.

"Yah, Vicky. You know who I am."

"And, who is your companion, Brian? I don't think I've ever seen her at school?"

"This is Lauren. Lauren, this is Vicky. She's not from around here."

Lauren smiled recognition, but was not met by any acknowledgment from Vicky.

"I suppose not. How far did you have to look for someone to go with, Brian, dear?"

Brian's face turned a tinge of red. First and foremost, he didn't like Vicky, in the least. Second, he was a little afraid that someone would tell her that Lauren was his cousin and he was fully aware of the ridicule Vicky could spew out. Last, Brian's sense of manliness was awakened as he felt the need to protect his "companion."

Vicky's eyes suddenly moved to Morgan. Her face initially showed disgust and scorn, but was quickly masked with a huge smile that all her cheerleader team could display at an instant's notice from long practice.

"Good evening, dear," Vicky's voice was syrupy and sickening sweet. "I don't mean to say that you aren't welcome here tonight, but after all, this is a grownup affair and not a tea party for children. Oh, and I hope you don't plan to find someone foolish enough to take you out on the dance floor in that pitiful rag. Did it come from the Goodwill? I certainly hope whoever asked you here tonight doesn't mind sitting with you by the sidelines."

The whole table was ready to explode, but before anyone could react, Patti rushed up and grabbed Vicky's arm.

"Come on, Vicky. The program is ready to start and we're all waiting for you to give your welcome speech."

"Can you believe it?" Vicky said in disgust as she hurried away. "Someone actually brought her here tonight. Just think of it. It's the senior prom and someone had the audacity to bring the retard. Whoever it is must be sick or something."

Ryan quickly rose from his chair and came over behind Morgan.

"Don't pay any attention to her, Morgan. She acts like that to everyone."

Morgan looked up into Ryan's reassuring eyes and became instantly aware of his protective hands on her shoulders.

Suddenly, Vicky's voice boomed out across the sound system.

"Good evening, everyone. Thank you all for coming out tonight. Most all of you know that my name is Vicky Hendricks and I thank you for voting for me as your prom queen. As you know, I'm not one for making long, drawn-out speeches, so let's all have a great time."

Patti jumped up and whispered something into Vicky's ear.

"Oh, yes. Silly me. I would also like to introduce the prom king, but of course, you all know who he is. He's our outstanding football team's quarterback, Tom Bodowski."

Tom stood up and sheepishly waved to the crowd which brought a light amount of clapping.

The band started, but only one or two couples filed out onto the dance-floor. Brian and Edward continued to shovel food into their mouths until all plates were completely empty.

"Think we can go back for seconds?" Brian asked Edward across the table.

Lauren put her hand on Brian's left arm, leaned over, and whispered, "Not right now, Brian. Remember, we're going out for dinner after the prom."

"Yah, Lauren. But, that's not for a couple of hours."

"You'll just have to starve along with the rest of us," Edward teased back.

Ryan stood up and took Morgan's hands.

"Shall we?" he said, and Morgan stood as quickly as she could.

Ryan guided Morgan out across the dance floor. He put his right hand on her back at the waist and reached out for her hand with his left hand.

Within seconds they were gliding across the floor. Even Morgan's left foot was behaving and only twice did she have to scoot her foot onto the top of Ryan's shoe to make sure it went where it was expected to be. Morgan's stomach was beginning to relax. The beat of the music, the graceful movements of the dance, and the strong support of Ryan made the whole atmosphere around her seem surreal.

Morgan smiled at Ryan when they watched Brian and Lauren go by. Through Lauren's guidance, even big, clumsy Brian was actually managing to dance.

The next number was a slow, romantic song that everyone knew. Ryan indicated with his eyes to look over to Morgan's left. There was Edward and Sherry. Sherry's head was leaning on Edward's shoulder and they slowly swayed to the soft beat of the music. Morgan liked that and wished she was bold enough to put her head on Ryan's shoulder. But, of course, she was not.

More music and more dancing allowed Morgan to almost completely relax, until she slowly became aware that almost everyone was watching her and Ryan. Morgan's gut immediately tightened.

"People … are watching … us."

Ryan looked up and smiled.

"They're not looking at us, Morgan. They're looking at you. You are so beautiful and your dress is the absolute talk of the prom."

Morgan instantly blushed and looked away. But, in her heart she loved Ryan's words. She wondered if he really thought she was beautiful.

Vicky and Tom stumbled by. Vicky complained constantly about Tom stepping on her shoes and having no rhythm at all.

"Oh, Ryan. There you are. Don't forget, I want to dance with you the rest of the night, just as soon as my duties as prom queen are finished."

"I'm afraid I can't," Ryan called back, but of course, Vicky wasn't listening at all.

"Oh, my God!" she suddenly shrieked. "Ryan. You're the one that brought her?"

Vicky's eyes filled with tears, but she instantly brought herself under control. She virtually dragged Tom to another part of the floor near the edge.

"Stay here and try not to step on yourself," Vicky snarled and stamped off towards the restroom.

The music ended and the lead singer said they were going to take a fifteen minute break. Edward and Sherry came over to where Ryan and Morgan were standing. Brian and Lauren joined the group.

"Wow, Morgan," Sherry smiled. "You sure zapped ol' Vicky, there. I thought she was going to break right down and bawl."

Morgan looked confused. For certain, she didn't understand Vicky's actions, but still, she felt sorry for her. Actually, she had never talked to her at all. But, on the other hand, she certainly didn't mean to do anything that would make her cry.

"Hey," Brian said to Edward. "Did you hear Vicky eat ol' Tom's ears off for stepping on her shoes?"

Edward laughed and said, "The last dance is the change partner one. Let's get all of us football players to be right where Vicky and Tom are and every time the partner change is called, it will be one of us. And, everybody knows how clumsy we all are. Not you, Ryan. You can't be part of this or she'll know it's all been set up."

Edward and Brian sped off to pass the word to the other members of the team.

"I ... think ... it's ... mean," Morgan said as she picked up a glass of punch from the refreshment table.

"Nothing she doesn't deserve, Morgan," Ryan smiled. "Don't worry. She won't be hurt or anything."

The music started up again and everyone found their partners and resumed dancing. The third piece turned soft and romantic and Ryan guided Morgan skillfully around and through the couples who were by now all smiling as they went by. Morgan relaxed and even her left foot behaved.

As the music went along, Morgan became enraptured by the haunting melody and slowly went into some of the ballet moves she was taught as a little girl. Ryan held her to perfection as she did an *Arabesque* which Morgan turned into a complete back layout position as Ryan's strong hand held her in support. The movements were in perfect timing to the music and most people stopped dancing, just stood, and watched.

The song ended and a beautiful love-ballad started.

"Why do I love you?" the lead singer's soft, male voice sang into the microphone.

Without even noticing or thinking, Morgan leaned her forehead on Ryan's shoulder. She loved the feel. She even noticed the slight chemical smell of the cleaning agent the tuxedo place must have used to clean the coat before Ryan picked it up. She became aware that Ryan was holding her very close and her breath came in short gasps.

The song ended and the singer announced that the last dance was going to be a change partner whenever he called out. The music started and everyone danced. Partners were switched and switched again. Everyone except Ryan and Morgan. Morgan wanted to go to the restroom before they left for dinner so Ryan told her he would wait by the punch table for her.

Morgan was standing by the mirror washing her hands when Patti came in.

"That's a drop-dead gorgeous gown," Patti said as she circled Morgan. "It must have cost a fortune."

Morgan smiled and reached for the door handle.

"Just so you know. Vicky is so jealous she's about ready to burst."

"Why?"

"She's about as envious of your gown as I've ever seen her. She had her mother take her into the city to a big department store to get her dress. You know, so no one would have anything close to it. Well, you certainly showed her up on that one. I'm here to tell you that no one has ever seen anything close to it and every girl here would just about give anything to be in your shoes."

"Why?" was all Morgan could say as she stood dumbfounded.

"And, to top it all off- you somehow took her boyfriend away from her."

Morgan was shocked. She had never realized that Ryan must have been Vicky's real boyfriend. He never said anything or acted like she was his old girlfriend.

"Oh," Patti said as she walked out with Morgan. "I know Vicky can be pretty mean sometimes, but don't put too much stock in it. She's actually really nice when she's away from school."

"I ... hope she's ... alright," Morgan struggled to say.

"Don't worry about her. She'll be just fine. She had planned all along tonight to dump Tom and end up dancing and showing off with Ryan, but it all blew up in her face."

"I'm ... sorry."

"Don't be sorry. She can be awful sometimes. Just like when she calls you a retard. She doesn't really mean it. It's just the most hateful thing she can think of to say."

When Morgan and Patti returned to the refreshment table the last dance was over and another Oakwood Heights senior prom was history. Ryan immediately came over and took Morgan's hand.

Vicky stumbled up to Patti and held onto her.

"Did you see that? Those buffoons stamped and tramped all over my shoes. My poor feet will never be the same."

Patti smiled caringly, but down deep thought Vicky deserved everything she received.

"Hello, Ryan," Vicky's attitude softened with a big smile. "You're going to the party at Bill Reynold's afterward, aren't you? His parents are out of town. Everyone is going."

Ryan smiled, but didn't have to answer as Vicky grabbed Tom's arm and walked away.

Brian, Lauren, Edward, and Sherry gathered around.

"Hear it's going to be a big bash over at Bill's tonight," Brian said matter-of-factly. "Word is they've got a kegger, too. Sounds like a real thing to avoid. Besides, we've got dinner reservations and I'm starved."

"You're always starved," Edward teased as he guided Sherry through the mass of kids out towards the waiting limo.

The trip to the Shelby Estate Restaurant took about twenty minutes, and was filled with constant chatter as each person reviewed what they liked best about the prom.

When the limo stopped right in front of the restaurant's main entrance, the doorman quickly opened the car door and helped each one out.

"Good evening," a man standing behind a little podium said and was undoubtedly the *maitre d'*. He was dressed in a black tux, had dark hair that was almost black, and a warm smile. "How may we help you this evening?"

Ryan stepped forward.

"We have reservations at ten, sir. It should be under Wakefield."

"Oh, yes. I have it right here. Table sixteen has been set for you. Would you all please follow me?"

They followed the man through the very intimate, luxurious dining area to a beautiful table set for six. The tablecloth was light tan with each place-setting immaculately set. Matching linen napkins, a large tan plate with the Shelby Estate logo on it, and a whole array of silverware were appropriately set on each side of the plates.

"Prom this evening?" the *maitre d'* directed his question to Lauren as he helped each one sit down and get settled.

"Yes it is," Lauren said with a big smile.

"I hope you all had a delightful time."

"We certainly did."

"But, we're certainly glad it's over," Brian sighed as he loosened his bow-tie a little and tried to relax.

The *maitre d'* smiled.

"Your waiter for this evening will be Hugo. I'll send him right over with menus so you can get started."

The *maitre d'* knew just who would be perfect for table sixteen and found Hugo.

"Hugo. I want you to take table sixteen under your wing. I know tonight's customers have been a little trying and I think, with your great care, it might really make our restaurant something pretty special for six kids from their high school prom. I think the three boys are trying to impress their girlfriends in coming here, but are probably way over their heads in what it's going to cost. So, my friend, handle them the way I know you can. Make them feel really special."

Hugo nodded and smiled. For some reason many of tonight's patrons had been really trying. The steak wasn't done enough. The potatoes were cold. The soup wasn't thick enough. The dessert wasn't big enough.

Hugo had heard it all. But, the most depressing thing of all was, complaints meant low tips and that was certainly the case tonight. Maybe six kids would be just what he needed.

Hugo came over and gave each person a huge menu. Each item was written in French with a little English note underneath.

"God!" Edward exclaimed. "Look at those prices."

"We should be okay," Ryan quickly said in an attempt to calm his friend. "Remember, we all pooled our money, so if no one gets too crazy, we should be alright."

"The Chef's Special for this evening is baked chicken with a thick wine-cream sauce. Everyone I've served it to tonight seems to have enjoyed it thoroughly. While you are deciding, may I take your drink order?"

Cokes and ice tea were ordered and Hugo left to get them. The six contemplated a huge selection of entrees.

"What do you think about the special, Morgan?" Ryan asked as he peaked around his huge menu."

"Don't ... like ... chicken ... much," Morgan said with a huge frown.

"How about shrimp? I remember you ordering that when we've been out sometimes."

Morgan smiled and nodded her head that she would like that.

Hugo came back and put the drinks around the table with great flourish.

"Now. May I take your order, madam?" He asked Morgan.

"She and I will both have shrimp," Ryan said in the most mature and grownup voice he could muster. "And, we'd like French fries and maybe some green beans, too."

"You all got green beans?" Brian quickly interjected.

"Certainly, sir. We have a wide variety of most everything."

Both Edward and Sherry ordered the Chef's Special and Lauren decided on chicken marcella. Now it was Brian's turn.

Brian called Hugo over and whispered, "Now, Hugo. Just so you know, and all. I'm not much on fancy places like yours here. Heck, I can't even read the menu and those words I do know, don't make any sense to me at all. Here's my problem. The others here have me half-starved. And, I don't mean a little bit. Can you tell me what's on the menu that is lots of food? Don't matter much what it is. I like almost everything there is. Quantity is what's important and the quality doesn't matter too much. I probably shouldn't be saying this, but you probably already guessed we don't have all that much money, and all. But, even so, can you tell me what to order?"

Hugo looked down at the huge young man and his heart went out to him. Even though he was considerably smaller than Brian, he clearly remembered going to his high school senior prom and the dinner afterward was a complete disaster. His date was not really a date, but rather someone that had just agreed to go with him at the last minute. At the dinner after the prom, she ordered the most expensive thing on the menu. He was in total shock and didn't know what to do. So, in desperation, he made up a story that he hadn't been feeling too well lately and would just have a Coke. He remembered another waiter who had taken pity. He smiled at him understandingly and said he was sure the chef could find something "complimentary" that might make him feel better. He brought soup and a large basket of bread and told him it might settle his stomach. And, now it was his turn.

"There is something that's quite special that's not on the menu, sir. It's called the 'Chef's Conglomerate' and might be just what you're looking for. I believe it's priced pretty reasonable, too. Let me look in my book here… ah yes, here it is," Hugo pretended. "It's $17.95."

"Perfect," Brian smiled with a grin that beamed from ear to ear.

"What did you order, Brian?" Edward asked as he handed the menus he had collected to Hugo.

"Can't tell. It's a secret and, the best part is it only cost $17.95. I'm the cheapest one here."

Everyone burst into laughter, even Hugo who then quickly disappeared.

"We got enough money, Ryan?" Edward worried.

"Should have. Should have enough for a pretty good tip, too."

"I've got some money," Lauren offered.

"Me, too," Sherry said. "My mom told me to never leave home without a few dollars."

"Ryan," Morgan said almost in shock. "I ... don't have ... any ... money."

Ryan smiled and told her not to worry at all. They had more than enough.

Hugo went into the kitchen and called Chef LaFontaine over.

"Tough night, Hugo?" the chef asked and smiled.

Chef LaFontaine was considerably older than Hugo. He was in his early sixties. His hair was gray, but he hadn't lost much of it. His deep blue eyes were always friendly and understanding, even though he was a highly respected French chef who usually carried the reputation of being offensive and explosive.

"I've got six kids out there that just came from their prom. Nice kids. The boss told me to really take care of them."

"We will, Hugo. Now, what do we have on their order?"

The chef read the order and then frowned.

"What's this, Hugo? Chef's Conglomerate?"

"One of the boys is afraid he won't get enough to eat so I made up this special order. He's huge and probably on the football team by the looks of him. I whispered to him that his order would be lots of food.

"They are probably pooling all their money just to be here and I noticed that one of the guys seemed to be totaling up an estimate as each one ordered and they are acting pretty scared they won't have enough."

"What about the two steaks that you brought back earlier? Remember, one was too done and the other was New York cut and the person claimed they ordered a rib-eye?"

"Oh, that'll work just perfect. Can you add some potatoes and lots of green beans?"

"Sure, Hugo. The kitchen stops taking orders soon, so we can dish up most anything we want. You just leave it to me."

Hugo smiled and knew from many years of working with Chef LaFontaine it would be perfect. He put six salads on his serving trolley along with a wide variety of dressings. He also picked up three baskets containing warm honey-buttered biscuits that were covered with linen napkins.

While serving the main course, Hugo used all his training and skills to make everything perfect. He first served Morgan and then Ryan. He followed up with Edward and Sherry.

"I've got to make another trip to the kitchen and will be right back," Hugo called as he swiftly pushed his trolley away from the table.

When he returned, his trolley was filled to capacity. He served Lauren first.

"Hmmm," Lauren smiled and lightly sniffed. "It smells divine."

Hugo then began to serve Brian. First, the chef had cut the two steaks into strips, which completely covered the plate. He had then drizzled a thick beef *bordelaise* sauce over it. Next, he set a huge serving bowl of mashed potatoes down along with a gravy boat filled with beef and mushroom gravy. Finally, Hugo set another large serving bowl down that was filled with green beans. He thoroughly enjoyed the shocked expression on everyone's face, especially Brian's.

"Is this for all of us?" Brian meekly asked when he finally managed to find his voice.

"Why no, sir. This is for you. The Chef's Conglomerate means whatever's left over and this is what we have."

Brian was elated. Everyone else was absolutely astonished.

Conversation dwindled down to a minimum. Hugo checked back with them from time to time, just to make sure everything was going alright.

"Don't forget to save room for dessert," Hugo smiled as he pushed his trolley which was now filled with decadent desserts. "Compliments of the chef." Hugo ducked down and whispered into Brian's ear, "they're free."

Brian groaned, but somehow managed to order one of the smaller items.

"Wow," Sherry said. "This is fabulous. I've never tasted anything like this in my life. It's like spice and cream whipped together that's so light it's like there's almost nothing to it."

"What do you have, Morgan?" Lauren leaned forward to see Morgan's dessert better.

"Chocolate," Morgan said with a big smile. "I … love … it."

"Everybody loves chocolate."

"Especially, … me."

Everyone laughed and they all agreed that this was probably the best meal they had ever had and ever would have in their entire lives.

Hugo presented the bill to Ryan who carefully took out their stack of cash and counted it out.

"And, a $20 bill for you, Hugo. For being so helpful and especially, kind."

"Before you leave, our chef would like to come out and meet all of you. We hardly ever get guests from any of the school functions and it's been said that we cater to the older and, well, I guess I must say wealthier people. Anyway, he would like to see how you are all dressed up."

Hugo disappeared, but soon reappeared along with Chef LaFontaine. He made the introductions and they all shook hands. They all complimented Chef LaFontaine on how wonderful the food had been

"Your 'Conglomerate' was the best thing I've ever eaten, Chef LaFontaine. But, why did I have to promise Hugo that I would keep it a secret? I want to tell everyone I meet."

"It's got to be our little secret," the chef smiled and put his hand on Brian's huge shoulder. "We only make it for very special people, so we must have your word."

Chef LaFontaine pulled each chair back so everyone could get up. He remarked on how beautiful Sherry's and Lauren's gowns were, which was very truthful. But when he pulled Morgan's chair back and she stood up, the old chef gasped.

"My word, young lady. Am I staring at royalty here? Could you possibly be a movie star? I am quite certain that you are the most beautiful young woman we've had in here in a long time. Am I not right on this, Hugo?"

Hugo agreed and smiled. He too had noticed Morgan's gorgeous gown, which he felt must have cost a small fortune.

Morgan blushed, looked down, and felt her face warming as it turned a scarlet tinge of red.

Everyone gathered outside the door while the driver brought the limo around. Hugo and the doorman helped them all get aboard.

The first stop was at Brian's parents' house. Lauren was staying all night and he would drive her home in the morning after church with his family.

The next stop was at Sherry's. Edward got out with her and walked her to the door. He stammered and stuttered. He stood on first one foot and then shifted his weight to the other. Finally, he put his arms around Sherry and hugged her.

"Come here," she said and leaned up and kissed him. "I had a terrific time. Thanks for everything."

Edward climbed back into the limo and was glad it was dark inside because he was sure his face was beet-red.

Edward was dropped off and the limo drove on until it turned into Morgan's driveway. Ryan's car was parked there, so when they got out the limo left.

They stood outside the door for a little while not saying anything. Ryan finally took both of Morgan's hands,

"You were wonderful tonight, Morgan. You're fantastic."

They looked up into a star-filled sky that appeared to be just made for them. Somewhere in the distance a dog barked. Then, there was silence. The breathing of both of them was all that was heard. Morgan's heart pounded.

Suddenly, Ryan moved close and kissed Morgan on the cheek. He quickly backed away with a huge smile. He turned and ran towards his car whistling. The spell was broken and Ryan left. Morgan stood outside the door for a few seconds and then finally went in.

Harlan looked up from watching television.

"Hello, Morgan."

Lillian had fallen asleep against Harlan's shoulder but woke up when she heard her husband talking.

"What? What is it?"

"Morgan's home."

"Hi, honey," Lillian said smiling trying to wake up. "Did you have a nice time tonight?"

"Fantastic," Morgan said and turned to go upstairs. "Tired ... and want ... to ... get ... ready for ... bed."

"I'll be up in a while to tuck you in."

"Interrogate her, don't you mean," Harlan laughed as he stood up, turned off the TV, and walked towards the stairway.

"Well, how would I ever know anything if I didn't work at it?" Lillian smiled and walked along with her husband while leaning her head on his shoulder and holding onto his arm.

Morgan went into her bedroom, turned on the light, and just stood in front of the mirror for a few seconds.

"Hi, Sissy," Karen's voice called out from the hallway. "So, how was your night?"

"Fantastic."

Karen came in and came over to her younger sister.

"Here. Let me help you out of the gown."

With some work, the two girls managed to get Morgan undressed and into her pajamas. Morgan climbed into bed and pulled up the blanket.

"So?" Karen said as she climbed into her bed.

"So?" Morgan replied.

"So? Did he kiss you goodnight?"

CHAPTER SEVEN
Graduation

A pillow flew across the room and buffeted Karen.

"He did, didn't he. Morgan's got a boyfriend."

"He's ... not my ... boyfriend."

"What is he then?"

"Just my friend," Morgan said softly.

"A kissin' friend."

Both of them were laughing when there was a soft tap on the door and Lillian came in.

"Did you get your gown off alright, Morgan?"

"I helped her, Mom. It's right there on the chair," Karen said and smiled like the cat that just ate the preverbal mouse.

Morgan glared a threatening stare at Karen warning her not to tell her mother, but couldn't hold it long and burst into laughter.

"What's so funny?" Lillian asked trying for an opening to hear all about Morgan's evening.

"Oh, ... nothing, ... Mom."

"Well, come on. Tell me all about your night," Lillian said as she came over and sat on Morgan's bed.

After a little more coaxing Morgan gave her mother a much shortened and highly edited version than she had just told her sister, but it seemed to satisfy her mother. She left out much of the "Vicky" details and of course, the "goodnight kiss" with Ryan.

Lillian got up and said goodnight and went into the master bedroom.

"Interrogation over?" Harlan asked with a huge smile as he clicked off the TV.

Lillian got into bed and relayed to Harlan what Morgan had just told her only edited a little further because she knew her husband was only interested in the overview and not the color of each girl's shoes.

"Sounds like she had a great time."

"Does."

Lillian pulled up the blanket and snuggled up to her husband's back.

"Harlan?"

"Hmmm?"

"What will happen now?"

"What do you mean?"

"Well. Now that the prom is over, do you think Ryan will still come over?"

"Sure. He seems to have a great time when he comes here."

"I'm really worried."

"About?" Harlan said and knew from years of experience that his wife was the worrier of the family.

"Ryan will be going off to college."

"It's time, Lillian. Like the lyrics of that old song- 'there's a time for everything.' I guess it's now time for Ryan to go off into the world."

"But, college, Harlan. He'll be away from home. He'll meet new people and, probably some of them will be girls."

"Probably, so."

"He'll probably find someone to date and I know it will break Morgan's heart."

"I didn't know Morgan's heart was so attracted to him."

"You can't be that blind, Harlan," Lillian said as she sat straight up in bed. "Haven't you noticed how they act together?"

"Have you had your 'little talk' with Morgan yet?"

"What? Little talk? Oh, for God's sake, Harlan. Of course I have."

Harlan could tell that Lillian was rapidly working herself up into a fever-pitch, so he tried, as best a man could, to defuse the situation.

"Young love is always tough, Lillian. Remember back when you were Morgan's age. Weren't you desperately in love with a new boy about twice a week?"

"Oh, you," Lillian suddenly smiled and snuggled back down. "You think you're so smart trying to change the subject. I'm on to you, but I still love you for trying."

Harlan held his wife close and soon noticed that her breathing was relaxed and regular. Lillian was asleep. He loved the warmth he felt when she snuggled up and loved to be held as she slept. In a way, it made him feel a little like her hero, her protector, and her partner. He loved it all.

Sleep didn't come quickly to Harlan. He laid awake for a long while thinking about his first love. Her name was Polly Hayes. His brain instantly brought up the image he liked best of her. She had auburn hair and green eyes. She was tall and very slender. Her voice was soft and hinted of a southern accent. He met her when he was a senior in high school. Her family had moved into the neighborhood during the school year and she was a junior. She didn't know anyone at school, so he immediately became her friend. They dated almost right away. Suddenly, he remembered the enormous pain he felt when he discovered that his best friend had moved in and was dating her behind his back. Stunned beyond belief and terribly hurt, he finally got up the nerve to confront her. She told him that she was waiting for the right time to tell him as she didn't want to hurt him. Funny, the words still hurt and that was over twenty-five years ago. Harlan wondered what ever happened to Polly. A few years ago he and Lillian went to his high school reunion and secretly he had hoped that she might show up. But she didn't.

Time passed and things got back to normal. Life centered around school and lots of homework. Ryan called Morgan frequently and usually came over on Wednesday nights to just hang out. On Friday nights they went with Morgan's family to a nearby restaurant for fish and Saturday evenings Ryan and Morgan usually went to see a movie.

The cold spring finally turned warm. Flowers bloomed and the trees leafed out. The warm days made everyone feel just glad to be alive.

Graduation was nearing and all the activity connected to it. It was announced that because Ryan's graduating class was one of the largest the school had ever had, each graduate would be limited to three tickets for the graduation ceremony. It would be just enough for Ryan's mother, dad, and sister to go, but unfortunately, not one for Morgan. Morgan told Ryan that she certainly understood and not to worry about it.

Graduation was scheduled to be held on Saturday morning which dawned clear and warm. Morgan got up early and called Ryan to wish him well and congratulate him.

"You're coming to the party tomorrow afternoon, aren't you?"

"Yes, … Ryan."

"Your family is planning on it too, right?"

"Yes."

"That's great. My sister told me she sure hoped your brother Charlie was coming. Otherwise, she would be bored and have no one to play with."

"We'll ... all be ... there."

"Wait a second, Morgan. Mom's waving at me. She wants to talk to you."

"Good morning dear. We don't have much time, so I'll get right to it. Stacey woke up with an earache this morning, so she won't be able to go to Ryan's graduation. Mrs. Jennings from next door is coming over to stay with her. Now, Morgan, with Stacey not going, it means that we have an extra ticket and would like to you go along with us, if you want to."

"Yes!" Morgan shouted enthusiastically. "Yes ... I would."

"Fine, dear. Now, you'll have to hurry. Ryan's already left so, we'll be by your house to get you in about twenty minutes. Can you be ready by then?"

Morgan told her she could. She told her mother that she was going to the graduation and only had twenty minutes to get ready. With the help of her mom and Karen, Morgan was standing in the driveway when Benjamin and Katherine drove up.

It was all like a dream. All through the ceremony she, for the second time in her life, again, felt like a real princess. She loved the pomp and circumstance. Ryan graduated second in his class so he wasn't the *Valedictorian*, but it didn't matter. Morgan clapped as loud as she could when the superintendent announced Ryan's name.

The program was long, but Morgan didn't mind. Finally, one of the local ministers gave a closing prayer which finished the ceremony. The 1965 graduation for Oakwood Heights High School was history.

Morgan stayed right with Ryan's mother and father as they made their way through the ocean of people; graduates, mothers, fathers, sisters, brothers, grandparents, and others milled about all looking for some missing part of their families.

"Over here," a male voice shouted above the multitude of voices.

It was Ryan. They made their way to him where he was standing with Edward, Brian, and Tom.

"Congratulations, all of you," Benjamin smiled widely and shook each of their hands.

"Pictures," Katherine shouted. "Benjamin, get the boys close together there."

Katherine took lots of shots. Pictures of Ryan, Edward, Brian, and Tom. Shots of Ryan and Edward, Ryan and Brian, Ryan and Tom.

"Here, Mrs. Wakefield," Brian said. "I'll take some of Ryan with you guys."

Brian took some of Ryan and Lillian, Ryan and Benjamin, and more of Ryan, Lillian, and Benjamin.

"I want some shots with Morgan and me," Ryan said as he came over to Morgan and put his arm around her.

Morgan loved the warmth of Ryan's arm around her and could feel her face warm as a little tinge of red showed on her cheeks.

"I brought an extra film just for it," Katherine smiled and put the new film into her camera.

Lots of poses were taken, but the one that Morgan loved most of all was where she and Ryan faced each other and they were looking into each other's eyes. *That said it all.*

The next morning at Ryan's house was a flurry of activity getting things ready for the party in the afternoon. Benjamin rented a huge tent that the rental company had set up yesterday. Ryan and his father were busy putting up tables and chairs while his mother rushed around putting on tablecloths and attending to the hundreds of other tasks that were required. Stacey's assignment was to meticulously comb the back yard for Roly-Poly's 'deposits' and use the pooper-scooper.

Even though Ryan's party was scheduled to start at two o'clock, many of his relatives started showing up shortly after noon, which threw Katherine into a tizzy.

Aunt Mollie, Katherine's older sister, and her husband, Uncle Robert, arrived first. Mollie was seven years older than Katherine and it showed. She and Robert married years ago and never had any children. Robert owned his own business and was quite successful. Mollie wore an almost 'see through' dress that floated upward with the slightest breeze. It might have been alright on her if she was thirty years younger, thirty pounds lighter, and was going to a rock concert. Her ensemble was finished off with four inch, white toeless high heels with a matching huge white hat with a purple feather plume. In Katherine's estimation, her sister looked like a circus clown.

Katherine and Mollie had never gotten along from as far back as Katherine could remember. Mollie talked constantly and evaluated everything, always with just a hint of sarcasm in her conversation, especially when she "counseled," as she called it, her younger sister.

Robert, on the other hand, was the exact opposite of Mollie. He was about ten years older, but always looked fit, tan, and successful. He had wavy white hair that was always perfectly trimmed, and he had dark blue eyes that sparkled when he talked. His demeanor was quiet, but very friendly and he loved telling jokes. Everyone that met him instantly liked him.

Robert immediately helped Benjamin finish setting up tables and then worked on getting the fires started in the three grills that he had set up.

More people arrived and Aunt Mollie floated around greeting them all as if she was the one giving the party. She directed people where to sit, where to put their gifts, and made a general nuisance of herself. Mollie found Ryan and threw her arms around him. She kissed him on the forehead and told him how she remembered him as a spoiled, little runt of a child that whined and cried constantly. She sincerely hoped that he had grown out of it. Ryan smiled but didn't say anything. Years of experience with Aunt Mollie had trained him. After all, she wasn't interested in anything he had to say anyway, even when she asked him a direct question. So, the best thing was to just smile and hope she would move on to some other unsuspecting person.

Stacey tried to avoid her aunt at all costs. She hated her hugging and kissing.

"Stacey, dear," Mollie called out as she approached her in the yard. "Come over here and let me take a good look at you."

Stacey was still on poop-patrol and hadn't even had time for a shower or to get out of her old jeans and sweatshirt.

"My gracious, but you're skinny," Aunt Mollie said as she hugged her niece. "Isn't your mother feeding you enough?"

Stacey squirmed a little to get loose from her aunt's death grip.

"Just look at those clothes. Don't you have anything better to wear today? It's your brother's party you know."

Stacey smiled sheepishly and wanted in the worst way to fib a little to her busybody aunt and tell her she was wearing the best she had. But she didn't.

"And, what are those pole things you're carrying?"

That was Stacey's opening and she couldn't resist.

"It's for picking up dog poop. You know, Aunt Mollie, so no one steps in it, like you just did."

Aunt Mollie shrieked and hopped around on one shoe when she noticed a thick, brown substance on the toe of her right white high-heel shoe.

Then, she hobbled on one foot towards the house. Stacey just couldn't help it and broke out into an all out laugh.

Uncle Robert was immediately assigned to removing the dog poop from the stained white high-heel followed by a thorough cleansing with almost half a canister of disinfectant.

Aunt Mollie stood in the kitchen complaining about Katherine's disgusting dog and couldn't understand why in the world anyone would have such a beast. Katherine pretty much ignored her older sister and continued to work getting things ready for the party. Robert finally came in and handed Aunt Mollie her 'sanitized' shoe.

More people arrived. Lots of relatives and friends of the family came. Many, Ryan had no idea who they even were. The large, fenced-in back yard filled almost to capacity. People stood in the large two car garage and on the driveway. Benjamin had three grills going and worked as fast as he could cooking hamburgers, hotdogs, and brats.

At ten minutes after two Harlan finally found a place to park. Morgan worried about being late, but Lillian tried to reassure her fretting daughter that graduation parties were open schedules and people just came and went as they pleased.

"Hi Stacey," Charlie shouted as he ran up the driveway. "Where's

Roly-Poly?"

"He's quarantined to the basement. Mama said he's doesn't have good enough manners to be at the party."

"Too bad. I brought a new tennis ball for us to play with."

"Maybe after most people leave we can let him out."

"I sure hope so."

Harlan saw Benjamin feverishly working and sweating at the grills and went over to help. Lillian went inside to help Katherine. Karen found one of her classmates and went over to talk to her for a while.

"Hi, ... Ryan," Morgan said as she found him standing by one of the food tables along with lots of friends and relatives.

It was as if the world stopped for a few seconds. Ryan immediately came over and smiled.

"Thanks for coming, Morgan. I've been watching for you."

"My ... dumb brother ... had to get ... a ... stupid ball ... to bring," Morgan smiled sheepishly and hoped Ryan didn't think she was the reason they were late getting there.

Ryan immediately took Morgan around and introduced her to his relatives and friends.

"Aunt Mollie," Ryan said as he came up beside his aunt. "I'd like you to meet a good friend of mine."

Aunt Mollie turned and took a few seconds to carefully scan Morgan from top to bottom.

"My gracious, but aren't you a pretty little thing," she said with a certain amount of suspicion in her voice.

She asked Morgan lots of questions, which of course, made her nervous. When Ryan realized that Aunt Mollie seemed to be asking too many questions, he immediately excused them to meet other people.

"She ... scares ... me," Morgan said as they walked towards the food table.

"Oh, she's alright. Just a little nosy, I guess," Ryan said as he picked up a plate and handed one to Morgan.

The party continued on. More people arrived and a few left. Ryan tried his best to meet everyone and thank them for coming, but made sure that Morgan was right with him.

Aunt Mollie came in the house and stood by the sink and offered no help at all to her younger sister who was dishing more potato salad up into a serving dish.

"Katherine. I've been meaning to talk to you about this girl that Ryan is hauling around out there."

"What's wrong?" Katherine responded and was a little shocked by her sister's voice, but not overly surprised by her criticism over anything.

"What's wrong with her? She sounds retarded. Good gracious, Katherine. Are you allowing your only son to associate with someone as afflicted as she is? I'll bet our mama is rolling over in her grave. God rest her soul."

Katherine carefully put the huge container of potato salad back into the refrigerator and didn't notice Charlie come in the kitchen. He picked up a ham sandwich off of a large serving platter that had just been refilled and walked over to the basement door. Charlie scrunched down and sat on the floor and smiled a little when he heard sniffing under the door jam.

"Roly-Poly," Charlie sang softly and pinched a small piece of ham from his sandwich and shoved it partway under the door. It immediately disappeared.

Charlie continued whispering to the dog and feeding him, not paying any attention to what was being said between the two adults nearby.

"You'd better stop whatever is going on between those two," Aunt Mollie said as she followed Katherine to the outside door.

Katherine had the bowl of potato salad in one hand and the platter of sandwiches in the other.

"Do you think you could stop your mouth for a few seconds and open the door?" Katherine hissed at her irritating sister.

"Well. You don't have to get short about it, sister dear. I'm only interested in what's best for your family. Lord knows, you seem to have lost track of it."

Aunt Mollie opened the door just enough so Katherine could get her toe between the door and the jam to push it open enough to get through. Aunt Mollie followed with non-stop yapping.

Meanwhile, Charlie continued to feed little pieces of ham by pushing it under the stairway door. He quietly sat on the floor and talked to his furry friend. He was answered by little whines and yips from the other side of the basement door. Charlie then told Roly-Poly that if he cracked the door open just a little he could give him a bigger piece, if he promised not make any noise. And, of course, Roly-Poly promised.

Charlie reached up, turned the door knob, and cracked the door open just a little. Suddenly, a huge fur ball breached the doorway, and mashed it completely open. The outburst knocked Charlie completely over on his back and the door hit the wall with a huge bang.

Roly-Poly burst through the doorway and managed to snatch what was left of Charlie's ham sandwich on the way by. He swallowed it without chewing it at all. The over-friendly, furry monster was on the loose. Out through the doorway he ran and sped into the backyard. People started shouting and when Ryan's father saw what was going on, yelled for Stacey to try and corral her runaway dog.

Roly-Poly sped from one throng of people to the next, snatching tidbits as he flew by. What fun he was having.

Katherine came outside to see what all the yelling was about and saw a honey colored burst of fur fly under the food table.

Aunt Mollie stood at the other end of the table talking to two long-lost cousins. Uncle Robert had just brought her the hotdog she had ordered. She held the plate in one hand and the catsup bottle with the other.

"I love dipping my hotdog in a little catsup," she said.

Roly-Poly burst out from under the table and right between Aunt Mollie's legs causing her to flip almost upside down with the hotdog tossed skyward. She landed flat on her back with her legs pointed straight up in the air. Almost in slow motion, the hotdog that was generously doused in catsup floated upward, and then stopped at the peak of its arc. It then started its downward plunge straight for Aunt Mollie. She saw it coming and moved her head just in time. It hit her hat, with its feather plume. At the same instant a huge furry beast tromped right up on her chest, grabbed the runaway hotdog, and rushed away, flipping his head trying to eat his catch in one gulp.

"I've been molested," Aunt Mollie shrieked. "That monster dog tried to attack me."

Katherine turned and went back into the house, but if anyone was watching, they saw a definite smile on her face.

Uncle Robert came to Aunt Mollie's rescue and helped her get up. Her thin dress was ripped, her hat full of catsup, and she was mad as all get out.

Charlie heard all the commotion and quietly let himself out the front door. He casually walked around to the driveway and innocently appeared to be looking for the cause of all the noise. When he went through the garage and out the door to the backyard he saw Stacey chasing Roly-Poly trying to catch him. He reached into his pocket and pulled out the ball he had brought along and bounced it on the sidewalk.

"Come on, Roly-Poly. Come and catch the ball," Charlie called out and continued to bounce the ball.

Roly-Poly couldn't resist a good game of chasing the ball and immediately came over to Charlie, wagging his tail and panting fiercely.

"Ready?" Charlie called out and acted like he was about the throw the ball.

Roly-Poly jumped up and down in anticipation of chasing the ball which gave Stacey just enough time to run up and grab his collar.

"Now I've got you," she said and Roly-Poly collapsed by her feet pleading for mercy. He knew the jig was up.

Order was restored. Roly-Poly was back in the basement and most everyone went back to eating and talking.

Aunt Mollie's pride was too dashed for her to stay. She announced with the loudest voice she could muster that she would never step one foot into this house again as long as her sister approved of having such a wild, uncontrollable beast living there. She grabbed Robert's arm and, in a big huff, left.

Benjamin came into the kitchen and found Katherine working on something at the counter.

"I don't think we need any more food out there, Katherine," he said as he came up behind her and put his arms around her.

"Probably not," she said quietly and continued working.

Benjamin noticed that she was working on filling Roly-Poly's dish with mashed potatoes and gravy, along with some beef and ham.

"Seems like a lot of good food there, for the hound."

"Well, he's got to eat, too," Katherine said with an ounce of satisfaction in her voice. She opened the basement door and took it down to the prisoner being held captive below.

Finally, the party was over and only a few people were still there.

Karen asked if it would be alright if she went to a show with a friend from school and Charlie asked if he could stay and play with Stacey and Roly-Poly who was now free at last to run around the back yard. Ryan said he would bring him when he brought Morgan home.

"Some party," Harlan said as he helped Lillian into their car.

"It certainly had some exciting moments," she grinned and tried her best to keep from laughing right out loud.

Harlan started the engine, put the selector into 'Drive' and drove away from the curb.

"Going to seem pretty quiet at home without any of the kids," he said as he looked into the rearview mirror.

"Guess that's the way it will be way too soon," Lillian said and leaned her head on Harlan's shoulder.

Harlan reached over and held her hand.

CHAPTER EIGHT
Is this real love?

Ryan's graduation party faded into history. Spring turned into summer and life got back into its regular routine. Ryan worked full time at the lumber yard, but always managed to come over to be with Morgan and her family on the weekends. He especially enjoyed going to church with her mom, dad, her sister Karen, and little brother Charlie.

The summer flew by and then it was time for Ryan to leave for the university.

Lillian worried about Morgan with Ryan gone. Would he find a new girlfriend? Would he forget about Morgan? Or, as Harlan had even warned her, maybe Morgan would find someone new in school. Things happen to teenagers.

Morgan was now a junior at Oakwood Heights High School. She not only excelled academically, but also seemed to be much more outgoing this year. She joined two clubs and worked in an afternoon program teaching little kids to read. She even found a job at the public library in town on Friday evenings and all day Saturday.

Ryan moved into a dorm on campus and started his classes. At first, he was a little apprehensive, but soon settled into a regular routine. He found a part-time job in the cafeteria to earn a little extra spending money. His routine consisted of getting up at seven for his daily workout and run. Then, he came home for a shower and got ready for his classes. He got to work at eleven and worked until two. He had one class in the afternoon and another in the early evening. Any spare time was spent in the library.

Karen started her senior year in high school and loved it. She was a good student and involved in lots of activities including the volleyball team. Her schedule was always jammed with things to do.

Each person's schedule melded into a routine which became the norm for the family. Ryan always called Morgan on the phone every Sunday afternoon and she always received a letter from him either on Wednesday or Thursday of each week. She wrote back the same evening she got a letter.

It was a week before Thanksgiving and Morgan hurried into the kitchen with her usual weekly letter from Ryan.

"Mom. Ryan ... wants me ... to come to ... his ... house ... for Thanks ... giving."

She went on to tell her mother that that they would have their meal around noon so that Morgan's family could have their meal in the late afternoon.

"Then, ... we will ... come ... here ... in the afternoon."

Lillian said that would be fine as she had customarily had their traditional Thanksgiving meal in the late afternoon.

"Mrs. Wakefield ... wants all ... of ... us to ... come ... to their house."

"Me, too?" Charlie shouted. No one thought that he was even paying attention. "That's great. I'll be able to play with Stacey and best of all, Roly-Poly."

"I'd better call Katherine," Lillian said and picked up the phone.

It was decided that rather than each family having separate meals, why not combine them and have one for all. Lillian would do the turkey and pumpkin pies and Katherine would bring everything else.

Karen and Morgan helped their mother clean the house from top to bottom. Everyone was full of excitement and anticipation. Everyone, except Charlie. He moped around and looked like he had just lost his last friend. Oh, he knew it would be a great time and lots of fun to have Stacey come, but knew full well that Roly-Poly's reputation would probably assign him to stay home.

Thanksgiving morning arrived along with a multitude of chores for everyone to do. The fragrance of roasting turkey that had been in the oven since early morning filled the house along with the wonderful aroma of spices from the pumpkin pies.

It was almost noon when Charlie spotted Ryan turn into the cement driveway followed by the Wakefield's Buick.

"They're here," Charlie shouted and ran towards the door.

Harlan stood and walked towards the door with a slight smile on his face.

"You're sure in a good mood this morning," Lillian said as she came over and put her arm through his.

"Charlie's in for a little surprise," Harlan whispered as they were joined by Morgan and Karen.

Pandemonium struck as a huge furry glob burst out of the Wakefield Buick. Charlie stood awestruck and his mouth hung open. Unbeknownst to anyone, Harlan had called Benjamin and told him that it would be fine for them to bring Roly-Poly along. They would all manage somehow.

"Roly-Poly!" Charlie shouted and ran outside to meet the fast closing steamroller. Charlie was knocked down and then greeted with lots of wet, slobbery kisses.

Everyone went inside. Stacey was being dragged along by Roly-Poly's leash.

"Just let him go, Stacey," Harlan bent down and said in a whisper. "He can't hurt anything."

Suddenly, Roly-Poly realized he was loose and began a complete examination of every corner of the house.

When dinner was served it was almost like something told Roly-Poly to go in the family room and snooze while both families enjoyed their Thanksgiving feast. Ryan told of his experiences at the university and how huge it seemed at first. Karen told of her senior year with Morgan adding things about her.

While the dishes were being taken to the kitchen and put into the dishwasher Harlan took Benjamin into the library to show him his collection of old handguns. Stacey and Charlie got to fill Roly-Poly's bowl with the dog food they brought along accented with lots of turkey scraps. Roly-Poly approved wholeheartedly and dove in.

Karen's new boyfriend, Jason, arrived and was introduced to everyone. He seemed like a nice kid, but Lillian told Katherine in confidence that she was very skeptical and wished Karen could find someone as nice as Ryan.

Ryan, Morgan, Karen, and Jason decided to take in a movie and left fairly soon after dinner. Harlan and Benjamin settled in the family room to watch a football game while Lillian conducted a tour of the house for Katherine. Charlie brought down one of his games and he and Stacey set up shop on the dining room table.

Almost without anyone noticing, Roly-Poly got up, stretched, and came over to the couch that Harlan was sitting on. He slowly oozed upward and ended up lying on the couch with his head resting on Harlan's lap. Harlan gently stroked Roly-Poly's ears which immediately put him to sleep.

Ryan went back to the university and the kids went back to school. The regular routine took over and the normal life-cycle of parents and kids resumed.

As Christmas approached, Lillian went crazy shopping with Morgan for just the right cardigan sweater for Ryan. It couldn't be too heavy, but of course, not too light. Then, there was the color. Ryan's favorite color was dark green and this year most all sweaters were in mauve, brown, red, or grey. They found one that was close to the right color at a shop at the mall, but after looking at other stores, when they came back to buy it, it was gone. Morgan was devastated.

Finally, Morgan found just what she was looking for on the main street of town in a little women's clothing boutique. It was on a male mannequin that was being used in a display. But, after some fast talking and the right amount of cash, Lillian was able to convince the owner to sell it.

Winter bloomed in full fury. The temperature dropped below zero and stayed in a bitter deep-freeze for two weeks on end. Then, it warmed up and snowed. It snowed and snowed again. On December 23rd it finally stopped with a record accumulation of 17 inches. The temperature then plummeted again.

Ryan came home from the university on the 20th and didn't have to be back for almost two weeks. He spent most of his time at Morgan's or he and she went shopping or to the movies.

On Christmas Eve both families went to church together. Stacey sang in the choir and even had a small solo which brought tears to Benjamin's eyes.

Afterward, they all went to Benjamin and Katherine's house for sandwiches and cake while the kids opened each other's presents. Ryan loved his sweater and immediately put it on. Morgan then opened her gift from him. Whether by happenstance or fate, he had bought her a beautiful maroon and brown sweater. He helped her put it on.

"Think of me with my arms around you," he whispered into her ear. "Every time you wear it."

It brought tears to Morgan's eyes.

Charlie gave Roly-Poly a new tennis ball which was a great hit. Roly-Poly wanted to play ball right away, but was relegated to lay on the floor and just chew it. He was fine with that and spent a long time chomping first on the right side of his mouth and then the left.

After dishes were done and put away, Lillian said it was time for them to go. Harlan helped her get her coat on while Charlie whined and said that he wanted to stay just a little longer. Karen wanted to go home so she could call Jason. Ryan said he would bring Morgan home, but they wanted to drive through the park and see the Christmas displays.

It was about 11:30 when Ryan drove into the Carter driveway. The two evergreens on each side of the porch were dressed in colored lights and the small overhead light by the front door was on. Ryan held Morgan's arm as they walked towards the door.

They stood close together facing each other in the bitter cold for a few minutes. Ryan's arms held Morgan and she loved the warmth and secure feeling she felt.

For some reason, she looked up into Ryan's eyes. She could feel his breath on her face. They were inches apart.

CHAPTER NINE
Time Moves Along

Their lips met. They had kissed before, but they were always just short and quick. This kiss was long and passionate. Morgan put her hands around Ryan's neck and pulled him down to her and nature guided her to press her body even closer to his.

The kiss seemed to go on and Morgan wanted it to last forever. She never wanted it to stop. Her heart pounded and her breath came in short gasps. Finally, Ryan's lips moved a few inches away from hers.

"Morgan," he whispered.

"Hmmm?" she murmured.

Her eyes were still shut and she was still basking in the afterglow of the kiss. Even though her nose was running, she noticed the warm, glowing fragrance of Ryan's coat. She could hear his heart beating as her head laid on his chest.

"I love you, Morgan," Ryan's voice said.

"Oh, … me, too, … Ryan. … Me, too."

Ryan went back to the university and the kids went back to school. Life got back to normal. Normal for the adults, at least.

Easter came along with spring-break. Ryan came home and Morgan was ecstatic. They spent almost all their waking hours together. But, as with most things, time moved along. They all went back to school and resumed their lives in academia.

Karen graduated and her graduation party was a terrific success. She had been accepted at the University of Colorado and planned to study geology. She also 'graduated' from Jason, much to the happiness of her parents.

Summer brought many hot days. Ryan worked full-time for the lumber yard and Morgan's job at the library expanded to a full, 40 hour workweek. But, it wasn't all work. Ryan and Morgan spent most evenings and weekends together. They went to the movies, tanned at the beach of a lake nearby, and went to church on Sunday along with both of their families.

Late summer finally called for the return to school. Morgan was now a senior at Oakwood Heights High. Ryan went back to school in Madison to start his sophomore year. Karen drove out to Colorado to start school out there. Both Stacey and Charlie started 6th grade.

Morgan's schedule was jammed full. She not only took honors classes, but soon became involved in virtually every extra-curricular activity she could possibly fit in. Her job at the library reverted back to Friday evening and all day Saturday. She was the editor of the school newspaper, one of the school photographers, a member of the Acapella group, and a member of the drama club. She even had a small part in the class play.

Lillian watched and worried about Morgan. She was a little afraid she had taken on too much. Whenever she was at home she spent studying, except Sunday afternoon when she talked to Ryan on the phone.

The winter had been fairly mild, but one afternoon in early January the temperature plummeted. Lillian fixed chili for supper and the family seemed to all enjoy the warmth of it on such a cold evening.

Lillian finished putting the dishes into the dishwasher, wiped the counter, and stovetop. She walked towards the family room and noticed that Harlan was watching television and laughing at the sitcom that was playing. Charlie was doing his homework on the kitchen counter. Everything seemed in order, except, where was Morgan?

Lillian made her way up the stairs and noticed that Morgan's door was ajar, so she tapped lightly on it and walked in.

There, leaning against the window, Morgan stood staring at nothing except the cold, dark landscape outside.

"You okay?"

Morgan didn't move or even to seem to realize her mother was talking to her.

"Morgan? Are you alright?"

Then Lillian noticed tears streaming down her daughter's cheeks.

"Oh, honey," she said, came over to Morgan, and took her into her arms. "What's the matter?"

Morgan started to sob and Lillian held her daughter. She just let her cry and didn't say anything.

Lillian suspicions turned on. Morgan got a letter from Ryan today and maybe it wasn't good. Maybe Ryan had found someone else at school.

"Is it something about Ryan?"

Morgan shook her head that it was.

"Is he seeing someone else?"

Morgan shook her head violently no.

"I ... miss ... him, ... Mom," Morgan sobbed.

"Oh, honey. I know. Your first love can be awful sometimes. Come on over here and sit on your bed. Here's a Kleenex."

Morgan sat down. Her face was red from crying and her nose was running. She blew her nose. She still made little honking sounds as she tried to keep from crying again.

"My first love happened when I was in high school. Just like you."

Morgan looked up with tear-soaked eyes.

"You ... mean ... it wasn't ... Dad?"

"No, honey," Lillian smiled and reached out for Morgan's hands. "As unbelievable as it may all seem, I was in love before him.

"His name was Roger Lewis. He was a senior and I was a junior. I had a huge crush on him, but he never paid any attention to me at all. Roger had the reputation of being a "bad boy," but no one ever seemed to know just why.

"One day in English class, we were assigned to write team papers and fate was with me. Roger was paired up with me. I was so excited I couldn't breath. Well, we met after school at the library and worked diligently. Or, at least he did. I mostly just sat and stared at him whenever I could.

"Sadly, it was all business. When our paper was finished and handed in, things went back to the way they were. I was heartbroken.

"Then, one morning right after math class, I had just opened my locker to change books when Roger came by. I hoped he couldn't hear my heart pound."

Morgan laughed a little. It all seemed funny to hear her mother talk about some boyfriend. Especially, when it wasn't her husband. It had never occurred to Morgan that her parents were young once, too, and had all the trials and tribulations she was going through.

"What ... did this ... Roger ...want?"

"Well, he asked me to go to a movie.

"I can't begin to tell you how shocked your grandparents were," Lillian laughed when she remembered the story. "Roger drove up the driveway on a motorcycle."

Morgan had stopped crying and was intrigued with her mother's confession. She wondered if her dad ever knew about Roger.

"My dad was furious. My mother absolutely forbid me to even go outside, but I did it anyway. I rushed out the door and in a flurry swung my leg over the back of the motorcycle and off we went."

Lillian left out the part of how the wind made her dress fly up around her waist and how she desperately worked at keeping it in place. It was a real fight. She almost needed both hands to keep her dress down, but she wanted to use both hands to hold on to Roger's waist. What a dilemma it was, but it solved itself because he soon drove into a parking lot by the theater and stopped.

"Funny. I can't even remember what the name of the movie was.

"After the show Roger took me to real "hangout" for burgers. It was kind of a bar I guess. I remember some real scruffy looking guys playing pool and there were some people sitting at the bar. Roger seemed to know most of them.

"When I got home both my mother and dad were waiting up for me, and boy, did they read me the 'riot act.' I was grounded for a month."

Morgan laughed and snuggled against her mother's right arm.

Lillian also left out the parts about how she sneaked out her bedroom window during the month she was grounded to go out with Roger.

"The funny thing was, though. He was always a perfect gentleman.

"We dated some after that and my parents even, let's say learned to tolerate Roger.

"I was madly in love with him, honey. He was my first love and my world revolved around being with him all that I could. I wrote his name all over everywhere- on my notebook and on my papers. All I could think about was Roger.

"Then, our dates became less and less frequent. I was heartbroken. My best friend told me that she had seen Roger with another girl. I couldn't believe it. I was crushed. My mother tried to get me to tell her what was wrong, but I couldn't. My world had come to an end. And, I was only a junior in high school.

"Roger was really a nice guy. He never made promises he couldn't keep and told me to never expect anything else.

"I didn't want to go back to school. I just wanted to crawl into a hole and be covered up. I wanted to die.

"It all sounds silly now, but it was so intense then, it was all that mattered."

"Did ... you ever ... see ... Roger ... after that?"

"Oh, sure. I'd see him at school sometimes, but, never to talk to him."

"What ... happened ... to him, Mom?"

"He graduated and then went into the Army. I graduated the next year and went on to college where I met the most wonderful person in the world, your father."

Lillian also left out the part that it was almost three years between Roger and Harlan. It wasn't that she had become a nun during those years at all. She dated now and then, but never anything serious.

"At first, your father and I were just friends. Then, we became really good friends. We fell in love and now, he's my 'knight in shining armor.'"

"Kind of ... like ... Ryan ... and me."

"Yes, honey. Sort of."

Lillian hugged her daughter and hoped she felt better. She had never divulged the story about Roger to anyone before. Not even to her own sister, or her best friend. Somehow, telling her hurting daughter made it all seem right.

"I know it all seems really hard right now. I also know how it is to be in love. In love with your first love."

Lillian put her arm around Morgan.

"Ryan may be the right one, honey, but it may not work out. I know that's not what you want to have happen, but sometimes even the best things just don't work out over time.

"It probably seems like an eternity to you right now, before you and Ryan can be together, but sometimes things just aren't meant to be. You are so young, honey. And, I know that's the last thing you want to hear from me. But, I can tell you from my own experience, that life goes on and most always for the better. Why, you may find someone else when you go to college next year."

Morgan shook her head no.

"I will … never … ever … find anyone … like … Ryan."

"No, of course not, Morgan. No one can ever replace anyone. Each person is completely different, and that's the way it should be."

Lillian stood up and held out her hand towards Morgan.

"Come on, honey. Let's get your face washed and go down and watch television with your dad for a little while. Charlie is almost done with his homework and I heard him say he wanted some popcorn when he finished."

"Thanks, … Mom."

Lillian smiled and knew that tonight when she was in bed, she would go back and remember all those things about Roger Lewis that were such 'life or death' issues she faced so long ago.

She was thankful that she had been able to talk to Morgan tonight. She knew, firsthand, the sharp edge of first love and really understood how Morgan felt. But, this was a great opportunity to make her aware that while it all seemed so perfect right now, time had a way to make a person realize how big the world really was. Although, not without the bumps and heartaches that happen along the way. At least she opened the door for Morgan. Just in case things didn't work out with Ryan, maybe it wouldn't be so earth-shattering to her daughter, as it was when it happened to her.

CHAPTER TEN
Graduation

Morgan continued her hectic pace right up until graduation. She achieved the highest grade-point average in her class. She was appropriately appointed *Valedictorian* which meant she had to make a speech during the graduation exercises.

Graduation morning was a whirlwind of countless things to do and worry about. Morgan had practiced her speech until she could recite it from memory. Karen arrived from Colorado two days earlier and Ryan got home yesterday.

The band played the traditional graduation march as the soon-to-be graduates filed into the gymnasium. This year's graduating class was smaller than Karen's last year's class and considerably smaller than Ryan's class, so there was plenty of room for parents, grandparents, relatives, and lots of friends to attend. Even Ryan's parents and Stacey were invited.

"Superintendent Oglby," Principal Smith said into the microphone. "Faculty, graduates, families, and friends, I would like to introduce the 1967 graduating class of Oakwood Heights High School."

The auditorium exploded with applause.

Speeches were given and finally it was time for the *Valedictorian* to address the class. Morgan was introduced by the school district's superintendent and everyone leaped from their seats and gave thunderous applause for her and chanted, "Morgan, Morgan, Morgan."

Everyone cheered, except one person. Oh, she stood all right so she wouldn't be noticed, but only lightly clapped. She was Miss Anderson. She was the one that gave Morgan her lowest grade- an A-. She internally scoffed at the idea that someone as handicapped as this girl was allowed to attend high school along with normal kids completely went against her principles, and, not only that, but she was *Valedictorian*, too. She began to wonder if the educational system was becoming a complete travesty.

"Everyone, please welcome the 1967 *Valedictorian*, Miss Morgan Carter."

The applause again cascaded throughout the whole building.

Morgan's stomach churned a little as she heard her introduction. She stood and walked to the podium. Suddenly, it was like a wave of confidence washed over her. The auditorium quieted down and Morgan's captivating smile radiated brightly, touching virtually everyone in the audience.

"What ... a great ... opportunity ... it is ... for all of ... us ... to be here ... today. We ... look back ... over our ... accomplishments ... and look forward ... to ... making our ... influence known ... to the world."

There was more applause. Miss Anderson instead fumbled to reach her pocket under her gown to find a Kleenex. She softly blew her nose.

"If ... you want ... to see ... budding ... enthusiasm ... ready ... to make ... opportunities ... happen, ... just turn ... and look at ... your neighbor ... seated ... next to ... you."

People turned, nodded, and smiled at the person next to them.

"Our ... graduating class ... will ... succeed and ... make a ... difference ... in the ... world. Thank you."

The whole gymnasium exploded in pandemonium. Graduates hats flew towards the ceiling as if a huge flock of birds was suddenly released.

Order was regained and hats were passed back and forth seeking the right graduate's head. The superintendent rose and announced that the awarding of the diplomas was the last order of business.

Each graduate was called by name which was always followed by some applause by their families as they walked across the stage, shook hands with the superintendent, and received their diploma.

"Morgan Carter."

Again, the applause exploded into a deafening roar. It was almost like a huge thunderstorm had let loose with all the lightning and thunder at one time. People clapped, whistled, chanted, and screamed.

Tears poured down Harlan's cheeks as he added his deep, baritone voice to the noise.

Ryan screamed and shouted until he was hoarse.

After the ceremony was over the multitude of people all moved outside for congratulations, handshaking, and picture taking. Both Morgan's mother and Ryan's dad took lots of "Kodak moments."

Morgan's graduation party was absolutely huge. Her invitations read from two to four, but people started to arrive a little after noon and continued until almost seven in the evening. Invitation or not, more than half the high school showed up and certainly almost everyone from Morgan's graduating class. This mass of kids and adults coupled with relatives and friends of the family filled the Carter house and exhausted everything they had set up for the party. Ryan had to make three trips to the large supermarket for more. The party was a fantastic success.

Morgan's job at the library went back to full-time for the summer and Ryan worked at the lumberyard. They still had lots of time to spend together and often took Charlie and Stacey with them.
In the fall, Morgan enrolled at the state university, but at the smaller campus much closer to home. This meant she could live at home while she went to college.
Secretly, Harlan had hoped that at least one of his girls would go to Northwestern where he went to school, but it wasn't to be.

Summer ended and Ryan went back to the university in Madison as a junior, Karen went back to Colorado, and Morgan started her first year of college.
Life got back to normal and regular routines formed in each person's life.
The year flew by and again, summer came with a vengeance. The temperature soared and stayed in the middle nineties for days on end. Ryan worked at the lumberyard, but the high heat made it brutal. He was thin by nature and genetics, but the high heat caused him to lose even a few more pounds. His mother quietly worried about him.

Fall came and the heat cycles snapped. Instead of the usual moderate temperatures and beautiful blue skies of autumn, the heavens opened up and rain poured down. Instead of the usual brilliant fall colors that everyone enjoyed along with the pungent smell of smoky burning leaves, the trees were bare, washed naked by the cold almost constant rain. Morgan was now a sophomore and Ryan was a senior.

"Let's have a glass of wine," Lillian said one evening after dinner as she reached for the bottle on the coffee table.

Harlan held up a glass and smiled.

"It seems like only yesterday that our house was full of kids and hustle and bustle. Now, it's so silent, it almost scares me."

"Hey," Charlie turned and called out from the dining room table. "I still make lots of noise."

Lillian and Harlan were both unaware that their son was listening, rather than working on a model airplane, or was even there for that matter.

"Maybe we should think about selling the house and moving into something smaller," Lillian murmured as she curled back up on the couch beside her husband and leaned her head on his shoulder.

"Maybe we should," he responded but didn't want to even contemplate the problems of selling and moving to another house.

Secretly, Lillian didn't want to move either. She was just making conversation. Conversation about a topic her husband wasn't adding much fuel to. She hoped Karen would find someone after she graduated next year, get married, and live not too far away. She let her mind explore a little further and hoped a little, no, even felt a little pang of longing as she wondered how it would be to hold and love a grandbaby.

In mid-April the university held a job-fair for prospective graduates on Wednesday afternoon. Ryan decided to attend. There were lots of large corporations represented along with some smaller companies and research groups.

"Hi. Welcome to General Turbine Corporation," a middle-aged man said as he came over to greet Ryan. "I'm Bill Gillison, vice-president of personnel."

"Ryan Wakefield."

"Where are you from?"

"Oakwood Heights, Wisconsin."

"You're graduating in May, Ryan?"

"Hope so."

"What's your major?"

"Double. Math and management."

"Impressive. How about your GPA?"

"3.85 on a 4 scale," Ryan almost whispered and his face tinged a little red. Even though he knew he should be proud of his achievements, it always sounded like bragging to him.

"Well, Ryan Wakefield. I can tell you that we're interested in you."

Bill Gillison gathered lots of information about General Turbine and handed it to Ryan.

"We're located just outside of Chicago. That's not too far from your hometown."

Ryan nodded and smiled. He took the materials handed to him and added them to the stack he had collected from other companies.

"I know you're probably going to visit all the booths here, Ryan. But, let me warn you. Be careful. Some companies will offer just about anything to recruit you. But, once they've got you, reality will set in. Their real offer won't be anything like what they tell you at first.

"Our company is not like that at all. We're straight forward in all respects. It won't do us much good if you come with us and then find out it was a big mistake.

"I'm here to find some really good managers and engineers, and you look like you could fit into either category.

"How about if you meet me for dinner tonight? I'll bring along one of our managers so the two of us can get to know you better."

Ryan agreed and it was decided that he would meet them at the Bull Terrier's Steakhouse at seven.

The very next booth was Helorn Electronics from Los Angeles. Their representative was John Baldwin and after a little conversation, it was clear he, too was interested in Ryan.

"What's your schedule, Ryan? Are you free for dinner tonight?"

"Can't tonight," Ryan said smiling to himself as he remembered how difficult it was to convince Mr. Phillips, the owner of the lumberyard, a couple of years ago how badly he wanted a part-time job. "Tomorrow night looks good, though."

"Fine, Ryan."

It was agreed that they would meet at an upscale Italian restaurant at seven tomorrow evening.

Both dinner meetings produced the same outcome. Ryan was invited to visit each company in the near future; all expenses paid, of course. Both representatives also knew how competitive it was to get good candidates and were ready to do whatever it took to give them the competitive edge.

Ryan couldn't wait to tell Morgan. He knew that she worked until nine on Friday and that he usually called her on Sunday afternoon, but this couldn't wait.

"Hello, Mr. Carter," Ryan said into the phone. "I know it's pretty late to be calling, but is Morgan home from the library yet?"

Morgan picked up the phone and Ryan told her about the two job offers.

She was happy about anything that made Ryan happy, but inside felt a little forlorn. Both jobs would take Ryan away from her, and one all the way to California.

During Friday of the next week Ryan drove to General Turbine in Chicago. Bill Gillison offered to make airline reservations for him, but Ryan said he would rather drive. He met a number of the key executives, all the way from the CEO down to some of the plant supervisors.

Later, he was taken out for dinner by Bill Gillison and two other vice-presidents in the restaurant of the hotel where they had booked a room for Ryan to stay the night. After dinner they sat at the table and talked. Ryan was given a formal offer. When he opened the folder he was shocked by the amount of the annual salary.

"I'll need to read this material over very carefully and then talk to the important people in my life," Ryan said and closed the folder. "You've been most gracious bringing me down here and taking time out of many people's busy schedules. I really appreciate it all."

Bill Gillison had recruited many new college graduates in his career and knew the importance of closing the deal as early as possible. He had hoped that his company's offer was good enough to convince Ryan to sign on. He also knew that Ryan possibly had interviews with other companies, so the quicker he could get him to agree, the less chance they had of losing him.

"Yes, Ryan," Bill fished a little. "I'm sure it is important to talk it over with your parents. But, wouldn't it end up being your decision in the end anyway?"

"Well, yes. I suppose," Ryan stammered. "But, there's…"

"Ah," Bill said and smiled slightly. "There's a special someone, is there?"

"Yes."

"Well, Ryan. We certainly understand. But, how about if you give us a tentative yes now and then call your special person from your hotel room later this evening and discuss it with her. I'm sure when you tell her about our salary offer and benefits, she will be delighted."

Bill's intuition told him that he was very close to reeling Ryan in.

"I really need a few days," Ryan held firm.

Now Bill smelled a competing company and his senses told him that if he pressed Ryan much further, he might lose him all together.

"How long do you think you might need," Bill asked and leaned back in the restaurant's dark green leather chair.

"Well, Mr. Gillison, I really hate to put you off, but this will be one of the biggest decisions of my life and, actually I didn't expect you to make an actual offer so soon. Plus, with finals and graduation coming up soon, I've got lots to do. I know this sounds pushy, but would it be alright if I called you in two weeks?"

"Ah, Ryan. Most grads we recruit sign on right away, but I respect your request to closely examine our offer. Now, if your lady has any questions about living down here in Chicago, let me know right away and I'll arrange for her to come down here for a tour."

Bill knew from lots of experience that the woman in a man's life had great influence over his career choice and geographic location. Sometimes even to the detriment. But, he also knew that if Ryan's special person would come down to Chicago, he would bring the full force of his company's capability to woo her.

It was agreed. Ryan stood and shook hands with his three hosts and bid them goodnight. He went up to his hotel room to immediately call Morgan.

"Well, Bill," one of the vice-presidents said. "Do you think we've got him?"

"I'm not sure. He'll certainly be a great catch, if we can get him. Wished I would have thought to invite his girlfriend to come along, though. It never occurred to me. I must be getting old."

"You think he's evaluating other offers?'

"Might be. But, I think if we give him a little breathing room, it might just do the trick. I don't think any company will match our salary offer."

The three men continued talking and worked out their strategy to counter any offers Ryan might get from other companies.

"I want that kid," Ronald Miller, vice-president of operations said. "Maybe we should've made the offer higher."

Monday morning came and Ryan had finals in his two hardest classes. Much to his surprise, they were both straightforward and fairly easy, so he was pretty sure had did pretty well on them. Tuesday brought two more tests and, to his relief, much easier than his Monday's exams. His fifth class didn't require a final, so all his class work was pretty much done.

Ryan was so excited he could hardly sleep. He had never been to California and could hardly believe he was actually going. The best part was that someone else was paying for his trip. He got up early Wednesday morning and quickly got ready to go. One of his classmates had a car and drove him to the airport before six. His flight was on Braniff Airlines on one of their new, colorful Boeing 707s. Ryan had never flown before and was very excited to get going. His flight was to depart at seven o'clock with an intermediate stop in Denver and arrive in Los Angeles at 10:31 a.m. local California time.

When it was time to board Ryan waited anxiously in line. He tried to act calm, like most of the people nearby, but inside his stomach was in turmoil. Finally, he stepped aboard and showed his ticket to the woman dressed in a pretty spectacular orange uniform. She smiled and told him how to find his seat. He made his way down the rather narrow aisle and was surprised at how beautiful and modern everything was. He found the row his ticket indicated and his assigned window seat.

Ryan moved into the seat by the window, sat down, and fumbled with the seatbelt. He finally got it locked together and leaned forward to look out the window while more passengers continued to board.

"Hello," a young, female voice said.

Ryan turned and was face to face with a very pretty, young woman. She sat down in the seat next to him and struggled with the seatbelt just like he had.

"I had trouble with the belt, too. Here, let me show you."

"Thanks. I've never been on an airplane before and I'm afraid it really shows."

"This is my first one, too." Ryan admitted. "But, I've heard that airline travel is very safe."

"I've heard that, too. Still, it's all pretty scary business."

A door shut somewhere and a soft, low whistle sound slowly grew in pitch and got steadily louder.

"My name is Nicole, but everyone calls me Nikki," the young woman said and held out her right hand.

"Mine's Ryan."

"Do you live in California?"

"Nope. I live here in Wisconsin. I'm graduating from college soon and am going out to Los Angeles on a job interview."

"Wow. That's pretty cool. I'm a junior and sure hope I get some good offers when I graduate."

"Do your parents live in California?"

"No. My aunt lives outside of Los Angeles and invited me to come out and spend a few weeks with her. I finished my last final yesterday afternoon, so here I am."

Ryan and Nikki talked like old friends which made the time go by quickly. They enjoyed the lunch that was served. Ryan found out that the women dressed in the orange and brown uniforms were called hostesses or stewardesses.

When they got off the plane in Los Angeles Nikki's aunt came rushing up to meet her. She waved goodbye to Ryan and walked away towards the baggage claim area.

Ryan looked around and then saw a man holding a sign that said "Wakefield" on it. It was John Baldwin.

"Hello, Ryan. How was your flight?"

They talked as they walked through the endless galleries and hallways until they finally came out into a huge parking garage. John led the way to his car.

"It's about an hour's drive to the plant," John said as he rapidly accelerated and merged into traffic on the freeway.

Ryan was bewildered. He, of course, knew what freeways and toll ways were and had even driven on them a few times near Milwaukee. But, these were different. There was so much traffic and there were so many roads it almost looked like spaghetti.

"Traffic is pretty light this morning," John said as he looked into his rearview mirror, quickly moved over into the left-most lane, and sped up.

Ryan noticed that they were going over eighty miles per hour and seemed to be just keeping up with traffic.

John chatted all the time asking Ryan about college, his interests, parents, and anything else that came to mind. Ryan's counselor had told him to play it close to his chest during these interviews and not tell them very much about his personal life.

John turned off on an exit ramp and slowed down. As they drove along, Ryan noticed that they were in a very upscale industrial park with most of the buildings made out of chromed steel and dark glass. There were many fountains and palm trees which made it look like each company was trying to outdo the other.

"Well, Ryan. Here we are," John said as he drove into a huge parking lot.

When they went through the main doors Ryan had to remind himself to keep his mouth shut and not gawk. The ceiling went up four floors. The walls were tinted glass and the floor was white marble. The whole ultra-modern motif was softened by plants everywhere.

They came to the guard station and John pushed his badge into a reader and the door unlocked.

"Our first stop is for you to meet the CEO of our company, Kent Ubans."

The elevator doors opened and once again Ryan was shocked. They faced an office suite that looked more like an apartment he had seen on television that millionaires live in.

"Good morning, Mrs. Collins," John said to the woman sitting behind a beautiful mahogany desk as they walked across the plush dark blue carpet. "We're here for our appointment with Mr. Ubans."

The woman was probably in her early thirties. She had dark brown hair that was perfectly done and dark brown eyes. She wore a tan blazer and looked like something that stepped right out of a fashion magazine. She smiled slightly to acknowledge they were expected, picked up the phone, and spoke softly into the receiver.

"You may go right in. Mr. Ubans is expecting you."

They walked into an office suite that made Ryan blink his eyes. One whole wall was glass. The room was spacious and airy with a high ceiling. Ryan scanned around and decided this one office was bigger than his parents' whole house. The office was decorated with what looked like very expensive antique furniture and accessories.

"Well, well, well," a small, thin, bald man said as he stood up and came out from behind his huge desk. "You must be Ryan. I've heard a lot of good things about you."

Ubans held out his hand and shook Ryan's hand. He was warm and friendly and ushered them all over to a table by the glass wall and told them to sit down so they could talk a little while.

"John, here, sure speaks highly of you. I've reviewed your course selection, transcript, and grade-point, and, Ryan, I must say, I'm impressed, too."

Ryan smiled a little and hoped his nervousness didn't show too much.

Ubans began a short history of Helorn Electronics. He was a master of human engineering and detected that Ryan seemed a little uneasy, although listening very intently.

"Ryan. One thing, here at Helorn. We all dress and act pretty casually out here in California. Why don't you take off that necktie? I think you will feel a little more at ease."

Ryan suddenly noticed that neither Ubans nor Baldwin wore neckties.

Ubans continued to talk about the products that Helorn made and that their main customer was the United States military. He talked about the numerous plants and facilities they had, which were located world-wide.

"We deal in very secret things, Ryan," Ubans said as he stood up. "Now, John will take you on a plant tour and show you around. We will all meet at the restaurant tonight at seven which is located in the hotel where you'll be staying."

Ubans stood up, so did Ryan and John. He reached out and shook Ryan's hand again.

John led the way out of the CEO's office, down the elevator, and out into the massive lobby. He motioned to a guard who disappeared for a few minutes, but returned just outside with an electric-powered vehicle.

"The plant is over that way," John pointed. "Little too far to walk."

Ryan enjoyed the ride and loved the soft, fragrant air of southern California.

The plant tour was interesting, but Ryan wasn't allowed to see very much because he didn't have the proper security clearance. Still, he enjoyed seeing the ultra-clean and modern factory and all its 'state-of-the-art' equipment.

It was about 5:30 when the tour was over. John drove Ryan to the hotel and told him they would meet at the restaurant at seven.

Ryan went up to his room and took a leisurely shower and tried to relax a little before getting dressed for dinner.

Promptly at seven, Ryan came up to the *maitre d'*.

"May I help you, sir?" the man dressed in a black tuxedo asked.

"I'm here to meet with a party from Helorn Electronics."

"Yes, sir. Right this way."

"Hi, Ryan," John Baldwin said as he stood up. "You remember Mr. Ubans, of course, and this is Arnold Snyder, our chief financial officer."

Ryan shook hands and sat down. Drinks were ordered. Ryan ordered iced tea. Ubans lead the conversation and talked about everything from professional sports to the political situation. He easily worked Ryan into the conversation.

They ordered dinner from a menu that had no prices. Ryan was confused and watched to see what the others ordered. He decided on baked cod.

Dinner came and was served with great elegance. Each dish had been very artistically prepared and, at first, Ryan thought they were too pretty to touch. But, when he saw the others dig in, he put 'art' aside and tasted his very unusual salad.

The baked cod was served and Ryan decided it was the best he had ever tasted.

The conversation was lively with lots of stories and jokes. Ryan liked everyone, but thought that Mr. Ubans was especially nice.

"They make a special dessert here, Ryan. They're famous for it. It's a concoction of chocolate cake, ice cream, and special sauces. Anyone that comes here has to try it."

Ryan agreed and Ubans ordered it for the whole table.

A waiter rolled a cart up to the table and a chef with a white hat came out and prepared the dessert right in front of them. When it was served, it was delightful to look at, but spectacular to taste.

"Now, Ryan," Ubans said as he pushed his plate aside. "I've had John and Arnold prepare a folder for you with an offer. We want you to come and work for us, young man."

Mr. Ubans smiled and pushed a magenta notebook over to Ryan with the Helorn logo embossed in gold on the cover.

"I think you'll have to agree that our salary offer will be considerably higher than other offers you may have received. We always try to hire the top people and are prepared to pay for it."

Ryan opened the notebook and was shocked to see the salary offer that was printed in bold numbers.

"But, there's more to life than money, Ryan," Ubans continued. "We feel that education is the key to all of our futures and success. We encourage our people to get advanced degrees. Naturally, our company will pay all expenses. But, there's more. We will pay half of any tuition, books, and fees for your spouse to continue her education."

Ryan was overwhelmed. Even though he thought the first offer he received in Chicago was way beyond his wildest hope, this offer was almost pure fiction.

"Well, son," Ubans smiled and sat back in his chair. "What do you think? Do we have a deal?"

Ryan hesitated. Sweat trickled down his back. Time seemed to stand still for a while.

"I'll need a little time to digest it all, Mr. Ubans. Your offer is very generous, but I want to look at all aspects."

Ubans knew not to press for closure. Too much pressure and he knew from experience that Ryan might bail.

"I understand, Ryan. It's a mighty big decision. How long will you need to think it over?"

"Maybe a week," Ryan said in a voice stronger than he had anticipated using.

"Well, that's quite a while," Ubans said and then fished a little. "Who else do you want to discuss our offer with?"

"Oh, my parents, and …" Ryan said, but quickly caught himself and remembered what his counselor had told him about giving out too much information.

Ubans' keen sense detected that Ryan had a girlfriend and wished he had known that earlier. He would have insisted that she come out with Ryan. He would have had his secretary spend the day with her and dazzle her with southern California and its advantages.

"I understand, Ryan. You analyze our offer and discuss it with those that are important in your life. Then, give John a call as soon as you reach a decision."

Ryan agreed and Mr. Ubans quickly led the conversation to a movie he had just seen. Arnold paid the bill and they all walked out into the lobby of the hotel.

Ubans came over and shook Ryan's hand.

"I'm really impressed with you, Ryan. Now, if you have other offers or an interview with another company coming up, please let us know what they are. Maybe we can make some adjustments in our offer, in case we are not quite competitive enough."

Ryan smiled and told Mr. Ubans he would carefully study everything.

"I think we've got him," John said as he held the door open for Mr. Ubans.

"Don't be too sure, John. Don't be too sure."

Ryan got up early and was waiting in the lobby when John arrived.

"Morning, Ryan," John said as he came into the lobby. "All set to go?"

Ryan said that he was ready and followed John out to his car.

"Looks like another nice day in paradise," John smiled as he started the motor. "Paradise except for a little smog, that is."

The trip from the hotel to the airport only took about twenty minutes and John chatted constantly. He pulled up to the departure doorways and stopped.

"Well, Ryan," John smiled and reached out his hand to Ryan. "Guess I'd better wish you a safe trip home. I can't stop out here for long or the cops will give me a ticket."

Ryan opened the door and got out. He thanked John for the trip and especially for the generous offer. He told him he would get back to him as soon as he possibly could.

He checked in at the ticket counter and walked leisurely out to the appropriate gate. He had lots of time as the flight was not due to board for another 45 minutes. He walked around and looked out the huge glass windows at the sleek jets moving around outside.

Ryan's flight was called and he walked to the gate. There were very few passengers that boarded. This was a direct flight to Chicago so the stewardess told him he could sit anywhere he wanted. He decided to sit in the very first row, right behind the first class section.

The big jet lifted into the sky at 8:31 a.m., right on time. The flight was smooth and uneventful, plus with very few passengers to take care of, one of the stewardesses sat and talked with Ryan for a little while.

They were twelve minutes early getting into Chicago so Ryan had almost and hour and a half to wait for his flight back home which was on a much smaller, two-engine propeller airplane that held about forty people.

Almost every seat was taken. The ride was fairly bumpy, but the flying time was only a little under an hour, so it wasn't too bad.

Finally, Ryan got off the airplane and came into the terminal building where his mother, father, and little sister were waiting for him.

"Ryan!" Stacey screamed as she ran to him and threw her arms around him. He hugged her back.

On the ride home, Ryan and Stacey sat in the backseat. He told them about California.

"Did you see any movie stars?" Stacey asked hoping that he had.

Ryan told her that he hadn't seen anyone famous that he knew of, but maybe there were some that he didn't know. That seemed to satisfy Stacey for the time being.

"Dad," Ryan said as he got out of the car. "I've got both job offers here and would appreciate it if you would look them over and tell me what you think about them."

Benjamin smiled and said he would be glad to.

They went into the house and Benjamin sat down in his big chair to read the two job offers. Ryan went into the dining room to call Morgan.

"Both look mighty lucrative, son," Benjamin said as he handed the two proposals to Ryan. "The one from California looks especially good. It appears to me like they're ready to promise you the moon. But, here's what I think. I think you should have Harlan look them over and give his opinion. He is a pretty accomplished lawyer, you know."

Ryan drove to Morgan's house and knocked on the door. The door flew open and he was greeted with an explosion of shouts and hugs by Morgan.

"I've ... missed ... you," Morgan said as she hugged him tightly.

"I've missed you more."

Morgan shook her head that there was no way he missed her more than she missed him.

"Hi, Ryan," Harlan said as he looked up from his newspaper. "How was California?"

"It was a great trip. I was wondering if you would mind looking over my two job offers and tell me what you think about them."

"Sure, Ryan. I'll take them into the library and have a look."

Lillian came into the family room and talked to Ryan about his trip to Chicago and then the one to Los Angeles.

"Isn't there anything closer around here, Ryan?" Lillian asked. "Seems like our companies must need good people too, you know."

"Well, Ryan, my boy," Harlan said as he came back into the family room. "Both of these offers are pretty spectacular. I especially think the one in Los Angeles hinges on being fantastic."

Harlan didn't go any further when he noticed the frown on his wife's face.

"Maybe you and I can talk more in depth about each one later on."

"Oh, and by the way," Ryan said. "I would like to invite all of you out for supper tomorrow night. It'll be all of you and my family, too. I've made reservations at the Red Rooster at six. Will that be alright with all of you?"

"You bet it is," Charlie shouted from the kitchen. "Is Stacey going?"

They all laughed and Ryan told Charlie that she would be coming, too.

"What's the occasion?" Harlan asked after he saw that he was supposed to from the look on his wife's face.

"Just want us all to get together and have a real nice time," Ryan said with a big smile.

It was agreed that six o'clock tomorrow night at the Red Rooster would be just fine for everyone.

Ryan and Morgan sat down on the couch to watch television. Harlan went out to the kitchen to get a soft drink and Lillian came up along side him when he had the refrigerator door open.

"Know what I think?" Lillian said with a suspicious frown and Harlan knew she was about to tell him without him asking. "I think he's setting us all up to drop the California bomb on us."

"Now, Lillian," Harlan said as he put his arms around his fretting wife. "We don't know that at all. Let's not get upset over something that's beyond our control."

"Well, you didn't have to say that you thought the California deal was so terrific."

"Didn't much matter what I think about it, Lillian. But, it really is a very lucrative offer."

Everyone arrived almost at the same time at the Red Rooster's parking lot. Ryan parked and went around to the passenger's side of his car to help Morgan get out. Benjamin drove in and parked next to Ryan and Harlan parked next to Benjamin. Even Karen was along. She had come home from Colorado in the morning. Stacey jumped out first.

"Hey, dumbbell," she shouted at Charlie. "Are they going to let someone as crude as you eat at a decent place like this?"

Charlie didn't miss a beat to tease back.

"Don't worry about me. I've heard you have to eat out in back with the dogs because you slobber so much."

Stacey punched Charlie's shoulder in a kidding soft hit.

"How come you didn't bring Roly-Poly along?"

They all went inside and were seated by the huge windows overlooking a manicured garden.

Drinks were ordered and everyone teased and laughed a lot after Ryan ordered a beer and Charlie said he would have one of those, too.

"You'd be on the floor if you even took a sip of one," Stacey teased.

Dinner was served with much elegance and fanfare. Each person remarked on how delicious their meal was. After everyone finished, the waiter came alongside the table with a dessert trolley. Making a selection was difficult because of the many choices.

Ryan whispered something in the waiter's ear. He smiled and quickly disappeared. When he returned he pushed another cart with a pan, bottles, and a little alcohol stove on top. He stopped right in front of Charlie and Stacey. The waiter lit the stove and heated the pan. He mixed a secret concoction of butter, brown sugar, and other special ingredients. He then sliced some fresh peaches into small slivers and put them into the pan. He poured some liquid out of one of the bottles into the pan, and a huge fire erupted. Stacey and Charlie sat mesmerized. After the flames had died down, the waiter scooped up some peaches and ladled some of the still flaming liquid on top He handed a plate to Stacey and one to Charlie.

"Hmmm," Stacey said as she carefully blew on her spoon and tasted the delectable concoction. "This is soooo good. What is this stuff, Mom?"

Katherine smiled and told her it was called *peaches flambé*.

"This would be time for a great cigar," Benjamin said to Harlan. "I hardly ever smoke, but after such a great meal, isn't it funny how a cigar would top it off just right?"

"Cigars stink," Stacey announced firmly with her arms crossed tightly against her chest.

"I've got some really good ones back at the house," Harlan said. "Why don't you all come back to our house for a while?"

Ryan took his spoon and clinked it on his water glass.

"Before we leave, could I have everyone's attention for a minute?"

They all turned and looked at Ryan who was standing. People at surrounding tables stopped talking and listened, too.

"First," Ryan continued. "I want to thank my mom and dad for everything they've done for me. They've always been there for me at every possible turn in the road. I just want you both to know how much I appreciate it."

Benjamin and Katherine were in shock. They both knew that Ryan had always been a very kind and considerate son, and that he always appreciated even little things. But, to actually hear him say the words was beyond touching. A tear streaked down Katherine's cheek.

"Here it comes," Lillian whispered into Harlan's ear. "He's going to California."

Harlan found Lillian's hand under the table and squeezed it to let her know he was there, as always, to support her.

"And, Harlan and Lillian, I want you both to know how much I appreciate all the things both of you have done for me. You've always been right there to talk and give advice, but more so, you've opened your hearts and accepted me into your family."

Now, it was Lillian's turn. Her heart opened up and tears streamed down her face. They were tears of happiness. She had come to almost love Ryan. In fact, she had often teased Morgan, that if she were younger and things were different, she would be out to get Ryan for herself. But, there were tears of sadness, too. She knew in her heart that they were all going to lose Ryan. He was about to announce that he had accepted the job in California and desperately hoped that Morgan wouldn't be crushed.

"Now, for the most important thing I've ever done in my life," Ryan said and put his hand into his pocket.

Lillian squeezed Harlan's hand so hard he thought she had cut off the circulation to it.

The whole room went quiet. Even the waiter stood and watched.

CHAPTER ELEVEN
The Restaurant Announcement

Ryan pulled his hand out of his pocket and sunk down on one knee in front of Morgan.

"Morgan? I think I've been in love with you from the first day I came to your house to be a tutor for one of your classes. Will you please marry me?"

The whole restaurant was silent. No one even seemed to breathe.

Ryan opened the little box he held which contained a diamond ring.

The words didn't make sense to Morgan for a few seconds. She just sat and stared. Then, almost as if something wiped away the clouds in her mind, like an eraser wiping a chalk board, her mind assembled the words and put meaning to them. Ryan stood up and Morgan leaped into his arms.

"Yes," she shouted. "Yes. Yes. Yes," and kissed him deeply.

Neither noticed that some of the people sitting at the surrounding tables started to clap and then the whole restaurant was applauding.

Morgan put the ring on and held up her hand so everyone could see it.

"Let me see that rock," Karen said as she came over and hugged her sister.

There was pandemonium everywhere. Everyone talked at the same time and the words just swarmed together in a huge fog in Lillian's mind. She was in absolute shock.

After paying the bill, Ryan and Morgan led the way to the parking lot. Karen asked to ride with Ryan and Morgan so she could catch up on everything that had led up to tonight's announcement. Stacey asked Charlie to ride with them, too.

Lillian was silent for a little while as Harlan started the engine and drove out of the parking lot.

"What in the world was Ryan thinking?" she mumbled so quietly that Harlan was not really sure whether he actually heard her or had somehow intercepted her thoughts.

Harlan didn't say anything and just kept driving.

"It can't happen," Lillian said firmly now with a much stronger voice.

Harlan was confused. He knew that Lillian liked Ryan a lot. She probably even loved him almost like her own son. He wondered what was causing her so much concern.

"We've got to stop it, Harlan."

"I don't think we have any say-so in the matter," Harlan said softly and held his concentration on the road ahead. "They're both of legal age, you know."

"But, what if Morgan gets pregnant? Did you ever think of that? She's not strong like other girls, you know. She's not like Karen. Remember what Dr. Haines told us when she was a little girl? He said that she would always be much more frail than other kids."

"Yes, Lillian. I remember. But, remember right after she was born and how tiny and frail she was?"

"Well, she was premature."

"I know. But, remember when we finally were able to bring her home? Dr. Haines advised against taking her home. He said she probably wouldn't live very long and it wouldn't be good if she happened to have problems where medical help wasn't right there. But, you were dead set against leaving her in the hospital and off we went with her."

"I am a nurse, you know. I could have done anything any of those people in the hospital could have."

"And, she did just fine. Remember when you realized that something was wrong when she didn't talk and didn't try to walk as quickly as Karen did? Dr. Haines diagnosed cerebral palsy and told you she probably would never be able to walk at all and would spend her life in a wheelchair. He also told you that she would never talk, either. But, she did both. And, she has done both very well. Then, remember when you met with the school board when it was time for her to start school? They wanted her in special education classes and you told them that she was as normal as any other kid, except she needed a little more time to get around. If you recall, my dear, when they balked, you had me threaten to file a lawsuit against them."

"Well, they needed it," Lillian said sharply remembering every detail about Morgan's struggles from birth until now. "But, this is different,

Harlan. Don't you see? Young couples have kids. We certainly did. Morgan's body could never carry a baby to term. She's just not strong enough."

Harlan continued to drive in silence for a little while formulating just how to tell Lillian something he knew.

"It's not a real problem, Lillian."

"Well, Mr. Magician. And, how do you know that? Accidents do happen, you know. We have Charlie to prove that. I don't care how good the birth control method is, they do fail sometimes."

Harlan smiled and reached out his hand to his fretting wife.

"He's had a vasectomy, Lillian. He can't make babies."

Lillian sat and digested the word.

"How in the world do you know that, Harlan?"

"Ryan told me when he was home during Christmas break. He went to a urologist near the campus and told him about Morgan and their plans to be married. Ryan, of course, was of legal age, so he had it done."

Lillian unbuckled her seatbelt, stood up on her knees, and hugged Harlan. She was now sobbing.

"Oh, Harlan," she cried. "I love them both so much. I now know for certain that God wants them to be together, no matter what."

Harlan loved being hugged, but finally told Lillian she had better get back into her seat and buckle her belt before they got pulled over by the police.

Lillian dried her eyes and sat quietly for a few seconds. Then, she suddenly sat straight up and faced Harlan.

"My God, Harlan. We've got a wedding to plan."

CHAPTER TWELVE
The First Attempt at Planning

Lillian called the church office and made an appointment for Morgan and her with Pastor Morris on Wednesday at 2:00 o'clock. Morgan had a half-day off on Wednesdays so Lillian told her that would give them time to have lunch first.

It was ten minutes to two when Lillian and Morgan arrived at the massive Church of the Divine Word and parked in the huge parking lot. Its membership was one of the largest in the whole area. The church itself was a tall building made of chrome and glass that seemed to reach for the sky. There were nine buildings in the complex and all were connected by glass walkways.

There weren't many cars in the lot so they were able to park fairly close to the office complex.

"Hello, Carolyn," Lillian said to the woman seated behind a beautiful deep red mahogany desk.

Carolyn Armstrong was Pastor Morris' secretary and was perfect for the job. She presented a perfect office image. She was about forty, had sparkly, light blue eyes, her hair was light brown, and coiffed perfectly. She wore a dark blue turtle-neck sweater accented with a small string of pearls. Carolyn always looked like she just stepped away from a photo fashion shot.

"Hello, Lillian. Hi, Morgan. Take a seat over there. The pastor should be ready to see you pretty soon."

Morgan smiled and sat down in the chair next to her mother.

Lillian and Carolyn were old friends. They grew up together and were friends all through school. They even went to college together. Both of their families were long-term members of the church. Carolyn and Lillian were active in church affairs, too, and often served on the same committees together. Presently, and over the last seven years, they were members of the finance committee.

Lillian flipped through a magazine and often made small talk with Carolyn. Morgan sat quietly and smiled whenever it seemed appropriate.

Time passed and Lillian periodically glanced at her watch. It was now ten minutes to three. She decided she wouldn't say anything for a little while longer, but was becoming very impatient.

"I don't know what's keeping him so long, Lillian," Carolyn said with a frown on her face. "I know he's in there. I can see by the light on my phone that he's still talking to someone."

Lillian smiled slightly and patted Morgan on the hand.

Finally, at twenty minutes after three the large oak door opened and Pastor Morris walked out of his office and over to Carolyn's desk. He really didn't ignore Lillian and Morgan. To him, they simply weren't there. They were no different than the two table lamps.

"Carolyn," Reverend Morris said as he plopped a folder on her desk. "I've jotted some notes down on a letter I want you to write to the Timmons family. This is the third time they're more than two months behind on their tithe and I want it brought up to date, with no excuses. You'll know what to say to soften the text, but I want the meaning to come through loud and clear."

"Alright," Carolyn said without looking up. She hated that part of her job, badgering parishioners for money. "Lillian and Morgan are here to see you. They had a two o'clock appointment."

Reverend Morris was a short man of about fifty. His hair was black with white streaks showing, perfectly trimmed and combed. He wore a tailor-made black suit and handmade tan, soft-leather shoes. His gray eyes flitted around uneasily until they found Morgan. They scanned her from head to toe and it was so noticeable that it made her very uneasy. She was glad her mother and Carolyn were in the room with her.

"Ah, Mrs. Colburn," he said and strutted over with outstretched hands.

"Carter," Lillian said as she stood and reached out her right hand.

"Yes, Mrs. Carter. And who might this lovely creature be?" Morris asked as he licked his lips.

"I'm sure you remember from last Sunday. This is my daughter, Morgan."

"Well, I do remember. Hello, Morgan. And, you have another child, don't you?"

Lillian was starting to burn, but held onto her temper. She reminded the pastor that she had an older daughter and a younger son.

Morgan smiled and immediately looked down, so she wouldn't make eye contact with the reverend.

"Come into my office, ladies. Carolyn. No interruptions, please."

Lillian and Morgan were taken into the depths of the reverend's office. Lillian had seen lots of plush offices before. In fact, her husband's office was considered very nice, but certainly nothing like this. In her whole lifetime and many committees she had served on, Lillian had never been allowed into this office before.

The wall behind the massive mahogany desk was glass windows that looked out onto a beautifully manicured flower garden. The other walls were lined with countless books that were so perfectly placed, they appeared to have never been disturbed. The beige carpet was so plush it was almost like walking in deep sand.

"Sit. Please, ladies. Sit."

The leather squeaked when Lillian sat in one of the chairs and almost made a chorus when Morgan sat in the other one.

"Now, Mrs. Colburn. What can your poor, old minister do for you?"

Morris sat behind his huge desk, folded his hands in a prayer-like form with his fingers pointing upward towards his nose.

"We want to see about booking the church for my daughter's wedding," Lillian said desperately trying to hold back her temper and again, she also wanted to remind the smug little man that her name was Carter and not Colburn.

"Wonderful!" Reverend Morris exclaimed. "Let me get the wedding schedule book."

He reached into his bottom drawer on the right side of his desk, brought out a large planner-book, and opened it.

"Now, when were you thinking?" he asked as he flipped through some of the pages.

"We'd like to see what's open for a late Saturday afternoon in June or July."

"Hmmm," the reverend said thoughtfully and then looked up over his reading glasses. "That's pretty soon. Is there a problem?"

"Problem?" Lillian said in a very surprised tone. "There's no problem.

At least not the kind of problem you're thinking."

"Thank goodness, Mrs. Colburn. You don't know how often that happens, though. I see that we have nothing open in June, July, or August. But, I see that the last Saturday in September and also, the second Saturday in October are both open."

Lillian wrote the two dates down in her little notebook that she always carried in her purse.

"Now, just so there's no surprises, here's a list of charges. It's $500 for the church and $500 for the minister, unless, of course, you would like me to officiate. Then, the charge would be $750."

Reverend Morris handed Lillian a paper that listed all the additional charges. She was a little shocked at all the high prices, even for the smallest items. She folded it up and put it in her purse.

"If I may be so bold, Mrs. Colburn," Morris said as he locked eyes with Lillian. "Usually it's the bride-to-be that comes to see me about the arrangements. Is your oldest daughter not home from college yet?"

Lillian had to process what was just said. It made no sense to her at all.

Finally, it came to her. Reverend Morris thought it was Karen that was planning to be married.

"It's not Karen. It's Morgan here."

Reverend Morris' eyes became mere slits. His face turned beet-red.

"Now, see here, Mrs. Colburn. That's just not possible. We don't allow the mentally retarded to marry in our church. Why, God, Himself, forbids it."

Lillian's temper was rapidly getting the best of her, but somehow she managed to appear calm.

"First of all, my dear man," Lillian's voice hinted a little of the fact that she was not impressed by the good reverend at all. "Morgan is not mentally retarded. She has cerebral palsy. There's a large difference, in case you don't know the difference between them. But, regardless, I've studied the Bible all my life and read it completely, cover to cover, many times. I don't recall any passage that even remotely refers to any prohibition at all. Please enlighten me as to the proper verses."

Reverend Morris was shocked. He hated uppity females, and this,

Mrs. Colburn, or whatever her name was, certainly filled the bill. He wanted nothing more than to rebuff her properly and put her into her subservient place, where all females should be.

"No need to be angry, Mrs. Colburn," Reverend Morris said softly. "I can certainly understand the strain you've been under raising such an afflicted child. But, you must try to understand what God's plan is for you and His test of your faith."

"Drop the bull, Pastor," Lillian said calmly, but with fire in her tone. "Just tell me the verse."

"There is no exact verse, my dear woman. But, by the divinely-inspired wisdom given to our church, it has become a rule of our congregation."

"So, you just made this ridiculous rule up?"

"We must think of the whole congregation, madam," Morris' voice rose. He was now getting tired of this testy female. "We simply don't allow anything that would raise the ire of any of our members. Is that clear?"

"Perfectly," Lillian snapped as she stood up and reached for Morgan's hand. "Perfectly."

"Good day," Reverend Morris called out as Lillian pulled Morgan along out the door.

They walked past so quickly that she said nothing to Carolyn on the way out.

"What a haughty woman," Pastor Morris said to Carolyn as he came out of his office and stood by her desk. "Demanding, too. Do you know that she wanted to have her mentally retarded daughter married in our church? Can you imagine that?"

Now Carolyn understood why Lillian dragged Morgan out the door without saying a word. She had known Morgan from the day she was born and watched her struggle and make something of herself. It also cemented how much she despised Reverend Morris. If she didn't need her job so badly, she would have walked out, too. That very day. But, of course, she couldn't. She was a single mom with a young child to raise and needed every dollar she earned.

Lillian got into her car and sat a minute to let her temper cool down.

-135-

She knew that otherwise, she would probably get a speeding ticket for sure. When she looked over at Morgan she noticed a tear streak down her cheek.

"Are you alright, honey?"

"Does ... this ... mean ... we ... can't ... get ... married ... now?" Morgan's voice quivered as she talked and her hands made quick, jerky movements that were so common when she was nervous or upset.

"Of course not. Reverend Morris is just a big ol' windbag."

They both laughed and it eased the tension.

"We'll figure something out."

CHAPTER THIRTEEN
The Second Attempt Turns Out Perfectly

When Harlan walked in the door, he could tell that something must not have gone right today. Lillian was slamming cupboard doors and talking to herself. He came up behind her and put his arms around her.

"Hi, beautiful. How was your day?"

"How can you say that?" Lillian said as she quickly spun around to face her husband. "How was my day? Let me tell you."

Harlan knew from lots of experience that whatever upset his wife, she had now worked herself into a tizzy about it, and she was ready to unload on him. That was fine, because it always created relief for her and through the blast of words, he could figure out what the real cause was. He went over to the counter and poured a glass of red wine for himself and one for Lillian.

"Do you have any idea what that pompous minister said?"

Naturally, Harlan had no clue what had happened, but knew that her question was rhetorical and she wasn't expecting an answer.

Lillian exploded and told Harlan the whole story. Even when she finished, unlike most other times, she was still mad.

"The gall of that man. If you remember correctly, I didn't like him right from the start. He's pompous, self-centered, only in it for the money...."

Harlan came over and put his arms around his still-fuming wife and held her. After a few minutes of sputtering, Lillian began to calm down.

"Where's Morgan?" Harlan asked as he let go of his wife and refilled his wine glass. "How's she doing?"

"At first, she thought that it was illegal for her to get married. Can you believe that? All the way home she didn't say much. Fortunately, Ryan came by right after he got off work and they went somewhere."

The next evening Harlan could hardly wait until he got inside the house.

"Hi, honey. I'm home," he said as he came into the kitchen.

"You're certainly in a good mood tonight," Lillian smiled and came over and kissed him tenderly.

"I just might have the answer to the problem you encountered yesterday."

"How so?" Lillian asked as she stirred the beef stew on the stove.

"You remember Donna who is Bill's secretary down at the office?"

Lillian nodded that she knew who she was.

"I was getting a cup of coffee this morning and Donna just happened to be at the coffee machine getting a cup too. I mentioned that Morgan was planning to get married soon. She asked me where, and of course, I told her it hadn't been planned out that far yet. She then suggested where she and her husband got married recently."

"Oh? Where was that?" Lillian responded and started setting the table.

"There's a little country church about ten miles out of town on County Highway M. It was a Lutheran church, but the congregation built a new building a few miles away. Regular church services are now held there only once a year, but they made it available for weddings the rest of the time. She said it was very beautiful."

"Hello, Daddy," Morgan said as she came into the kitchen.

"Hi, darlin'. Just get home from work?"

Morgan shook her head that she had and went to the refrigerator for a bottle of juice.

Harlan told Morgan about the little church and watched her eyes light up.

"I've … got to … call … Ryan," Morgan said and hurried out into the family room to the phone.

Harlan called Charlie for supper. He saw that Morgan was still on the phone and whispered that supper was on the table.

"Ryan … is coming … right … over," Morgan said as she sat down in her usual place at the table.

It was a little after six when Ryan knocked at the door and came in. Morgan quickly told him the news and was literally shaking with excitement. At first, Ryan had trouble piecing together what she was saying, but finally figured it out.

"Sounds perfect," Ryan said. "It's still going to be light outside for another few hours. Let's drive out and see it."

Morgan clapped her hands and opened her arms to hug her future husband.

"Come with us," Ryan said to Lillian and Harlan.

"I can't Ryan," Harlan said. "I have to wait for a phone call from one of my clients, but there's no reason you can't go with them Lillian."

It was settled. Ryan drove with Morgan sitting in the front by him and Lillian in the back.

It was a beautiful early evening sky. The temperature was warm and they had the windows down to let the air in. Ryan drove out County Highway M for a while, and then they saw it. Off in the distance rose the high spire of an old, typical country church.

"There … it is!" Morgan shouted.

Ryan turned off the blacktop road into the parking lot. They got out and walked up to the entrance.

The church was painted white and seemed to be in excellent repair. The sides had huge stained glass windows and the spire on the bell-tower seemed to be reaching to heaven.

Ryan held Morgan's hand as they walked around inspecting the quaint, yet very beautiful vision of tranquility and peace.

"Hello," a friendly voice said which caused all three to turn around and look.

A young man dressed in an old tattered tan shirt, Levis, and cowboy boots smiled and came up to the three with his hand extended to shake Ryan's hand. He appeared to be in his mid-thirties, rather thin, and glowed with friendliness. His face and arms were deeply tanned and his sandy brown hair seemed to have a mind of its own and strands of it stood straight up.

"I'm John Bierhoff. Came to look over our jewel in the country, did you?"

Ryan shook John's hand and told him they just heard about the church and came to see what it looked like.

"Well, come in. Come and see the inside," John said as he led the way. "Are you two planning a wedding?"

Morgan was the first to say that they were as they stepped inside the sanctuary. Morgan's mouth dropped open. They all stood silently and stared.

The inside of the little church was beautiful with the deep blues, greens, reds, and violets from the late afternoon sun flowing through the huge stained glass windows. Cages with canaries lined each wall and they twittered back and forth to each other in the excitement of people coming into the church.

"You should hear them sing when the organ's played," John said as he noticed the three looking at the canaries.

"Are you the caretaker?" Lillian asked as she came back to stand where John was and watched Ryan and Morgan stand in awe about halfway down the aisle.

"Yep. Could call me that, I guess. I'm the appointed reverend, too. Guess you could call me Reverend Caretaker John."

John laughed and his sparkling brown eyes laughed with him. His face wrinkled up with ecstasy as he seemed to enjoy his joke to his very soul.

"Let me show you something," John said as he walked down the left side aisle.

He came to the console of the organ, sat down, and turned it on. A soft whirring sound came from somewhere behind them. Suddenly, the whole sanctuary came to life in loud music that only a pipe-organ could make. John was not only the assigned minister to the church, but an expert musician as well. He and the organ played the Toccata in Fugue in D minor. The room virtually shook with the low notes and high pitched pipes. Coupled with the dazzling hues from the stained glass windows it all coupled into an ethereal vision that only God Himself, could have created.

Then the multitude of canaries burst into song to sing along with the massive organ.

Morgan and Ryan just stood and stared trying desperately to take it all in.

When Reverend John finished he sat back and listened to the canaries for a few seconds while they continued their song. They followed no written music made by mere man, but sang the song God gave them.

"Oh, Ryan," Morgan said softly. "This … is the … place where … we are … going … to be … married."

Reverend John got up from the organ console and came over to the group that was reveling in the afterglow. Still partially stunned by the whole vision.

"Let's go into my study and see what's available."

Reverend John's study was more like a closet at the back of the church. It had one small window and a desk that looked like an old school teacher's desk. Especially compared to the one Morgan and Lillian had seen in Pastor Morris' office. There were only two chairs so Ryan stood by the door.

"Now, let me see," Reverend John said after he put on his reading glasses and opened a schedule book. "When were you thinking?"

Morgan spoke up with no hesitation.

"Next ... Saturday afternoon ... or as ... soon as ... possible."

Reverend John looked up over his glasses and laughed, which was very contagious.

"I see that the last Saturday afternoon in July is open. How's that sound?"

Lillian saw by Morgan's wonderful smile that it would be perfect.

"Now, as to the business side of things," Reverend John said as he reached into his only desk drawer and took out a paper. "We charge $25 for the church and a $25 ministerial fee. That includes the rental for the wedding and time for a rehearsal the night before. We also have a lady from our regular congregation who plays the organ and another who will sing for you. They charge $15 each."

Lillian was shocked after finding out the horrendous amount her church charged and reached inside her purse for her checkbook.

"You don't have to pay anything right now," Reverend John said with his typical warm smile. "You can write a check when everything is set, unless you just want to get it out of the way now."

Lillian didn't hesitate at all. She wrote out a check for $80 and handed it to Reverend John.

"Great," he said as he wrote Ryan and Morgan in his schedule book. "I'll contact the two ladies and have them here the Friday night before your wedding for the rehearsal."

Morgan was so excited and elated. She talked most of the way home.

CHAPTER FOURTEEN
The Planning

It was noon on Saturday and Lillian and Karen were waiting for Morgan to get off work.

"Hi, Mom."

"Hi, honey. How was work?"

"Usual."

Lillian started the engine and drove off. They stopped at a fast food place, but went inside to eat.

"I thought we'd plan our strategy while we eat," Lillian said as she unwrapped a hamburger. "After we eat, let's go to the bridal shop over on Glidden Parkway. I've heard they have some really pretty things."

"What about that place you got Morgan's prom dress, Mom?" Karen asked as she sipped her chocolate shake. "That dress was drop-dead gorgeous."

"Your father told me some time ago that after winning more prestigious awards, Mr. Ferrolli moved his business and his family to Los Angeles. The building is now an office complex."

Morgan was almost too excited to think about eating anything, but did manage to pick over a few French fries.

Lillian led the way into the bridal shop. The shop was quite large and there were several women looking at the huge array of gowns that they had available hanging in long rows.

A middle-age woman came up to them. She was dressed in a black pants suit that was just a tad too tight and pulled the buttons almost to their limit. She said that her name was Mrs. Lutz and she was part-owner of the shop.

"Now, dear," Mrs. Lutz said as she scanned Morgan carefully. "What sort of gown do you have in mind?"

Morgan struggled to say that she wanted something that was floor-length and just covered the tops of her shoes, but, not any longer. She also didn't want a huge train.

Mrs. Lutz showed them a number of samples, but while Lillian and

Karen found one or two fairly favorable, Morgan didn't like any of them.

"We do have some catalogues over there at the table. Possibly, you could find something in one of them that you might like."

Mrs. Lutz had grown a little impatient, but certainly didn't let on to her possible customers. Her anxiety grew a little more when two more ladies came into the shop.

"I ... don't ... like anything ... here, Mom."

Lillian smiled and stood up. She gathered up her brood and told Mrs. Lutz they would possibly be back.

"The only other good bridal shop that I know of is the one I went to when your Aunt Elva got married two years ago. I was one of the bride's maids and at that time, they had some pretty nice things," Lillian said as she drove out of town towards the outskirts of Milwaukee.

The bell tinkled when they opened the door of a much smaller bridal shop than the one they had just come from. Inside, the main salon was bathed in brilliant sunlight from the massive skylight above. The white light virtually paled the dark green carpet, but made the white gowns appear to glow from their racks that surrounded the room.

"Good afternoon ladies," a slim lady with gray hair said as she came to greet them. She appeared to be in her mid-sixties, had a captivating smile, and dancing blue eyes. She wore a very tailored tan skirt and a dark brown turtleneck sweater. "I'm Ms. Kaplan," which explained the "K" in the name of the shop- "K's Bridal Shoppe."

Ms. Kaplan asked lots of questions about the wedding and how many attendants Morgan was going to have. She showed them a number of gowns that she thought might be appropriate.

Lillian thought the third one was a possibility until Morgan tried it on. When she came out of the dressing room she wrinkled up her nose and told her mother she didn't like it very much.

"I ... might ... trip ... on the ... skirt."

More gowns were brought out. Karen picked out two that she thought looked very cool, but her younger sister turned thumbs down on both of them.

Ms. Kaplan was beginning to sense that maybe the gowns she had been showing them were too expensive. She hadn't noticed the designer clothes each of the three women wore, or the BMW parked in her parking lot. She hated to lose a sale and wracked her brain for something they might like. Just when she saw that the ladies were about to walk out, she remembered something in the back room. She told them to wait just another minute and she rushed back to find it.

"Now, here's something I've had for a while. It was specially made and quite expensive. But, at the last minute, the almost-bride-to-be backed out and never even tried it on."

Ms. Kaplan urged Morgan to try the gown on. She knew that it would fit her almost perfectly and, she also really wanted to sell it. It had been in her racks for over two years, but of course, she didn't say anything about that.

Lillian could see by the huge smile on Morgan's face that she liked the gown and she had good reason. The gown was spectacular and fit Morgan almost as if it had been made for her. The bell of the skirt was hand-embroidered with flowers and white doves. The bodice was chantilly-lace with a high collar and plunging neckline. The hem came down almost to the floor, but not low enough to interfere with Morgan's stiff gait.

Karen rushed to her sister and raved at how cool it looked.

"It appears that this gown has been waiting just for you, my dear," Ms. Kaplan smiled and made little adjustments here and there. She was pretty sure this might be just the thing, if it was priced right.

Lillian walked around Morgan to see how the gown looked at all angles.

"This certainly looks like a possibility. What's the price?"

Ms. Kaplan's brain whirled into a spin. This was the first time anyone had even considered the gown, or appeared to be really interested. She also knew that originally, when the person placed the order for the gown, her deposit completely covered Ms. Kaplan's cost, plus some extra for her effort. So, whatever she could get for it was really pure profit.

"Well," Ms. Kaplan appeared to be mentally calculating. "You must remember that this gown is a one-of-a-kind and was quite expensive to make." She noticed the frown on Lillian's face and incorrectly interpreted it as having to do with the price. Instead, Lillian's real concern was the very daring, plunging neckline. "I think I could be persuaded to let it go for $400. Providing, of course, that we do the dresses for the two bridal attendants."

Lillian looked at Morgan's smiling face and knew that it was settled, and for a lot less than she thought it was going to be. But, of course, Lillian also knew that she and Harlan would pretty much allow Morgan to pick out whatever she wanted, within reason of course, and price was not the deciding factor.

There was a big discussion over the color for the bridesmaids' dresses. Karen thought that one of the new electric colors, such as blue, green, or magenta would be striking and cool. Lillian thought that they should be a pale color; such as light yellow or pink. Ms. Kaplan suggested light tan or a pale gold.

Morgan was dead-set on pale purple and would not be swayed. Finally, she won out and everyone agreed. Dresses for Karen and Stacey were going to be made in light violet.

Ms. Kaplan busied herself making marks for the minor alterations needed for Morgan's gown. Next, she measured Karen. Karen stood on the raised platform while Ms. Kaplan measured and wrote what seemed to be a hundred things.

Lillian decided on a design for herself that was in one of the large books that lay on the nearby table. The dress was chic, slender, and quite formfitting. Lillian worked out everyday and her body showed it. Everyone agreed that it would look very elegant on her, but yet, not overshadow the bride. It was to be made of ivory colored silk.

Harlan was all sweaty. He had just finished mowing the lawn and drove his power mower by the side of the house to hose it down when the girls came home. He shut the water off and walked over to the driveway and was immediately inundated by the three women, all talking at once. He saw their excitement and smiled appropriately. He knew that his wife would fill him in on all the details later on in the evening.

That evening, Lillian called Katherine and made a list of things that needed to be done.

"Katherine and Stacey are going over to the bridal shop Monday afternoon for measurements," Lillian said and made a checkmark on her now four-page list.

The next two weeks were a whirlwind of activity. Guest lists were developed, revised, and rewritten so many times that Morgan said she wanted to elope. Invitations were ordered, received, and addressed. Everyone worked on them as Morgan wanted all the envelopes handwritten. Katherine took home enough for Ryan's side and she, Stacey, Benjamin, and Ryan worked on them until they were in the mail.

It was Tuesday evening after supper. Benjamin was watching his favorite television program, Stacey was working on her homework on the dining room table, and Katherine had just finishing up her work in the kitchen.

Suddenly, the phone rang.

"I'll get it," Stacey yelled and jumped up so quickly that her chair fell over backward. She secretly hoped it was Charlie. "Hello."

"Hello, Stacey," a very curt female voice said. "Let me talk to your mother, please."

"Mom. It's for you."

"Who is it?" Katherine asked her daughter softly as she came into the dining room wiping her hands on a towel.

Stacey shrugged her shoulders to tell her mother that she had no idea.

"Hello."

"Don't you try and act so innocent to me, sister dear," the voice at the other end of the line snarled. "Just what do you think you're trying to pull?"

"Hello, Mollie dear," Katherine said as sweetly as she possibly could, but felt her temper rapidly rising just from the few words she had heard.

"Are you trying to put us all down on the lowest rung in town?"

"What in the world are you babbling about?"

"You think I believe for one second that you innocently have no idea?"

"None."

Well, then. I'll be more than happy to clarify your feeble brain from solid rock into something softer."

"I'm listening."

"You know full-well why I'm calling. I just received this unbelievable invitation in the mail just now."

"If you are referring to Ryan's wedding invitation, I should think you would be happy to have been invited."

"You should have put your foot down and stopped it long before it ever got to this point."

"It doesn't matter what you think, Mollie."

"It seems to me that if you were too weak-kneed to have stopped it, then Benjamin should forbid it."

"Ryan and Morgan are both grown adults of legal age, Mollie. They can do whatever they choose to do."

"Don't you know what people will think if you allow poor, innocent Ryan to marry a girl with such an affliction? Have you no shame?"

"If you put it that way, I guess I don't have any shame. Not in your eyes, at least. I still don't understand why this should make you so upset."

"My dear sister. You know full well that weddings lead to babies. And with Morgan's deformity, aren't you even a little concerned with what your grandbabies might turn out like? People like her, should never be allowed to marry and propagate these awful abnormalities. Now, you know that I'm not prejudiced in any way, but, it's a scientific fact that those afflictions are carried in the genes. You know that we don't have anything like that in our family."

Katherine's temper suddenly let loose.

"I've had more than enough of your narrow minded, bigoted, small minded thinking. Don't feel for a second that I'm concerned in the least. Morgan is a fine girl. She's very intelligent and wonderful. Ryan loves her dearly."

"But, for how long?" Mollie interrupted. "It won't take long for him to lose interest and stray. Most men do that anyway, let alone someone that has to live with, well pardon me for saying so, a freak."

"If there's any freak, Mollie, it's definitely you. I never thought even you would stoop to such a low level, but now, I guess you have. My recommendation to you and Robert is to stay home. Avoid the wedding at all cost. And don't think that anyone believes that your reputation is so lily-white and spotless either. People know, Mollie. People know."

There was a distinct 'click' on the line from Mollie hanging up her phone. Katherine smirked and smiled a little. Just maybe, she had finally been able to stand up for herself against her older sister for once.

Benjamin overheard a little of Katherine's conversation and had surmised that she was talking to her sister, judging by her body language. He also knew, from long experience, that she would tell him what their conversation was all about, but probably not for a while. Katherine would have to cool off a little first.

CHAPTER FIFTEEN
Taking a Few Feathers Along the Way

One Thursday evening in early July Lillian was busy working out the few remaining details for the upcoming wedding. Things were going along fairly well and her list of things to do had shrunk from the original four pages down to one. You would think that the wedding she was working on so diligently was her own, but in fact, it was for Morgan.

If the details had been left up to Morgan, very little would have happened. She just wanted to go down to city hall and get married and forget all the formalities.

But, of course, that's not the way it was going to happen. Lillian took command, as she always had, and became the wedding-planner.

Harlan was out in the kitchen pouring each of them a cup of coffee when Lillian's concentration was interrupted by the telephone.

"It's for you, dear," Harlan poked his head into the family room.

"Hi, Lillian. It's Carolyn Armstrong. You know, from church?"

"Yes, Carolyn. Hello."

"I've hesitated calling you because I know how busy you are with the upcoming wedding."

"Carolyn, this sounds serious."

"I'm afraid it is, Lillian. I had lunch with Nancy and Mavis yesterday. We think that we have something that needs discussing between all of us and, with your husband, too."

"Harlan? What in the world would he have to do with anything?"

"He's a lawyer, Lillian. And, not only a lawyer, but one of the best anywhere around."

Lillian was shocked, but intrigued. Carolyn wouldn't discuss anything more on the telephone, so she invited them to come over the next night around seven o'clock which would give Harlan time to get home, changed, and calm down a little after his usual stressful schedule at work.

That night in bed, Lillian told Harlan about her conversation with Carolyn.

"Sounds like secret stuff," Harlan said as he pulled the sheet up and clicked on the television.

"It's our church, Harlan. What in the world could be secret about that? It's all completely on the up and up and out in the open for everyone to see."

Harlan teased her a little, but quickly realized that she was dead serious and in no mood for kidding or teasing.

"You can't do anything about it tonight. Let's get some sleep and worry about it tomorrow."

"Still makes me wonder. Let me see. I'm on three committees this year; mission planning, finance, and building scheduling."

"Are all of you involved in anything together?"

Lillian thought a few seconds and told Harlan that all three served on two of the same committees; mission planning and finance.

Harlan continued to scan the multitude of channels until he grew tired and clicked the TV off. He kissed Lillian goodnight and rolled over. He was sound asleep in a few minutes, but Lillian lay beside him with her eyes wide open and her mind working a hundred miles an hour.

Lillian worried and thought about her phone conversation with Carolyn all through the next day and was glad when Harlan came home from his office a little earlier than usual.

"Hi, honey. How was your day?" he said as he came into the kitchen.

"Fine. I've got supper almost ready."

"We've got lots of time. It's not even five-thirty."

"I know, but I want to have supper out of the way and the dishes in the dishwasher when the girls get here."

Lillian had just finished putting the last dish into the dishwasher when the doorbell rang.

"Hello, Carolyn," Harlan said when he opened the door and saw that Mavis and Nancy were just coming up the driveway. "Hi, girls," he called out and waved. "Come right on in."

Lillian rushed into the foyer, welcomed her friends, and directed them into the family room.

Each of the three women carried a large notebook closed with a zipper so nothing would fall out.

"There's coffee in the carafe and cookies on the counter over there.

Everyone help yourself."

They all gathered around the counter and Harlan poured cups of coffee for everyone. They all made small talk about the weather and Morgan's upcoming wedding.

Harlan set up TV trays for each one and Lillian got everyone into chairs and situated.

"Well, Carolyn. You certainly have piqued my curiosity."

"I suppose we should start. Mavis and Nancy, is it alright if I begin?"

They nodded their approval.

"I've been Pastor Morris' administrative assistant for the past nine years and in the same position for Pastor Walker for three years before that."

Everyone nodded that they knew.

"I began to notice some irregularities more than five years ago. That was when there were big changes in our board. All of the new members were friends and associates of Pastor Morris.

"I first noticed something strange almost right away. Pastor Morris told the board that he wanted fairly large raises for all the assistant pastors and, a really huge one for himself. He had me put into the minutes that he thought that way, all the members of the clergy would be freed up from worrying about the money for their services, especially for weddings and funerals. Instead of receiving payment directly, all the money would go directly to the church.

"Sounded like a good idea and the board immediately went along with it.

"Over time, I talked to Mavis, who has been the finance chairman for the last four years and Nancy, who keeps the church calendar and schedules all the weddings and funerals.

"Because none of us do the whole process, I guess that makes it a good audit safeguard. But, one day over coffee, Mavis asked me if Pastor Morris had stopped doing special events. When I told her that his calendar was always full, she said that it was funny, but she never saw any money from his work.

"Well, this concerned us, so we talked with Nancy one afternoon when Pastor Morris was out. We saw a very definite pattern.

"We put together a spreadsheet on large columnar paper. Nancy wrote in her schedules and Mavis then copied on her cash receipts. Every event for each of the assistant pastors was accounted for. Every event for Pastor Morris was not."

Harlan looked up and asked Carolyn if she possibly had a copy of Pastor Morris' contract.

"Yes, I do. We all made copies of everything we thought might be important, and then some."

Carolyn dug through her notebook, found what she was looking for and handed a copy to Harlan.

Harlan put on his reading glasses and began to read.

"Excuse me for interrupting, Harlan. But, if you'll turn to Clause 41, which was added over four years ago, it seems to exempt Pastor Morris from turning in any money."

Harlan flipped ahead to Clause 41 and carefully read.

"It certainly does. How did he ever get the board to approve such a change?"

"I'm sorry to say, but it seems he can do anything he wants and the present board will automatically approve it."

"Hmmm. Looks like any money Morris generates himself is his to keep."

"What?" Lillian exclaimed and jumped to her feet. "You mean that he just pockets everything he does?"

"That's not all. He keeps the fees for the church rental, chairs, food service, and transportation, too."

"Harlan, isn't that downright illegal?"

"Doesn't look like it. He's got it pretty well covered here in his contract."

Lillian was now noticeably upset. She had grown up in her church and had loved and protected it since she was a little girl.

"There's more," Mavis added. "I take care of the payroll and he usually gets a bonus every month that's loosely based on the amount of money he collected."

Carolyn chimed in. "That's why he has me writing and telephoning members for money all the time. He even goes after some of our members that can hardly even pay their rent and you should hear the guilt trip he smothers them in."

"Doesn't any change in payroll have to be approved by the board, Mavis?"

"Look at Clause 74. It grants all power to make raises and payments to Pastor Morris."

"One thing for sure. He covers his tracks very thoroughly," Harlan said as he flipped to the next page of the contract.

"I'm in charge of the church schedules and also, the appropriations for the new building complex fund," Nancy said quietly. "We've received some pretty big donations along the way and the account had grown to a considerable amount."

"What do you mean 'had,' Nancy?" Harlan stopped reading and looked up over his reading glasses.

"It was about a year ago when the board approved Pastor Morris taking complete charge and the first thing he did was to make an automatic pathway to a new, special account that only he has access to."

"How does this automatic pathway work?"

"All deposits are placed in the normal account, but when it reaches a balance of $10,000, half of it is transferred."

"Hmmm. That must mean that lots of money must have been moved. I think I remember that account having over $300,000 in it back when I was a board member, and that was more than five years ago."

"Any idea what he uses the money for, Nancy?"

"I'm afraid I don't, but Carolyn does."

Carolyn dug through her notebook again and retrieved some stapled papers and handed them to Harlan.

"Here's copies I made from bank statements I found in his office one day when he had me looking for something else. I made copies of them while he was out for his usual three hour lunch."

"Well this is interesting. Here's a huge check written to Castor Motors for a Bentley. I've never seen him drive anything but the black Cadillac the church provides for him. I wonder what that's all about?"

"I've seen him in it," Mavis said and she dug through her records. "He keeps it parked in a private storage building the church rents for him. I write the check every month to pay for it, but never knew what it was, so last week I drove by it just to see it."

"Wonder what else is in there?"

"I'm afraid I can't help much there, Harlan. I've never seen what's actually inside. But, look further down the bank statement at all the checks written to Bigalow Travel Agency. Carolyn checked his schedule to see where he was for each entry."

"They say they're for training or spiritual symposiums. And, they're always in exotic places in the Caribbean, Hawaii, and even Fiji. But, here's the real kicker. He always takes a huge travel advance and then, the church pays for everything on his expense voucher afterward. And, it never shows that he's ever paid for anything with his advance."

"Looks like he's double-dipping," Harlan chuckled a little and continued reading the contract.

"Don't be flip, Harlan," Lillian snapped. "This really infuriates me. I've never liked that fat little weasel. I thought he was disgusting right from the start. Remember, Harlan? There was just something about him that didn't ring right."

"Actually, there's more," Carolyn said. "Harlan, please go back to the set of bank statements I just gave you and look at the charges made directly to that account. I've tracked them down and those $1,100 charges each month are for apartment rent at the Ashland Towers for a Ms. Rhonda Danion. She's the one that all those airline tickets to the same places that Pastor Morris attends those conferences are for."

"How long has that been going on, Carolyn?"

"I've found records for the last four years where we've been paying her rent and all travel, plus incidentals."

"It even goes farther," Mavis added almost immediately. "Pastor Morris put her on our payroll two years ago."

"Good grief," Lillian expounded. "I can just imagine what her job title might be. This all really makes me sick."

"Her job title is 'spiritual advisor' at a salary of $600 per week."

"Oh, please. I've heard enough. What can we do, Harlan?"

"Here's what I think we should do. If it's alright with all of you, I would like to take all of these papers to work and have one of my partners look them over. One especially comes to mind. He works on all kinds of contract fraud, so he is probably much better equipped than I am to make real sense out of all this.

"I do think that our secrecy is key, though. Don't whisper anything to anyone and then, let's all meet back here one week from tonight and we'll see where we go from here."

Everyone agreed and thanked Harlan for looking into the situation.

That night in bed, Harlan was doing his usual channel surfing when Lillian finally came to bed. He shut off the TV and turned out the light.

"Harlan?"

"Yes, dear?"

"If all is true that came out tonight, what can they do to the pastor?"

"Don't know for sure."

"Don't give me any of the lawyer talk. Just tell me what you think."

"On the surface, I don't think too much can be done. Morris has been very careful and made sure his contract allows him to do what he's done."

"But, hasn't he broken any laws?"

"Here's the thing, Lillian. Our church is a 'not for profit,' tax-exempt, religious enterprise. What Morris seems to have done is certainly unethical, but probably not illegal. Even if we find something that is illegal, have charges brought, and he is found guilty, he probably would get off with nothing more than a slap on the hands."

Lillian didn't respond for quite a while and lay silently by her husband.

"Well, I hope we can find something really outlandish that we can get him for."

"I do, too. What would you like to see happen to him? Jail time?"

"Jail is too good for him. I want him crucified."

"I think they outlawed that a couple thousand years ago," Harlan quietly chuckled and put his arm around his fretting wife.

The next week would have dragged, but there were lots of things to still get organized for the wedding. So, time actually flew by.

It was late Tuesday afternoon when Lillian finally got home. Charlie looked up from the kitchen table where he was working on his homework.

"What's for supper, Mom?"

"I haven't even thought about it, Charlie. Do you have any ideas?"

"Let's order a pizza."

"Pizza sure sounds good to me," Harlan said as he came through the door from the garage and came into the kitchen. "Hi, gorgeous. Where's the rest of the brood?"

"Morgan said this morning that Ryan was going to pick her up from work this afternoon. So, they should be here pretty soon."

"Guess we better order two large," Harlan said as he thumbed through the phonebook.

It was a little after six when Ryan and Morgan came in and Karen arrived about ten minutes later.

"Boy, Dad," Charlie worried. "Sure hope you ordered enough."

Lillian and Karen had the table set when the pizza arrived.

"Hmmm," this is really good," Charlie said with his mouth full and put another piece on his plate.

Everyone was finally full of pizza. Lillian, Karen, and Morgan picked up the dishes and put them in the sink to be rinsed before putting them into the dishwasher.

"So, Ryan," Harlan said as he picked up his coffee cup to see if there was anything left. "Have you made a decision on which job you're going to take?"

Harlan's question took Lillian by complete surprise. She whirled around so fast that she almost lost her balance. With all the things she had to do for the wedding, she had completely forgotten all about Ryan's job offers. She immediately sifted through numerous scenarios before she decided on what was probably about to happen.

Oh, my God. They're going to move to California right after the wedding. I just know it, Lillian thought and tears formed in her eyes.

Ryan stood up and moved behind Morgan's chair. He tenderly put his hands on Morgan's shoulders. She immediately put her hands on his, looked up, and smiled lovingly into his eyes.

"Morgan and I have talked it over very carefully and made our decision yesterday."

"Come on, kids. Don't keep us in suspense. Which job did you decide on, Ryan? Chicago or Los Angeles?"

Oh my God, oh my God, Lillian's mind raced. *Let it be Chicago and not Los Angeles. At least Chicago isn't so far away.*

"Neither."

"Neither one?" Harlan's voice sounded very curious.

"We're staying right here in Oakwood Heights."

"You're not planning on working for ol' man Phillips down at the lumberyard all your life, are you?"

"No, sir. Not at all. You see, there was a third offer that Morgan and I were considering all along.

"Mr. Albright, from Albright Investments and Securities came up to school to talk to me some time back. It's one of the biggest financial organizations in the Midwest. Anyway, he made me a really good offer to come to work for his company at their corporate office in Milwaukee.

"While his offer wasn't nearly as good as the one in Los Angeles or Chicago, it would mean that Morgan and I could live right here in Oakwood Heights and I could drive back and forth every day. Besides, that way, Morgan could finish school right here, too."

"Oh, my God," Lillian exclaimed and rushed over and threw her arms around Ryan, and then Morgan. "I'm so happy you two are going to stay right here."

That night, Lillian literally crawled into bed. She was exhausted. Her nerves had been strained to the limit. Harlan turned off the TV and she snuggled up to him and he put his arms around her. She fell into a deep sleep, secure in the arms of her knight in shining armor.

Wednesday afternoon came and Lillian had hoped that Harlan would've been able to come home early, but it turned out that Carolyn, Mavis, and Nancy got there first.

"Hi, gorgeous," Harlan said as he came into the kitchen from the garage and kissed Lillian on the lips. "Sorry about being late, but had some last minute things to do before I could leave."

Just then, the doorbell rang.

"Hi, Josh," Lillian said as she opened the front door. "Come on in. I didn't know you were coming tonight, but I'm glad to see you."

Josh Newman was tall and slender. He had almost black hair which was perfectly trimmed and every hair was immaculately in place. His dark brown eyes radiated friendliness. He wore a dark blue suit with a light blue shirt which was finished off with a blue floral necktie. Josh was the firm's youngest partner. He was just thirty and had already developed a reputation as one of the best contract lawyers all over the state.

"Everyone. This is Josh Newman. He's one of the partners in Harlan's firm."

Mavis smiled and held out her hand to Josh. He smiled warmly.

Nancy stood up and smiled. She held out her right hand and said that she had a friend that Josh had represented a few years ago and won his case.

Carolyn looked up and their eyes locked for just a few seconds. She smiled warmly and then immediately looked down. Josh quickly reached down and shook her hand and told her he was pleased to meet her.

Lillian poured coffee for everyone and Harlan came into the family room to join in. He had no sooner sat down when the doorbell rang.

"Hi, John," Harlan said as he opened the door.

"This is John Eubanks, everyone. John, this is Carolyn, Mavis, Nancy, and that lovely creature over there is, of course, my wife, Lillian."

John walked around the room and greeted everyone. He was shorter than Josh and a little older, probably near forty. He had sandy colored hair and brown twinkling eyes. His suit was an off-the-rack light brown model from Sears. He was warm and very personable.

After some small talk and coffee, Harlan asked for everyone's attention.

"I took all the information you gave me last week and had Josh and his team work on it. They really know contract law and criminal law as well, so I thought they would be the appropriate ones to analyze everything. Josh? Would you bring us all up to date?"

"Sure," Josh said as he stood and came forward to face the group. "First, it certainly looks like your pastor has taken you all for a very expensive ride. He's very careful, though. He's made sure that his contract grants authority for everything he's done. And, he's done a lot. We've only had time to analyze the last five years, and it looks like he's milked the church coffers out of almost $800,000."

Everyone gasped. While they all felt that Pastor Morris had committed some improprieties, none of them had ever considered that it had reached such an enormous magnitude.

"Let's get him," Mavis spoke up. "Do we have enough evidence?"

"I'm afraid," Josh paused while he pulled out some papers from his briefcase. "As I said, he's covered his tracks very well. While what he's done may be considered highly unethical, it's not illegal in the eyes of the law. We probably could pressure a court case, but I don't think we'd have a prayer of winning. This is a pretty well thought out plan."

"Isn't there anything we can do?" Carolyn spoke up.

"My wife wants him crucified," Harlan said to ease the tension which caused everyone to laugh.

"I didn't mean it literally," Lillian quickly said, but down deep she thought he deserved it.

"Bottom line," Josh smiled warmly. "Yes, there are things that we can do. That's why I asked John to come along with me tonight."

"Hello, again," John said as he got up from his chair and stood in front of the group. "I work for the federal government. I'm what's known as a special prosecuting investigator for the Internal Revenue Service. After reviewing the information Josh showed me, I went to my superior and we believe that we have more than adequate reason to charge Pastor Morris with tax evasion. While this may not seem like a very serious thing, let me assure you that it is. Especially in the magnitude we are dealing with here. It looks like he's cheated the federal government out of approximately a quarter of a million dollars in income tax. Now, Uncle Sam takes a very dim view of that kind of thing and the law has real teeth in it to prevent people from trying to do it. It's a good thing that most people pay their taxes. And, it's often a good thing when people like your Pastor Morris, after taking such careful precautions to make sure his contract grants all his moves, forgets all about paying taxes on his gains. Further, whenever we file charges against someone for tax evasion, the state then usually follows suit for their portion of the pie. In large cases, such as this one, and of course, if he's found guilty, he will have to pay full restitution and, there will usually be pretty hefty fines, punitive penalties, and possibly even prison time. All in all, I think we've pretty much got this guy red-handed.

"Also, after meeting with Josh and his people, I had my team do some checking on Pastor Morris. I don't mean to criticize your organization, but when you interviewed him, you must not have checked him out very thoroughly."

"We didn't, John," Harlan spoke up. "I was on the search committee at that time and we were desperately looking for a pastor to replace Reverend Walker. I am as guilty as the others on the committee for our hasty decision. Morris was a very charismatic person and had some really glowing credentials."

"I can understand your haste, Mr. Carter. But, if you would've checked into his background, you would have found that he had recently escaped prosecution by a church much like yours, in Dallas, Texas."

Everyone gasped.

"It appears that Morris and two of his partners from the Dallas church, who by the way, after checking into it, are members of your board today, seem to be very good at draining large amounts of money without anyone realizing what is going on. "

Carolyn called for a quick huddle with Mavis, Nancy, and Lillian.

"We want that no-good guy taken down," Carolyn said firmly and the other three nodded their heads affirmatively. "How do we go about it? How do we take our church back?"

"First, and foremost, is secrecy." John said firmly. "No one outside this room can know what's going to happen.

"I'll apply for a search warrant tomorrow morning, just to make sure we've got everything lined up legally.

"Then, Friday morning, I'll come to your office, Carolyn, along with two auditors. We'll tell you we're there to audit your institution for compliance with federal law for nonprofit entities, and do a payroll audit. All, certainly within the authority of my office to do so.

"You, Carolyn, will then call Pastor Morris and tell him that we're there and why. I can tell you from lots of experience that the first thing that will happen is, he will tell you that he will be out in a few minutes. Next, if you have a multiple-line phone, you'll see a line light up while he calls two people. First, he'll call his lawyer and second, your accountant. They will tell him that we're on the up-and-up and the best way to deal with us is to give us *carte-blanche* which will get us on our way as fast as possible. He'll then copy any files he considers sensitive onto some form of removable media and delete them off the main-frame. Finally, he'll then come out to meet us with all his charm and charisma and tell you that you are to give us anything and everything we need for our audit.

"Our audit will take about three days and we'll tell Pastor Morris that we've pretty much completed everything and will notify him in a week or so about our findings.

"Oh, yes. By the way. I also predict that he'll try and take my team out for lunch every day we're here."

Carolyn asked more questions which John quickly answered.

"Also, Carolyn. Are you the last to leave each day?"

"Yes. My last task is to do an auto-save on the main-frame computer. I usually set it up a little after five and leave at 5:30."

"How long does it take to complete?"

"I think it takes about an hour. I know when I've had to work late, it's always done before I leave."

"What about Pastor Morris? What time does he usually leave for the night?"

"He always leaves early. Usually, about 3:30."

"Does he ever come back for an evening meeting?"

"Never. If there is anything going on, he'll always assign one of the assistant ministers to come back."

"Fine. Tomorrow night I want you to stay until the save is complete. Take the tape cartridge home and keep it for us.

"Mavis and Nancy? Are your terminals connected to the same main-frame as Carolyn's?"

Both women said that they were.

"We don't want Pastor Morris to have any clue that we've copied anything. Then, do the same on Friday night as you did on Thursday.

That way we can compare the two and see what, if anything, the good pastor deleted."

"What happens if it all somehow falls apart?" Nancy asked with a worried look on her face. "I really need this job."

"I don't want to mislead any of you. If it does fall apart, all three of your jobs will be in jeopardy. He wouldn't fire any of you immediately because that would bring suspicion. But, over time, he will find ways to eliminate your jobs or begin a campaign to make it appear that you are not doing your job. The bottom line is, he'll have you all replaced over time."

"But, what about our church?" Lillian asked. "How do we get control back from him? Especially, when he's got the board filled with his people."

"I think I can answer that," Josh said as he reached into his briefcase an brought out a large stack of papers. "I read over your original charter and found it has just what you're looking for."

Josh handed the charter to Harlan and pointed to the appropriate clause and asked him to read it out loud.

Harlan put on his reading glasses and adjusted the floor-light. "It says, 'If an occasion arises where there is corruption in the clergy, or in conjunction with the governing board, or both; the congregation, as a whole body, may grant themselves authority to suspend the minister and the board while a complete investigation takes place.

" 'Causes for such action against the clergy are things such as murder, inappropriate behavior, adultery, neglect of the congregation, stealing church funds, and other deeds that may take the church into perilous pathways.

" 'If such a condition either exists, or it is suspected to exist, a lay-leader will stand before the congregation and state the reasons for such action. The congregation present, as long as it represents more than fifty percent, will then be asked to vote. If the vote is favorable, the clergy and board will be suspended until they are either charged legally or proven innocent.' "

"Do you think we'll have to actually do such a thing?" Mavis asked softly. "It all scares me."

"Possibly," Josh spoke up. "Pastor Morris having a mistress will certainly be a real good starter in getting your church back. But, remember. The better we plan this all out, the better our chances are for success."

"Also, remember," John quickly added, "secrecy is key. The timeline is to start on Friday when we arrive at your office, Carolyn. We'll finish our work by noon on Tuesday. We'll then go back to the office and do our work. I'll keep Josh informed so he can keep all of you posted. If we find what we think is there, warrants will be issued and I'll be back the following week with the federal marshals to arrest Pastor Morris."

"It should be on the following Sunday," Josh turned and said to Harlan, "when you, or whoever you think appropriate, will need to face the congregation and tell them what has happened."

The plan was once again laid out so that there would be no misunderstanding on anyone's part, no matter how small the issue was. Finally, total agreement was reached and their secrecy promised.

"Well, I'm certainly glad we're finally doing something about all this," Lillian said as she put cups into the dishwasher.

Harlan smiled warmly, but knew that things were bound to get lots worse before they got better and desperately hoped it would all work out according to their plan.

Then, out of the dimly lit stairway, they heard a voice.

Lillian spun around so fast that she almost lost her balance and fell against the island in the kitchen.

CHAPTER SIXTEEN
Catching an Ol' Alley Cat

"What is it, dear?" Lillian asked as she hurried towards her daughter and realized that Morgan must have overheard her and Harlan's conversation.

"Does … this mean … that … Ryan … and I … will … have to … get … married … in our church … now?"

"No, of course not, honey," Lillian said as she put her arms around Morgan to reassure her. "Everything for your wedding will be just as we planned. Nothing will change."

"Thanks, … Mom."

Harlan came up and put his arms around both his consoling wife and concerned daughter. He, too, reassured Morgan that nothing had changed and that her wedding would go on just as they had all planned.

"One more thing," Harlan said to Morgan who had by now started up the stairs. "What you heard your mother and I discussing must absolutely be kept between us three. Is that understood?"

Morgan said that she understood.

Thursday was a blur for Carolyn. She was sure that Pastor Morris was suspicious, but then realized that it was nothing more than her imagination. Thursdays were packed full because Morris always left early for 'personal study.' But, Carolyn knew it was to be with his mistress.

It was a little after five in the afternoon when Carolyn initiated the daily backup procedure. But, instead of copying just the normal files, she issued the command to do a complete save. It was all done by 6:30. She put the tape cartridge into her purse, shut everything off, and went home.

Friday morning started out as every day always did. Carolyn got to work at 7:30, turned on the lights in the office, powered up the mainframe computer, and made coffee.

It was five after eight when Pastor Morris strutted in.

"Good morning," she said looking up from her typewriter.

As usual, she was completely ignored. Morris went into his office and shut the door. Carolyn noticed that the light for line #2 on her phone lit up. He was probably calling his mistress. The light for line #3 lit and Carolyn's phone buzzed.

"Yes, Pastor?"

"Coffee. A donut would be good, too."

Pastor Morris' demeanor had always galled Carolyn, but today it seemed to really get to her. She got up and went over to the coffee machine. She poured a cup, and then went to the donut bag that she was told to bring every day. It wasn't that the donut shop was out of her way on her way to work, but more that she was expected to go there and buy them. And, to top it all off, she was expected to use her own money.

It was just nine o'clock when John Eubanks, along with two other men, walked into Carolyn's office.

"Good morning," John said never letting on that he had ever met Carolyn before. "I'm from the Internal Revenue Service. This is Bill Hastings and that's Will Brown."

Bill Hastings was the shortest of the three men and looked to be about fifty. He wore a brown suit that was neat and pressed along with a solid brown necktie. Will Brown was considerably younger. He looked to be about thirty. He was the heaviest of the three, but not fat. He wore a gray suit with a gray and magenta necktie. He had a warm and captivating smile and his eyes sparkled when he laughed. Both men nodded as they were introduced.

"We're here to conduct a normal audit of your records to insure that your non-profit, tax-exempt status is appropriate and also to audit your payroll records. Would you please notify," John hesitated as he looked through his official papers for the senior minister's name. "Please notify Pastor Morris that we are here."

Carolyn immediately picked up her phone and buzzed Pastor Morris. She buzzed again. She saw the light on line #2 start to blink, which meant that whoever it was that Pastor Morris was talking to, was put on hold.

"Yes?" Morris' voice was terse and impatient.

Carolyn explained who was in the office.

"Tell them I'm on the phone and will be out shortly."

Carolyn did. She then watched and saw the light on line #2 go out for a few seconds and then relight.

Just as Mr. Eubanks predicted. Probably calling his lawyer right now, Carolyn thought and smiled to herself. The light on line #2 went out and then came back on. *Calling Dave.* Dave Roberts was the church accountant.

Carolyn keyed some commands into her computer terminal and was now able to monitor the main-frame computer. She couldn't see exactly what was going on, but could tell that Morris was on his terminal.

Suddenly, Pastor Morris burst out of his office all smiles. He extended his right hand towards Eubanks.

"Gentlemen. Sorry to keep you waiting, but I was on the phone with one of our board members. I'm Pastor Morris."

Introductions were made and Eubanks told Pastor Morris the reason for their visit.

"Just routine," John smiled. "I know it probably all sounds pretty boring to you, Pastor, but it keeps the three of us off unemployment.

"Not a problem at all. Carolyn, please set these three gentlemen up in our pastoral conference room and give them anything they need."

Carolyn got up from her desk and motioned for the three men to follow her.

"Anything you need, gentlemen. Just ask Carolyn and she'll get it for you. We've got coffee right over there and donuts, too. Make yourselves right at home."

Carolyn was nervous as a cat on the proverbial "hot tin roof." John Eubanks gave her a list of things they needed initially, which she immediately noticed included "the latest computer backup media," but she told herself that it stuck out like a sore thumb only to her and to anyone else, it would have been almost unnoticeable.

She busied herself collecting the items requested from the huge walk-in vault and placed everything onto a cart

"Please place the backup media in this case," John said as he looked up when Carolyn came into the conference room pushing the cart and handed her a small black leather case.

Carolyn went to her locker, unlocked the door, and took out her purse.

-169-

She softly closed the door and went back to the conference room. She carefully pulled the backup tape cartridges out of her purse and placed them into the leather case.

"Everything on here?" John asked in a very non-threatening way as he looked up over his reading glasses.

"Yes, it should all be there."

"Excellent." He didn't say anything more, but locked the case and placed it into his huge briefcase.

At 11:30, Morris bounded out of his office and went into the conference room.

"How about lunch, gentlemen? I know a wonderful place not very far from here. Surely, you can take a little break. Even government employees get a lunch hour."

John thanked Morris for the generous offer, but told him that it was against policy, but more importantly, they needed to work straight through so that they could finish their work as soon as possible.

"We'll be out of your hair no later than Tuesday noon, if everything goes well," John reassured Morris. "We've got a large church downtown Milwaukee that we have to be at first thing Wednesday morning."

It was just as Pastor Morris' lawyer had told him. Interfere as little as possible. Let them do what they have to do and they'll be gone before you know it. Morris could still hear his lawyer drone on about how heavy their caseload was, so there was not going to be a very in-depth analysis. Also, the government had cut the budget for the field agents over the last few years, so there weren't very many to do the job. Just stay calm and they'll be gone soon, he kept telling himself.

All day, Morris would pop out of his office and look around. He often went to the church library saying he needed a book or magazine for his sermon on Sunday. Carolyn knew that wasn't true because yesterday afternoon, just before Morris left for the day, he threw a pile of papers on her desk and told her to bind it for his sermon. Morris always wanted his sermons spiral-bound to keep everything together.

But, Carolyn knew something else about Pastor Morris' weekly sermons that probably no one else knew, except the pastor, himself. The church subscribed to a sermon service and Carolyn knew that he often used one of theirs, rather than writing his own.

Pastor Morris stayed later than normal for a Friday night. Usually, he left around four, but today, he stayed until five o'clock.

"Any idea how long those auditors are going to stay tonight?"

"They told me a little while ago that they wanted to stay at least until six, and then get an early start tomorrow."

"Lock up when they leave. I've got to run."

Thanks for asking, Carolyn thought to herself sarcastically.

Morris left.

"Any danger of him coming back for anything?" John asked standing in the doorway.

"I don't think so. He always has an important date on Friday nights."

"That's nice of him. With his wife, I assume."

She shook her head, no.

"Oh. That's too bad. Come on and I'll help you do the backup we need."

Carolyn rarely worked on Saturday unless there was some special program going on. This Saturday was different. She got to the church parking lot at 7:30 and noticed that the auditors were already there and waiting at the door.

"Good morning," they all said in unison. Carolyn unlocked the door, turned on the lights, and busied herself making coffee.

Sunday morning's worship service always brought out a huge crowd and this Sunday was no exception. Almost every seat was filled.

When it came time for Pastor Morris' sermon, he rose slowly in front of the congregation in his extremely expensive purple robe and walked to the podium.

When Carolyn remembered how much the robe cost, she almost choked and even this morning, it churned acid in her stomach.

"Friends," Morris began with his amplified voice booming across the congregation. "During the past week I worked diligently, hour after hour, on a sermon that I thought would be appropriate for today. But, almost at the last hour, I had a vision." Morris paused for dramatic effect and a few people gasped. "A vision came to me and told me to cast aside all my hard work. It then filled my mind with thoughts and words that came so fast I could hardly make sense out of it all." More people gasped. Some said 'amen.'

"I wrote as fast and furious as I could. I stayed up all night. I worked and worked. Sweat poured down my forehead, but I could not stop working. When I finished this morning, I was completely exhausted and my tired body wanted to rest. But, the Spirit kept pushing me onward. It told me that there would be time to rest later, but right now, my congregation desperately needed me.

"So, my friends. I stand before you this morning as your humble servant of God and will try to enlighten you to the words that were given to me."

Murmurs of approval went through the crowd. Morris was a master performer and was in fine form this morning.

"The title of my sermon this morning is, 'The importance of being there for God, as he is for you.'"

Carolyn instantly recognized that this wasn't something that had just came to Pastor Morris. It was the one she had bound for him earlier in the week.

Pastor Morris railed on for almost two hours on how important it was for every church member, no matter how rich or poor, to give to the cause of God, and give until it hurt.

The congregation gave. They gave until it hurt. When the collection plates were passed, they were filled to overflowing.

When the service was over, Pastor Morris stood outside the sanctuary and greeted each person as they came out. He was talking to the mayor and his wife when Carolyn came out.

"Yes, my friend," Morris said to the mayor. "I would be nothing if it weren't for dedicated, hardworking people, like my right-hand person, Carolyn over there."

Everyone around nodded their approval at the pastor's humbleness and recognition of his employees. Especially the mayor's wife, who was a friend of Pastor Morris' wife.

Unfortunately, Carolyn knew just how hollow those words were, but she kept quiet and smiled graciously.

Tuesday came and the auditors finished their work right around 10:30. They told Pastor Morris that everything appeared in order, but if they needed anything they would come back. Otherwise, they would send him a report in a few weeks. He bid them goodbye in his typical overfriendly manner. Carolyn was glad that the auditors seemed to pay little attention at all.

"Well, I certainly hope that's over," Morris said as he strutted into his office. "Those things certainly put a strain on everything. Coffee, Carolyn. And, a donut, if you please."

Thursday morning came and Carolyn was working on a departmental budget when the office door opened.

"Good morning," John Eubanks said as he came in along with two federal marshals. "Please tell Pastor Morris to come out here."

Carolyn did as she was asked.

"What do they want, Carolyn? Isn't it something you can handle? Otherwise, see if you can get them to come back next week. I'm a busy man, you know."

"I think they mean now, Pastor."

Pastor Morris' office door opened and he stepped out into the lobby.

"Well, hello, John. Sorry about the wait. Did you need something else for your audit?"

"I'm afraid so," John said with a much more commanding voice. It was the voice of a federal agent rather than an auditor. "Eugene Dobson Morris. You are being charged with tax evasion, fraudulently reporting income to the federal government, appropriating church funds to political campaigns through secondary accounts in violation of your tax-exempt status, and embezzlement of church monies.

"You have the right to remain silent …."

Pastor Morris stood in shock as his rights were read to him.

"Do you understand your rights just read to you?"

"I think I need to call my lawyer."

"You'll have time to call your lawyer later. Now, if you'll just come along with us."

"I'll do no such thing. I'm an innocent man. I'm just a poor man of God, trying to look out for my flock," Morris said as he started to back away.

"You can either come along peaceably or in handcuffs."

Eubanks had no sooner uttered the words when Morris bolted back into his office, slammed and locked the door.

He dashed across his spacious office and unlocked the back door.

"Going somewhere, Pastor?" The second marshal with dark sunglasses who was about the size of a defensive lineman asked.

Within a few seconds the second marshal brought Pastor Morris, now in handcuffs, into the front office.

"He tried to slip out the back door," the marshal smiled. "Just as you predicted."

CHAPTER SEVENTEEN
Yes, My Love, I Do

Pastor Morris was taken away. He was booked and placed in a holding cell for further processing. He was allowed one phone call to his lawyer, which, by the sound of it, was quite heated.

Harlan stood in front of the congregation on the following Sunday and presented his case. He then asked for a vote to immediately suspend Pastor Morris and the complete board. The vote was unanimous.

As the wedding drew closer, there seemed to be a hundred things that needed attention. Both Ryan's and Morgan's households were whirlwinds of activity.

Friday evening arrived and everyone gathered at the little country church for the rehearsal.

Reverend John introduced everyone to Mrs. Tixlor, the singer, and then tried to get things organized so they could practice.

"Now," Lillian said as she stepped forward taking command. "I've got a complete list of how the ceremony should go."

She started putting people into their places and told each one what was expected of them. Reverend John nodded occasionally and smiled.

"No, ... Mom. Stop."

The church got instantly quiet and everyone looked at Morgan.

"It's ... all ... too complicated."

Lillian suddenly realized that Morgan was right. What she had planned were her ideas, not her daughter's. She remembered back to when she and Harlan got married and how her mother took complete command of the whole thing. She resented it to this very day.

"I'm so sorry, Morgan. In my quest to make everything perfect for you, I guess I got a little carried away. Tell us how you want it."

Morgan outlined what she wanted. It was one she and Ryan had discussed a few days earlier and was much simpler.

Reverend John ran through the process with lots of fun and laughter. Once, even Mrs. Tixlor had to laugh right out loud.

"Looks good, Morgan," Reverend John said when they finished. "What do you and Ryan think?"

"We both love it."

"And, Reverend John," Benjamin said as they were walking out of the church. "We want you and Mrs. Tixlor to come with us to the Shepherd's Lamb for dinner."

After all the stress of planning, and then going through the rehearsal, the dinner afterward was a joyous occasion.

Finally, desserts and coffee were served.

An older man and his wife, both dressed very elegantly came over to the banquet table.

"Please excuse my intrusion, everyone. I'm Jake Timmons and this is my wife, Margaret. We've been enjoying your charm and fellowship while we sat and ate our dinner. Even though we've never met, I must say that you've all brought joy to the hearts of both Margaret and myself."

Introductions were immediately made.

"Oh, don't need to introduce us to Reverend John. We know him well. He's my nephew, you see."

Reverend John's face tinged a little red.

"Now, John's too modest to offer, but he's a real musician. Plays the piano and organ wonderfully. Why don't we all see if we can persuade him to play something for us."

"Oh, Uncle Jake."

But, Reverend John had no choice and, when Jake found out that Mrs. Tixlor was a singer, he talked her into accompanying his nephew.

Reverend John began playing and the restaurant became quiet as people listened. First, he played something classical, which he then turned into jazz. Then, he suddenly burst into modern pop songs and Mrs. Tixlor stood by the piano and sang. It was all a wonderful ending to a very busy day.

It was Saturday morning, the day of the wedding, and it was cloudy with a light drizzle.

Lillian, Karen, and Morgan parked in the large lot in front of Maggie's

Salon and went inside. Katherine and Stacey had just finished and were ready to leave. They excitedly chatted for a few minutes and then went their separate ways.

"Well, at least it isn't searing hot," Benjamin said as he drove towards the little church in the country.

"Look," Stacey pointed at the car in the parking lot. "They're already here." Harlan's gray BMW was parked near the side entrance of the church.

The dressing room was a small room off to the right side of the main church and had probably served as a pastor's study when the church was active. Within a matter of a few minutes the room became a flurry of clothes, makeup, hairspray, and lots of excited talking.

The photographer arrived and came into the dressing room and took lots of pictures.

"Hey," Stacey shouted. "Get that guy out of here. I'm standing here in my underwear."

Everyone laughed and Katherine ushered the photographer out the door while he continuously apologized and said that he hadn't taken pictures of anybody not completely dressed.

Benjamin, Harlan, and Charlie gathered in a small white tent that was nothing more than a canvas roof set up near the left side of the back of the church.

"People are starting to show up," Reverend John said as he walked up to the little tent. "Let's hope the rain is over."

Almost on cue, everyone walked out from under the shelter of the little canvas roof and looked skyward.

Reverend John looked at his watch and smiled. "Hey, we'd better get this show on the road. I'll go round up the mothers so they can be seated. Benjamin, you need to meet Katherine at the back of the sanctuary so we can get you two seated.

Of Ryan's three closest friends, he asked Edward to be his best man and Brian and Tom had been selected as ushers. They were dressed in tuxedos that matched the groom's party. People were pouring in from the parking lot so they had lots of work to do getting them seated.

"What in the world are those little birdcages for?" Mollie asked her husband as Brian escorted them in and got them seated. "It looks like we're attending some sort of gypsy's' hoopla."

Robert didn't say anything. He knew from long experience that most of Mollie's questions were rhetorical and she wouldn't listen to an answer anyway.

"My God, Robert. There's real birds in those cages. Look closely and you'll see them jumping around in there."

The organist began playing a soft prelude as more people came and were seated. The canaries began to chirp and sing. The little church rapidly filled beyond capacity, so Tom and Brian quickly set up folding chairs along the outside aisles.

Benjamin and Katherine came down the aisle with Katherine on Brian's arm. They were seated on the right side in the first row. The murmur of the crowd settled down to an occasional whisper.

Lillian came down the aisle on Tom's arm and was seated in the front row on the left side.

The organist played one of Morgan's most favorite love songs and Mrs. Tixlor, dressed in her white choir-robe, stood and sang.

Almost immediately, all the canaries burst into their joyous song to accompany the singer.

The door opened on the right side of the little church near the front and Reverend John led Ryan, Edward, and Charlie down to the alter.

The organist paused. The sanctuary was silent except for the occasional chirping from a few of the canaries. Then, the pipe organ began playing a march with a slow beat. Virtually, as a single voice, all the canaries burst into a heavenly chorus. Almost as if that was their cue, people turned and looked towards the back of the church.

Slowly, with perfect tempo, Stacey began her march down the aisle. Her slow, timed steps made a stunning beginning to the wedding. Stacey was now 15 and had matured from a little girl into a beautiful young woman. Her face glowed in the warm afternoon light. She smiled slightly and to all, except the trained eye, she appeared calm and collected. The only giveaway to her nervousness was the tiny quiver in the brim of her hat as she made her way down the aisle.

Morgan's maid of honor, her sister, Karen, began her slow walk down the aisle. She was radiantly beautiful and people smiled at her as she came by, but she kept her eyes fixed on the altar.

Once again, the organist paused. Then, the organ boomed out playing the more traditional Wedding March. Everyone stood and faced the rear of the church.

Morgan was holding on tightly to Harlan's arm. Her gown was absolutely stunning and her beauty radiated everywhere, even though her face was slightly shrouded by her veil. Morgan and Harlan began their slow walk towards the alter. The old pipe organ played, the birds sang, and Morgan smiled. She and her father floated down the aisle like a vision from heaven. Her eyes locked with Ryan's and the plague of her left leg seemed to disappear. Each row of the congregation turned towards the front of the church to watch Morgan and her father walk onward. When they reached the front of the church the organist finished, but the music seemed to continue. It was almost as if the walls had remembered the notes and echoes rebounded, accompanied by the continuous song of the canaries who were certainly not aware that the music had ended.

Reverend John motioned for everyone to be seated. "Dearly beloved," he began as the birds continued their song. "We are gathered here this afternoon, in the presence of God to join this man and this woman in marriage."

The canaries continued their serenade.

"Who gives this woman here today?"

"Her mother and I," Harlan said in his clear baritone voice dusted with just a tinge of nervousness. Harlan reached up and lifted Morgan's veil. He kissed her lightly on the cheek. "We love you, darlin'," he whispered.

"I love … you, too, Dad."

Suddenly, Harlan's eyes filled with tears. He turned and quickly found his place beside Lillian.

Lillian had been able to keep her composure right up until her husband sat down beside her and she saw tears dripping off his cheek. She was no longer able to hold back. Her eyes filled with tears and she struggled desperately to keep from sobbing. After all, their little girl was ready to be married.

Reverend John began his traditional essay about marriage and ended with a prayer of blessing for such a joyous occasion.

Mrs. Tixlor sang one of Ryan's favorite love-songs and held the last note for a long time. Suddenly, she was taken aback by the massive burst of colored light that bathed the whole church.

It was almost as if God decided to bless the wedding in a way that only He had the power to do. The late afternoon sun had come out in all its glory. Deep reds, greens, blues, and purples poured into the sanctuary through the old stained-glass windows. But, most impressive was the purplish blue light that shown directly on Ryan and Morgan. It was so brilliant that even Reverend John stopped and looked up.

Katherine choked up and sobbed which seemed to be very contagious. Many in the congregation now had eyes filled with tears. Even the usual stoic Benjamin couldn't hold back and reached for his handkerchief.

"Ryan Martin Wakefield. Will you take this woman to be your lawfully wedded wife? To have and hold, in sickness and health ..." Reverend John continued until he said, "If so, please answer, I will."

There was a slight pause.

"I will."

"Morgan Lynn Carter. Do you take this man ..."

Before Reverend John could finish and ask Morgan her answer, she said, "Yes, I will. I do. Yes."

A titter of laughter rippled across the whole congregation.

"The giving and receiving of rings is a symbol for all ..." Reverend John explained and told the story of how the ring is a circle with no beginning or end. "Now, Ryan. Please place your ring on Morgan's finger and repeat after me. I, Ryan ..."

"Morgan, I ..., I... " Ryan stammered, "Morgan, what I want to say to you is not repeating some ancient vow, but rather, I want to tell you what's in my heart."

Tears streamed down Morgan's face. Lillian sobbed softly and Harlan tried to console her, but tears dripped off of his nose. Karen put her right hand to her mouth and cried. The birds stopped singing.

"When I first met you, I knew there was something special about you.

I couldn't figure out what it was or put a name to it. But, I immediately realized that I felt very different just being around you.

"As we got to know each other, I realized that every time I left your house, I couldn't wait until I would see you again.

"One day I realized what it was. I loved you. Morgan, I've always loved you. My love for you spans beyond the here and now. It has always been and it will always be. From now on, we will be together, forever.

"I can't remember a time when I didn't love you, and there will never be a time when I don't love you.

"Morgan Carter, I promise that I will love you forever," Ryan said as he slid his wedding ring over her finger. Morgan fell into his arms sobbing. Reverend John stood with tears streaming down his face. Katherine buried her face in Benjamin's shoulder. Even Aunt Mollie was crying.

Reverend John and Karen came over and helped Morgan regain her composure.

"Morgan. Please repeat after me. With token and pledge,"

Somehow, Morgan managed to get through her vow and giving of her ring to Ryan.

"What God has joined together, let no man put asunder," Reverend John said as he held his right hand over the heads of Ryan and Morgan. "With the power vested in me, as an ordained minister of the Gospel and the civil authority granted by the State of Wisconsin, I now pronounce you husband and wife. Ryan, you may kiss your bride."

Morgan put her hands up and held on to the back of Ryan's neck. She stood up on her tiptoes as he bent down to meet her. Their kiss was long and passionate. They held their kiss so long that a little snicker sneaked through the congregation. The colored light through the stained-glass window behind the alter was absolutely breathtaking. God was truly blessing this marriage.

"Ladies and gentlemen. I would like to present to you Mr. and Mrs. Wakefield."

People jumped to their feet and applauded. The organist played and the canaries sang. Morgan put her right hand on Ryan's arm and they walked to the back of the church.

"In the name of the Father …" Reverend John smiled and said almost as an afterthought. "In case anyone wants to hear the end. In the name of the Father, the Son, and the holy ghost, Amen."

People lined up and congratulated everyone in the wedding party. Everyone, except Mollie. She absolutely refused to acknowledge the fact that her nephew had married a person with an "affliction."

Ryan held Morgan's hand and they walked towards the waiting limo under a shower of white rice.

"Wait," Charlie and Stacey shouted as they ran up to Morgan and Ryan. They handed each one a small white cardboard box. "Open them together."

On the count of three, Ryan and Morgan opened their boxes. A white dove flew out from each box, found each other, and soared skyward together. Morgan clapped her hands in joy.

"It's … like our … marriage. Always … together … forever."

The wedding party got into the limo for a drive around town with horns honking while the guests made their way to the VFW for the reception.

After about a half-hour, the limo came to a stop back at the little country church. Everyone got out and went back inside for the more traditional wedding photographs.

Karen had met a team of volunteers early that morning to decorate the VFW. Streamers hung from the ceiling and each table was decorated with fresh flowers and full table settings.

People started showing up and looked around with amazement at how their plain-looking VFW had been transported into such a delightful reception hall. Most made their way to the bar, and then found seats at one of the tables.

The highly prized band called the **60's Boys** had been hired and were busy setting up their equipment and instruments.

When the wedding party arrived there were cheers and lots of applause. Ryan and Morgan led the way to the head table.

Edward and Karen stood by the head table for a few seconds while people found their seats. Edward pulled the chair out for Karen and helped her get seated. He then reached for his empty water glass and clinked his spoon against it.

People shushed each other and quickly found chairs. Edward picked up the microphone that was placed by his plate.

"May I have everyone's attention?"

The murmur of the crowd died down.

"There's wine or grape juice on each of the tables. Please take a few minutes and fill your glasses so we can make a toast to the bride and groom."

Activity and conversation spread across the room as bottles were passed and glasses filled.

"I've known Ryan for most all my life," Edward's voice boomed out of the speakers in the ceiling. "We grew up together. We've been inseparable.

"My earliest memory of Ryan was when he and I played like we were pirates up on ol' Benson's bridge. Our hats were made out of old newspapers and our swords were sticks, but it didn't matter. We still were able to fight off any force thrown at us.

"We learned to play baseball together at the park and were on the same Little League team. We played Pee-Wee football together.

"We even learned to drive together. Ryan's dad took us both out on old country roads and let us practice. We probably scared him half to death, but he never seemed to get upset or scold us. We both took our driver's test on the same day, one right after the other.

"I have to admit that when it came to school, Ryan excelled and, well, I just got along.

"What I'm trying to say is, that I'm talking about a guy that is not only my best friend, but more than that. He's a brother to me.

"I met Morgan in a class in high school. Ryan and I were seniors and she was a sophomore. I can't say that I really noticed her at first. I remember one time when Ryan told me that he was going to take on the job of being a tutor for a student. I also remember when he brought her around and we were all introduced to Morgan.

"I noticed that she was a very pretty girl right away. Of course, all us red-blooded teenage boys would notice such a thing, and I was no exception.

"At first, she was shy and didn't talk very much, but with Ryan's help, it didn't take her long to become part of our group.

"It also didn't take long for it to become pretty plain to all of us that these two should be together. And, I don't mean like friends going out on the weekends. I mean these two should be together, forever.

"So, not trying to drag this out any longer, here's to a wonderful life, Ryan and Morgan. We love you!"

Everyone stood, raised their glasses, and sipped their wine or grape juice. Ryan set his glass on the table and turned to Morgan. She immediately put her arms around his neck and gave him a very passionate kiss, much to the delight of the audience.

Salads were served followed by dinner which consisted of an elegant presentation of roast beef, mashed potatoes, and green beans. Dessert was a delightfully decadent pastry shell filled with a strawberry compote.

The band started to play and lights dimmed. The lead singer picked up the microphone and asked Ryan and Morgan to come out on the dance floor for the traditional bride-groom dance.

The band played softly and the lead singer crooned while the newlyweds swayed beautifully to the music for the traditional bride-groom dance.

The next dance was dedicated to the father of the bride, so Harlan went out on the dance floor to his daughter.

"We love you, you know."

"I ... know, Daddy. I've ... always ... known."

Ryan came over to Lillian and asked her to dance. Soon, the dance floor was filled with couples swaying to the well-known gentle music.

Charlie asked Stacey to dance.

The band played and people danced. There was a short interruption for the cutting of the cake, and then many people went back out onto the dance floor.

The band was great. They mixed pop, country, and romantic numbers. They played old favorites and asked everyone to sing along, which most did. As the evening went on, more and more people danced. Most just stayed out on the floor in between each song and waited for the next one to start. People stayed and stayed.

The lead singer sang the number one country love-song. This was one of Morgan's most favorite songs and she and Ryan virtually stood still in each other's arms and just swayed to the lovely, high tremolo of the singer.

Charlie and Stacey had danced almost every dance together. Charlie was certainly glad that he had learned lots of the steps from Ryan and smiled to himself when he remembered how much fun it was listening, learning, and the endless hours of practicing in the family room.

Stacey loved the song, too, and easily moved closer to Charlie as his arm put pressure on her waist. She snuggled her head onto his shoulder.

CHAPTER EIGHTEEN
What's This? A New Job?

Charlie moved Stacey as far away as possible from the band to the corner that was closest to the bar. It wasn't completely dark back there, but almost. There were a few other couples slowly dancing nearby as the mood of the romantic songs wove its spell of love.

Charlie moved back, looked down, and was surprised to see Stacey looking up at him.

He moved closer and she moved upward.

The lead singer's voice sang soft and clear through the loudspeakers and one of the female backup singers sang harmony that blended so well it sent a shiver down Stacey's spine.

Charlie and Stacey moved closer. She reached up and put her hands behind Charlie's neck and pulled him closer. Their lips touched. Life seemed to stand still. Their hearts for an instant beat as one heart. Was it two lost soul-mates that had suddenly found each other? Or, was it just the mood of the occasion and the words from the music? None of it mattered as Charlie held and kissed Stacey and she held and kissed him back.

Morgan told Ryan a long time ago that she had always wanted to go to Disneyworld, and that's what he arranged for their honeymoon.

They flew out of Milwaukee to Orlando. It was Morgan's first time to fly. She was so excited, but just a little scared. The flight was beautiful and smooth. She sat at the window and was mesmerized as she watched the tiny landscape pass before them.

They stayed for four days at the Polynesian Resort right on the Disney property.

They rode every ride and thoroughly enjoyed every exhibit. They swam in the pool and even laid out a little while in the hot Florida sun.

Too soon, it was time to go home. Morgan and Ryan promised each other that they would come back for their tenth anniversary.

Ryan and Morgan came home and moved into their new home. They bought a small, two bedroom brick bungalow that was right on the edge of town. During the first year they worked diligently painting and renovating the whole house. They completely redid the kitchen and bathroom, complete with new appliances and fixtures. They painted the walls and sanded the hardwood floors in all the other rooms.

Morgan had special ideas for the outside. Their backyard was large, but she didn't want any grass. Instead, she rototilled the whole thing. She ordered huge quantities of day lilies of all colors and planted them everywhere. During the first two years, they grew, but didn't bloom very much. But, after that, the whole back yard became a cacophony of color. Newspapers carried color pictures of the glorious cascades of color and people from miles around drove by, just to see it.

Life developed a more regular routine. Morgan loved being in love with Ryan. She loved her little home and most of all, she loved life.

Ryan's work schedule was somewhat erratic and he often had to conduct meetings and seminars in the evenings, but had the weekends off.

Morgan's work schedule was Monday through Saturday with Friday off. Her normal day was morning classes at college and then, work from noon until 5:30PM, except Wednesday, which was her long day having to work until close at 9:00PM.

It was more than six months after the wedding on a Friday afternoon and Morgan's day off. She had been shopping with Stacey and went into the house with her for a while. Stacey was showing her mother a new pair of jeans she had just bought when Aunt Mollie happened to drive up the driveway.

"Hello, everyone," Mollie said as she came into the kitchen and plopped into a chair. "Good gracious, Katherine. You certainly aren't going to let Stacey wear those awful jeans, are you?"

Morgan smiled to herself as she watched fire flash in Katherine's eyes, but she quickly squashed it back.

"Oh, Mollie. This is what the girls wear these days. They're not so bad."

Stacey quickly retreated taking her new jeans down to the basement to the washer. Katherine put the teakettle on.

"Well, young lady. I suppose you are still living in marital bliss?"

Morgan was completely taken by surprise. Mollie had never, ever talked directly to her before. And, she was asking about marital bliss? What should she say? She loved being married. She loved everything about it. So, instead of saying anything, Morgan just smiled.

"Won't last, you know. Just wait a few years. The romance wears away by all the washing, ironing, and housecleaning. Won't be long and you'll be glad to just drop into bed exhausted, and hope your man will leave you alone so you can get some sleep."

"Leave Morgan be, Mollie," Katherine quickly interjected firmly as she poured tea into cups for each of them.

"Well, I suppose you and Benjamin are still behaving like young frisky high school kids, are you?"

"My dear sister. First of all, that's absolutely none of your concern. Second. You would be the last person I would ever talk to about Benjamin's and my love-life. So, change the subject."

Morgan excused herself and went downstairs to find Stacey. She told Stacey what Mollie had said and they both laughed almost hysterically.

"She's just a mean old woman. It's funny how Uncle Robert has put up with her all these years."

Morgan's life fell into a regular routine of working, cooking, eating out, laundry, housework, and most importantly, loving Ryan.

Time went by. Karen graduated from college and accepted a job with a large petroleum company in southern Texas and moved to Galveston.

More time went by and before anyone knew it, another year had passed. Morgan graduated with a double major degree. The first was in secondary education with emphasis on special education and the second was in elementary education.

Much to everyone's surprise, she went back to work fulltime at the library.

More than two years passed. It was a Thursday morning and Morgan was busy working on books that had been returned to the library the night before. First, she scanned the bar code and then placed the book onto a four-wheel cart so that she could work on putting the books back onto the shelves in the afternoon.

"Mrs. Wakefield?"

Morgan looked up and saw a man standing on the opposite side of the counter. He was short and had thinning black hair that was peppered with gray. His blue eyes twinkled as he talked and he had a captivating smile. He wore a very trim dark blue suit, white shirt, and a necktie with bold red and blue stripes.

"I'm Chester Simmons." He extended his right hand out towards Morgan. "Perhaps you've heard of me? I'm the president of the public school board."

"Yes, ... Mr. Simmons, I've ... read ... about you ... in the newspaper."

"Please call me Chester."

Morgan wondered what the president of the local school board wanted with her and her brain mentally scanned what she had read about him in the newspaper recently.

"I've played golf with your husband on a number of Saturdays."

Morgan remembered Ryan telling her, on occasion, who his golfing partners were, and somewhere in the back of her mind she recalled the name of the person standing across the counter from her.

"Anyway, Mrs. Wakefield. I was talking with Ryan last Saturday about some of the more aggressive plans we were trying to work out. I guess at first, it was just more for conversation. But, when I'm excited about something, I virtually explode with enthusiasm I've been told."

Morgan smiled. Chester Simmons was openly friendly and animated.

"Anyway, when I mentioned one of our newest thoughts, well I dare say, your husband told me that I should talk to you as soon as possible."

"Oh?" Morgan asked as she checked out a book for a young girl that came up to the counter.

"Mrs. Wakefield. Is there anywhere we can talk that would be a little more private? What I have to say won't take long."

"I can ... ask ... Mrs. Carlyle ... to take over ... for a ... little while ... and take ... my break. I ...think the ... conference ... room is ...

vacant."

Morgan called Mrs. Carlyle and asked it she would take over the front desk while she took her morning break. Morgan then led the way back to the conference room, unlocked the door, and turned on the lights.

"Mrs. Wakefield. Ryan told me that your degree was in secondary education with special emphasis on children with special needs. Is that correct?"

Morgan nodded that it was.

"The school board urgently knows that we must be integrating more children with special needs into our regular classes. Does that make sense to you?"

"Yes, certainly. I … am … one of … those … people."

"You mean … I don't mean to pry, here, but do you mean that you had special needs as a student?"

"Yes. I … have cerebral … palsy. When I … first … started school, my parents … got the … school board … to allow me … to enroll … into regular classes."

"Oh, my gosh. You must be the Morgan Carter that I read about in the records from a long time ago. Isn't that right? Your father threatened the school board with a law suit if they didn't allow you to attend regular classes. I'm sorry I didn't put two and two together here. I didn't realize that Morgan Carter is actually you, Mrs. Wakefield."

Morgan smiled.

"Did it all work out okay for you?"

"Yes. It … pretty much … worked … out just fine. There … were … a … few teachers … that seemed … uncomfortable with … me … being in … their classes, but … it wasn't … much … of a problem."

"Oh, Morgan. I think you might be just what we're going to need. What the school board is ready to do is to start an aggressive program to integrate kids with special needs into our regular curriculum this coming school year. What would you see as one of the major issues that need immediate attention?"

"Teacher education," Morgan said after some definite consideration.

"I think your husband is absolutely right. I think you just might be the perfect person to fill the role of coordinator. What do think about that?"

Morgan was stunned. Yes, she knew, first hand, what many of the problems were because she had been a kid with special needs. But, in her case, the only special need she really had was, a chance to prove that she was just as capable academically as any of the other kids. And, she did. She had not only been a good student, she was the top student in her class.

"I would like to ask if you would come to a special meeting and talk to our search committee. This is all still pretty preliminary and must be kept under tight wraps until we have a signed contract. I hope you understand."

Morgan nodded that she did.

"Here's a short synopsis of what we're planning along with a preliminary job description. Please look it over and make any comments, changes, or additions you feel necessary. Oh, and before I forget. Here's the most important part of all. This is what we are prepared to offer as the starting annual salary." Chester wrote a number on the paper and put a large dollar sign in front of the amount.

Morgan sat in disbelief. The number seemed astronomical to her, especially in light of her salary at the library. It all seemed like a dream to her.

"Talk it over with your husband and I'll call you with the time and place for our meeting. And, if it all goes well, which I can't see any reason it wouldn't, we will make an official offer to you."

Chester Simmons smiled, stood up, and left. Morgan sat for a few minutes to let it all settle in. Finally, she got up and went back to the front desk to relieve Mrs. Carlyle.

The rest of the day dragged, which was almost unheard of for Morgan. She loved her job at the library. But, this afternoon was different. She couldn't wait to get home and talk to Ryan.

"Wow, Morgan!" Ryan said as he read over the material Simmons had given her. "This seems like the perfect job for you, and I think you'd be terrific at it."

"But, what ... about ... my job ... at the ... library?"

Ryan took Morgan into his arms and held her close.

"I know how important the library has been to you, my love. But, sometimes you have to look beyond and see where you can do the most good. Think of it as chapters in a great book. The chapter you just read was your job at the library. This new opportunity is the next chapter. And, what a wonderful chapter it could be. Especially, with your knowledge, training, and insight. I can see why Simmons thinks you'll be the perfect candidate."

"So, you ... think ... I should ... accept ...the job, ... if they ... offer it ... to me?"

"I think whatever makes you happy is what's important here, Morgan. You know I'll be standing right here beside you not matter what you decide."

Morgan hugged Ryan tightly.

"But, you know what? Let's run over to your folks' house and have your dad read this over and see what he thinks."

Within a few minutes they were in the car and drove towards her parents' house.

"Well, good gracious, Morgan," Harlan said. "This almost looks like the perfect job for you. You know, honey, it's pretty rare when any board has the forethought to put someone in command of any sort of program where they actually have firsthand knowledge of it."

"You ... think it's ... okay, then, ... Dad?"

"I think it's a great opportunity, honey. But, it's your decision. I know how helpful you are at the library and how much the people you work with like you. But, that's not the real issue here, is it? This new opportunity allows you to make a real difference in the lives of so many kids that just need a chance."

Morgan and Ryan stayed for dinner and talked until after ten o'clock.

On the way home, Ryan stopped for the traffic light at Elm and Center streets and waited for the light to turn green.

"Ryan?"

"Hmmm?"

"I ... think ... I'll ... take the job."

Ryan smiled. The light turned green and he drove towards home.

"Is that ... alright ... with you?"

Ryan drove up to the curb and stopped. He leaned over and put his arms around Morgan and said, "Whatever makes you happy, my love, makes me happy. But, this isn't about being happy. I believe this is about you making a difference. So few ever get that chance. I'm so glad you decided to take the job."

"Do … you think … I can … do it?"

"I have no doubt. You can do anything you put your mind to."

"You're … just saying … that."

"Because I love you?"

"Maybe."

"No maybes about it. First, I know you can do it, and second, yes, I will always be there for you, no matter what. Last, I love you more than you could ever imagine."

Ryan put the shift lever back into *drive*, pulled away from the curb and drove home.

"I want … to … do it, … Ryan. I … want to … make a … difference."

Ryan reached out for Morgan's hand and held it. He smiled in the darkness as he drove onward towards home.

Chester Simmons called Morgan the next night and arranged for a meeting the next Tuesday evening at seven o'clock in the administration office building. He said it would be great if she could bring her husband along, too.

CHAPTER NINETEEN
Here's What I Want

Morgan was relieved to have Ryan with her, but she was still very nervous. They arrived promptly at seven o'clock and went into a large conference room. There were five board members already seated at the meeting, and Mr. Simmons. Three women and three men. Morgan was asked to sit at the front of the table so they could all ask her questions, get her comments, and ideas.

It took a while before Morgan began to calm down and feel at ease. She answered all the questions clearly, competently, and thoroughly.

Ryan sat at the back and watched. He never ceased to be amazed by his wife's capabilities. He knew that once she set her mind to something, she could and would accomplish it. He smiled as he heard her next comment.

"I think ... the real ... issue ... is ... teacher training. Help ... them understand ... that many ... handicapped kids ... need ... nothing more ... than ... a chance. But, ... foremost, ... there must be ... training ... on just what ... the special needs ... and ... handicaps are. Myths ... must be ... erased. Caring ... must be ... foremost. The other ... kids must be ... led. Then, ... real integration ... will occur naturally. Of course, ... not without ... problems, ... but problems ... can be solved."

The committee suddenly applauded.

"I've heard enough," one of the women committee members said firmly. "Let's put this to a verbal vote. I move that we offer this new position to Morgan Wakefield."

It was an immediate, unanimous vote.

"Well, Mrs. Wakefield," Chester Simmons said as he quickly got up from his chair and came over to Morgan. "The job is yours, if you will accept it."

Tears welled up in Morgan's eyes, but she nodded her head that she wanted the job.

Morgan dreaded giving her notice to Mr. Foxbie, the director of the library. She worked on her resignation letter for two nights before she was satisfied that it said exactly what she wanted to say.

The next morning she was up early and was ready to leave before Ryan was even out of the shower.

"Can't go to work before they unlock the door, can you?" Ryan tried to joke with Morgan as he wiped his wet head with the towel.

Morgan made up her mind to take her letter directly to Mr. Foxbie's office just as soon as she got to work.

"Hi, Morgan," Julia Fallon, Mr. Foxbie's secretary said as she was filling the coffee maker.

"Good ... morning. Is ... Mr. Foxbie ... here?"

"Not yet, but ..."

Julia was cut short by Foxbie coming through the door.

Foxbie was a tall, thin man and about forty-five years old. He always dressed perfectly and in the latest fashion. All the women at the library talked about how much money he must spend just on neckties. Everyone talked, except Morgan, of course. She tried to never enter into any of the office gossip.

Raymond Foxbie had sandy colored hair that was always trimmed to perfection. His shoes were always shined. Today, he wore a tan suit with a light yellow shirt and a bold stripped necktie. "Good morning, Julia. Oh, and good morning, Morgan."

"Morgan would like to meet with you for a few minutes."

"Sure. Come on into my office, Morgan."

Morgan followed Foxbie into his office. She handed him her envelope.

"What's this, Morgan?" Foxbie asked as he sat down and picked up his reading glasses. He opened the envelope and began to read. "Good, God, Morgan. You're leaving us?"

Morgan told Raymond Foxbie about her new job. She promised herself that she wouldn't let herself cry, but when she tried to tell him how much she had loved her job at the library, she just couldn't hold back. Tears ran down her cheeks and she struggled hard to keep from sobbing.

"Well, Morgan," Foxbie said and folded his hands. "We're certainly going to miss you."

Morgan sobbed a little and reached into her purse for a tissue.

"But, it sounds like this new job will be perfect for you. Not only will it be a great opportunity for you, but just think of the doors you can open for some kids that really need it."

It took less than an hour for the news to reach every person in the library. Everyone came over to congratulate Morgan on her new job.

Her last day was Saturday. When she got to work she was shocked. Everyone was already there, including Ryan.

"Surprise!" everyone yelled out together.

There was food on every available surface. There was even a line of crock-pots.

When it was over every employee came up to Morgan, hugged her, and told her how much they would miss her.

The scheduled workers then went back to work and the others left to do whatever else they had planned on their day off. Morgan took up her normal post at the front desk.

It was the longest day she had ever had at the library. There were very few patrons and not much to do. The large clock on the wall facing her seemed to be operating in slow-motion.

Morgan took no time off between jobs and started right in on her new position Monday morning. Her first day was filled with meetings and interviews with candidates for her assistant.

"I had … no idea … how … tiring it all is," Morgan said to Ryan when he came home from work. "It … seems like … there's no end … to what … needs … to get done … before … I can start … doing … what … I was … hired … to do."

Ryan smiled and hugged his fretting wife.

Over the course of the next four days, Morgan interviewed twelve candidates for the job as her assistant and decided that the job should be offered to Janis Cleaver. Janis was about Morgan's mother's age. She was a single mom and had two children. She was three courses short of completing her degree, most of it done at night. Janis was full of energy and a self-made person. But, what impressed Morgan most was when she found out that Janis' oldest child, William, was twelve years old and had Down's Syndrome. When she checked the school system records she found that William had always been denied admission to any class. Janis had home-schooled William, and some teachers even petitioned the State that the form of home-schooling he received was invalid.

Morgan dove right into her new job. She and Janis worked tirelessly all summer.

First, she met with community leaders and people leading various groups that supported kids with special needs to determine the scope of the issue. She made lists of everyone she could identify that had children with some type of disability, and then went out and met with the parents.

During each meeting with the parents, together, they reached a consensus as to how their child could best be served by the school district. In many cases, it was very clear that their child would best be served by home schooling or special education classes. But, a number of kids were identified that should, and could, fit right into regular classes. Eleven children that were classified as special needs Morgan felt could go into regular classes, with no special accommodations. Their disabilities ranged from physical handicaps, to Down's Syndrome, to cerebral palsy. There were four that were appropriate for classes one to five, three for grades six through eight, and four that could be in high school.

She met individually with the superintendent of the school district and each school board member for their input, opinions, and questions about the new initiative. Next, she met with the three grammar school principals and finally, the principal of the high school. All were very enthusiastic.

Morgan developed training materials for the teachers and met with each one that would have a handicapped child starting in their class in the fall.

The superintendent placed Morgan on the agenda of the teachers training meeting that was always held one week before the start of school.

"Ladies and gentlemen," Chester Simmons addressed the teachers assembled in the high school auditorium on the second day of teacher training. "Please take your seats so we can begin this afternoon's program."

People moved around and found their seats. The noise calmed to a murmur that rose and fell until most everyone had found their place and sat down.

"As you all know, the federal government has notified school districts that they will be enforcing the new laws and guidelines that were passed a few years ago. In order for our district to be in compliance, we have hired a special needs coordinator to help guide us.

"Her name is Morgan Wakefield. Morgan is a product of our school system. Her degree is in special education. Some of you have probably already met her by now and know she is a very personable and capable young woman.

"So, I would like to present Mrs. Morgan Wakefield."

Morgan stood up and walked to the podium. There was a small, courteous amount of applause.

"Thank you, … Mr. Simmons."

Morgan's speech was well prepared and rehearsed. She told about her own disability and her experiences which everyone listened to intently. She read the federal guidelines and then told about the eleven children that not only could go to regular public school, but should.

"Many people … shun … those of us … with handicaps … because we are … considered … different. But, we're not … different at all. We don't … want special … treatment, … just fair and … equal opportunities.

"Take for instance, … my assistant's son, … William. He is … twelve … and has … Down's Syndrome. Other … than that, he's a … normal kid. He's … smart and … academically, is almost … a grade … ahead of other … kids his age. Every year … his mother … has … applied … for admission … to regular classes … for him … and has … always been … denied."

Morgan continued telling about other children that should be in regular public school classes. Most everyone listened intently nodding in agreement from time to time.

"In closing, I … know there … will be challenges. Please call … me

"... any time, at my ... office ... or home. Thank you."

There was a fair amount of applause and some even stood as they clapped to show their approval.

"Thank you, Mrs. Wakefield. We have a few minutes left, so if anyone would like to ask a question or make any comments, please raise your hand."

A murmur went across the crowd as people talked to each other. Finally, one of the fifth grade teachers raised her hand.

"My name is Janet Fitch. I teach fifth grade at the Crossing Elementary School. One of the new students will start my class in a few days, and I just want to say that I think it's high time they do. It will be good for our new student, certainly, but a real learning experience for the rest of the class, and, for me, too. More importantly, it's the right thing to do."

People applauded and a few shouted their agreement.

Another hand went up and was recognized. A thin, middle-aged woman stood.

"My name is Miss Anderson and I teach high school classes here in sociology. I've had, over the years, plenty of first hand experience with some of these kids you are trying to ram down our throats. Fortunately, there haven't been too many over the years."

The whole assembly instantly grew silent and listened.

"What you aren't being told is how much they disrupt the class. They make funny noises and often wave their hands uncontrollably. The kids make fun of them. And, as far as learning and keeping up- ha! Most of them could barely be taught to tie their own shoes.

"I'm not without compassion, for heaven's sake, but, they have no place in a regular classroom. They all need to be in special education classes where properly trained people can, well I guess there's no other way to put it, baby sit them.

"Every semester that I've had to put up with one of them, I've complained to our principal, the school board, and even filed a few grievances to our union. All my complaints were totally ignored.

"I even remember back about ten years or so when I complained about one of the special needs students, someone threatened the school board with a law suit, which of course, caused them to cave in totally.

"While my opinion may be unsavory, just wait. In a few years, you'll all come to the same conclusion."

A few people applauded their agreement, but more booed and hissed their disapproval. Miss Anderson sat down, her face tinged in red, but she desperately tried to hide her anger.

It was clear that she didn't recognize Morgan as one of her former "special needs" students, but Morgan immediately recognized her. She wondered if it was her that Miss Anderson was talking about.

The superintendent immediately stood up and came up to the podium.

"Miss Anderson, I thank you for your concerns and experiences. The decision has already been made, both at the federal and state levels. What we all need is to learn how best to proceed. That's why we've hired Mrs. Wakefield."

More people raised their hands and asked questions.

"I'm George Griggs and I teach eight grade. I've had a few kids in my eighth grade class that have been handicapped. In fact, I remember one, a few years back, by the name of Tim Stanton. He was confined to a wheelchair, but, as I remember it, he was a great student. The kids all seemed to like him, too. So, I guess I would like to ask, what's the big problem?"

A considerable number of people clapped their approval.

When the meeting was finally over, many of the teachers crowded around the podium to take brochures and talk to Morgan and her assistant. Most were very upbeat and accepting. Morgan was bombarded with questions which she tried her best to answer.

Miss Anderson's casual bombshell of a law suit being filed about ten years ago caused Morgan to wonder if possibly her father was somehow involved in it. She couldn't remember any mention of it before.

She put the keys in the ignition of her car and decided to stop and ask her mother about it.

"Hi, Mom."

"Hello, Morgan," Lillian said as she came out of the laundry room to greet her daughter.

The two women talked casually while Lillian put the teakettle on to heat.

Morgan told her mother about the meeting she had just left and about Miss Anderson's comments about a law suit.

"I remember we threatened the school board when you first started school, but I don't think anything ever came of it. Besides, that was longer than ten years ago."

"How ... did it ... happen ... that I was ... accepted into ... regular school, Mom?"

"We put you into daycare when you were four. The next year you started right into kindergarten, in the regular school system. You went right on from there. No one ever thought anything of it as far as I know. It's just the way it was. You never had any problem making top grades, in fact you were always pretty close to a straight A student all through school."

Lillian poured a cup of tea for each of them and they talked for quite a while.

"Hey, beautiful," Harlan said as he came in the back door, went over and put his arms around Lillian, and gave her a kiss. "Hi, Morgan. It's, sure good to see you. You and Ryan must be avoiding us lately."

Morgan and her dad kidded back and forth for a few minutes. Then, Morgan gave him a rundown on her meeting with the teachers.

"Isn't it funny how people can feel so threatened by a person that's a little different from the norm? Especially, when it's about kids."

Morgan finally got up the nerve to tell her dad what Miss Anderson had said and wondered if it was him that had filed a law suit to allow her to go to school.

"For you, honey?" Harlan laughed out loud. "Oh, I threatened the school board a time or two, but never anything too serious.

"But, I think what this teacher is talking about was the action I did file about ten years ago for a kid that was in eighth grade. Funny, too. It was when a few teachers in the high school found out about him, they tried to block his admission as a freshman the next year. Remember him, Lillian? Nice kid."

"Derrick Stevens?"

"Yep. That was his name."

"Why, … did they … try to … keep him out … of high … school, Dad?"

"He had some kind of physical disability, if I remember correctly, and was confined to a wheelchair. The coalition of high school teachers tried to show that the building was not properly equipped to deal with wheelchairs, so he shouldn't be allowed admission."

"What … happened?"

"I had our firm file a legal brief with the court against the school board for blatant discrimination. After all, he went all through grammar school with no problems, and that school was considerably older than the high school."

"But, that wasn't all, was it dear?" Lillian smiled and put the tea cups into the sink. "You were quite unpopular around town for a little while?"

"Why … was that?"

"Well, honey. It seems like that year had been a tough year on the football team. Turns out that two boys had broken legs and were in wheelchairs. Another one was on crutches because of a broken foot. Plus, two girls had been in a car accident which left one in a wheelchair and the other using crutches. Our suit claimed that if the Stevens boy was denied admission because the building could not properly accommodate him, then the only fair thing to do was to immediately expel all students using wheelchairs or crutches."

"Wow, Dad. You … never … told me … anything about that."

"Your father went before the school board and told them that he was prepared to take it all the way to the State Supreme Court, if necessary. And, possibly, beyond that into the federal courts."

"What happened?"

"The school board was shocked, to say the least," Lillian added as she rinsed out the cups.

"Yes, they certainly were, Lillian. Not only did they allow Derrick to be admitted with open arms, but they wrote searing letters to each of the teachers that tried to block his admission to be placed into their personnel files."

"That's when the newspaper got wind of it and they ran article after article about all sorts of problems in our schools."

"Guess any organization needs to be aired out once in a while. Anyway, Morgan, the whole thing got dropped and life went on. Most people forgot all about it in a few weeks and went back to worrying about their kids, jobs, and paying their bills."

All the way home, Morgan felt proud of what her father had done. She knew he was a man of honesty and principle, but always thought it was because he was her dad. But, now she knew his principles ran deep and she admired him all the more for it.

School started and the eleven kids were accepted in. Morgan worked with each of their teachers and with the kids. She even tutored them, on occasion.

After six months, all eleven had excelled and were doing very well. The other kids had accepted them exceedingly well, even better than some of the teachers.

Morgan's program and guidance had become a great success.

It was summer between the second and third year of Morgan's new job. She went to her office every day and worked with her administrative assistant on plans for the coming school year, which would start within a few months.

But, Morgan occasionally had trouble concentrating. Often, when she was alone in her office, she would just sit and stare out the window and let her mind run.

It was on a Tuesday, in the middle of July and one of the hottest days of the summer so far. Morgan had made up her mind.

She called Ryan's office and asked if he could come home early.

"What is it, Morgan? Are you sick?"

"No. Not ... sick. Just ... want to ... talk."

Ryan was really worried. He knew that she had been working too hard lately and hadn't been feeling well. Maybe something was wrong with her.

He told her that he would leave right away.

Morgan got home first and was sitting at the kitchen table when Ryan drove up the driveway and screeched his tires to a quick stop. He jumped out and ran inside."

"What is it, Morgan?" Ryan asked as he immediately came over to her and hugged her.

CHAPTER TWENTY
I Want One of Those

"I want ... one ... of those."

"What those, are you talking about?"

"Baby," Morgan smiled and looked into Ryan's eyes with all the love he had ever seen in her eyes.

"Baby? Morgan," Ryan stammered as the shock settled in. "You know ... I ... that is ... we've ... talked that all out. Remember? It would be terribly dangerous for you to get pregnant. The doctor told us that. And, I can't make you pregnant. I've had a vasectomy."

"Not me ... pregnant, ... silly. Adopt."

Ryan rushed to his wife and held her in his arms. He had secretly always wanted children, but his love for Morgan was too deep to ever risk it. The doctor had told them that it would be too risky for her to carry a fetus, so he decided long ago to have the sterilizing operation. The thought of adopting had somehow never entered his mind.

"I love you, Morgan Wakefield. With all my heart and soul," Ryan said as he kissed her and tears streamed down his face.

Morgan told him about her research into adoption. She had even contacted two agencies that were within fifty miles of where they lived and said they were ready to meet, face to face, with them. Morgan took a folder out of her briefcase and showed Ryan the brochures and materials both had sent her.

"I should have known, Morgan. You've certainly done your homework."

Morgan smiled and moved Ryan through every one of the pages. Her enthusiasm was contagious and it wasn't long before he was completely captivated by the thought of them becoming parents.

Over the course of the next month, Morgan and Ryan met with numerous adoption administrators, counselors, clergy, and lawyers that specialized in adoption. The whole process seemed extremely complicated and time consuming.

Then, came a long period of many months of just waiting. Nothing.

Morgan made notes on her calendar and called the agencies on the tenth of each month just to make contact. She was always assured that everything was proceeding as fast as possible and to never give up hope.

It was a Thursday in mid-September and a new school year started. It was Morgan's fourth year in the school system. She started eleven kids her first year. This year there were thirty one. It was not quite four o'clock when Janis knocked on the door and stepped in.

"Sorry to interrupt you, boss. Telephone."

Janis had turned out to be an extremely valuable employee. Not only was she completely competent, but had become Morgan's right-hand person. But, it was a two-way street. Morgan had delegated lots of authority to Janis and even allowed her to take time off during the day to finish her degree.

"Morgan Wakefield."

"Hello, Mrs. Wakefield. This is Mrs. Baxter at the adoption agency."

"Yes?"

"Are you sitting down?"

"Yes," Morgan said but wondered why Mrs. Baxter would wonder if she was sitting or standing.

"We have a newborn baby."

Mrs. Baxter didn't say anything and let the news settle in.

Suddenly, Morgan shouted, "What?"

"Could you and your husband meet me at University Hospital Saturday morning at ten?"

Before Mrs. Baxter had been able to get the whole sentence out, Morgan was shouting.

"A baby? Baby! Janis, ... it's ... a baby!"

Morgan hurriedly wrote down the details making sure she had everything straight.

Janis rushed in and the women hugged and cried as Morgan tried to tell her what Mrs. Baxter had said.

"Is it a boy or girl," Janis asked.

Morgan thought for a few seconds and then said, "I ... don't know. Don't care ... either."

She called Ryan and told him the news between sobs.

Morgan was still in shock. She was going to be a mom. Finally!

"Do you have anything to take care of a new baby, Morgan?"

"Everything … we need. Had it … all for over a … year."

Friday was a whirlwind of activity. But, even in all her excitement and elation, Morgan had learned over the almost two years of dealing with adoption agencies, there was always the looming cloud of disappointment. There had been lots of "hurry up and wait" months. There had even been two, halfway promises of babies, but both fell through.

This time seemed different to Morgan, though. As much as she tried to keep her emotions reined in, she would suddenly have a burst of excitement.

Ryan was having the same emotional ride, but tried his best to appear calm and collected. His charade certainly didn't work, though. Whenever Morgan got excited, even over the littlest things, like rearranging the furniture in the baby's room for the thirtieth time, her emotional high immediately captivated him and took him along for he ride.

Neither Morgan nor Ryan slept much Friday night. It was just five a.m. when Morgan declared that it was useless to stay in bed, so they both got up.

Morgan made another trip into the baby's room for a last minute check and made a list of things she thought they might need. It was ten minutes to six when they went out the door and, hopefully, the start of a life-long dream as parents.

The world wasn't on their time, however. Ryan drove around town for a while, but found nothing was open.

"Let's … drive … towards … the city, … Ryan. Maybe we … can find … a restaurant … so we … can have … breakfast."

Ryan smiled and turned onto the main highway leading out of town. He noticed the excitement in Morgan's voice, especially because of the more exaggerated hesitation between some words. Ryan smiled to himself.

They found a restaurant that was open and tried to take as long as possible to burn off some time. Breakfast only took fifty minutes.

The waitress told them that there was a K-Mart that opened early and was only about twenty minutes away, so Ryan wrote down the directions.

Morgan found everything on her list and added to it as they browsed the aisles. The K-Mart diversion took up almost an hour.

The drive time to the hospital would have normally taken about an hour, but today, it seemed like forever.

Ryan drove into the hospital parking lot, found a parking space, and shut off the engine. It was five minutes after nine.

They got out of the car and had just started walking towards the main entrance. Suddenly, Morgan looked over at Ryan with a big smile.

"I'm ... going ... to be ... a mom, ... Ryan, ... and ... you're ... going ... to be ... a dad."

As they continued walking towards the main entrance they heard someone calling. "Mrs. Wakefield, is that you?"

Ryan and Morgan turned around and looked back towards the ocean of parked cars and saw a woman running towards them. Morgan immediately recognized her. It was Mrs. Baxter. Morgan's heart sunk as she thought it must be bad news.

"Glad you're here early. Hello, Ryan."

Ryan smiled and said hello.

"We can get the rest of the paperwork out of the way," Mrs. Baxter said as the three went inside the main lobby of the huge hospital.

Mrs. Baxter directed Morgan and Ryan into a small conference room. She put her briefcase on the table and asked them to sit down.

"Alright. Let's begin. Now, I know you have both requested not to be told the sex of the child as you wanted to be surprised, just as if you gave birth.

"If you'll both sign this document," Mrs. Baxter pointed to the appropriate lines. "This notifies the State of your acceptance of the child."

Morgan immediately signed. Ryan looked the document over for a few seconds, and then signed.

"This paper grants authority to our agency to act as intermediary."

Morgan and Ryan signed it, along with four more documents.

"Last, this document has been signed by the birth mother releasing all rights and claims to her child and grants to you all rights and authority forever."

Tears streaked down Morgan's face as, for the first time, she realized that a woman was giving up her child to Ryan and her. Morgan touched the mother's signature reverently. It was almost as if she could feel the unbelievable pain in the birth mother's heart.

"This is the only time you'll ever hear or see of the child's real mother," Mrs. Baxter said as she noticed Morgan lingering over the scrawled signature.

"What … about the … birth mother?" Morgan asked slowly. "What caused … her to … want to … give up … her … baby?"

"All I can tell you is that she is very young. She was thirteen when she got pregnant. Her mother and father are divorced and her dad lives in California somewhere. She has two younger sisters. I know it seems very hard to imagine and probably even cruel, Mrs. Wakefield," Mrs. Baxter said as she touched Morgan's hand, "But, the world we live in can be a very cruel place sometimes. She really had no choice at all and, I can tell you that she is very grateful that the baby will be placed in the loving arms of you and Ryan." Mrs. Baxter was careful not to identify the sex of the baby to distance the child further from its birthmother.

Tears streamed down Morgan's face. The tears were of joy for her and Ryan, but there were tears of pain and heartache for the baby's birthmother, too.

Three more documents were signed and then Mrs. Baxter excused herself for a few minutes.

Ryan and Morgan didn't say anything to each other. Ryan held Morgan's hand and they both stared into space.

The door opened and Mrs. Baxter came in carrying something wrapped in a baby's blanket.

"Well, here she is. Mr. and Mrs. Wakefield, you have a three day old, baby girl."

Mrs. Baxter carefully handed the baby to Morgan's outstretched arms. Morgan carefully pulled the newborn close to her breast and swayed gently. The baby was sound asleep and snuggled close to the warmth of Morgan's body.

Ryan's heart was filled with joy as he put his arm around Morgan and looked down at their new daughter. He noticed tears streaming down Morgan's face and felt warm inside as he saw the mothering glow shine all over her face.

"Have you decided on a name for her?" Mrs. Baxter asked with a big smile. "I need it for the birth certificate application."

CHAPTER TWENTY ONE
The Growing Years and Mending Fences

Without any hesitation, Morgan whispered, "Beth Anne."
So it was that Beth Anne Wakefield was born and became part of Ryan and Morgan's hearts and their very souls.

Morgan had no doubt that she wanted to be a fulltime mom and immediately resigned from her job with the school system. She recommended that Janis be promoted to take over, which was unanimously approved by the school board.

Time passed and Morgan found only joy in being a mother. To her, there was no downside. She never minded getting up in the middle of the night to feed and change Beth Anne. She loved the feeling that only a mother can know, of holding her baby close to her heart. Even when it was Ryan's turn to get up at night, Morgan always got up with him.

Both sets of grandparents were completely captivated with their new granddaughter and were competitive at taking care of her. They always offered and made suggestions that Morgan and Ryan needed to get away for the weekend, but it never happened. They had to settle with holding her and taking care of her in short bursts whenever they came over or Morgan stopped at their house for a while.

As Beth Anne grew and more time passed, she did spend nights with both sets of grandparents. She especially loved her Aunt Stacey and Stacey was captivated by her.

It was Beth Anne's fourth birthday and a big party had been planned in the backyard of Ryan's parents house. Many relatives were invited. There were lots of games, food, and cake. Beth Anne had a real fondness for cake, and there was plenty.

"Where's Beth Anne?" Katherine suddenly asked noticing her absence. "I haven't seen her for quite a while."

Stacey volunteered to make a full search of the house and was off in a flash.

"Well, I'm not surprised," Aunt Mollie said to Katherine in a sarcastic tone. "The way you all dote over her, it's no wonder she's so spoiled. Actually, she's pretty much a brat, if you ask me. She's probably just gone off somewhere."

If looks could kill, Mollie would be dead. Katherine's frown told Aunt Mollie not to press it any further, but of course, she couldn't resist.

"I suppose it's all we can expect being a child of ... well, you know what I mean. A child of a misfit, and all. Lord only knows where she's wandered off to."

Suddenly, Katherine exploded into a seething rage. She grabbed Mollie by the arm and marched her into the house and once they were alone, unloaded on her with both barrels.

"You ignorant ingrate. If you're calling Morgan a misfit, you're an absolute ignorant, ingrate. Morgan had cerebral palsy, for God's sake. It left her with some minor disability, that's all. She's a brilliant girl and a terrific mother."

Mollie was a little shocked by her younger sister's outburst, but didn't show it in any way. She was right, and she knew it.

"Further, Sister. I'm tired of being ridiculed by your stupid remarks. How Robert puts up with you, only heaven knows."

"Well, all I can say is, like mother, like daughter."

"What the hell is that supposed to mean?"

"If her mother is a little crazy, I suppose it's only natural that the daughter would follow suit."

"Have you no understanding or compassion at all? Are you really that stupid?"

"I'm holding to my impression, that's all."

Katherine was just about to tell her sister about the adoption, but decided against it. She decided to let Mollie continue to think that Morgan had given natural birth to Beth Anne and would never tell her otherwise. Hopefully, she wouldn't ever find out for the rest of her life. After all, she had some knowledge that Mollie wasn't privy to, and that was power in the sisterhood battle.

"Hey, Mom," Stacey said as she came into the living room where her mother and aunt were still making stabbing remarks to each other. "I found Beth Anne. She's sound asleep upstairs on my bed."

Katherine laughed almost hysterically. She was relieved to know where her granddaughter was and she basked in the light of how stupid it made her sister look.

Beth Anne was almost the complete opposite of Aunt Mollie's description. She was cute, bright, and most of all, very polite. Especially for an only child and grandchild.

Another year went by. Beth Anne grew and longed to start school. Morgan set up a little schoolroom for her in the basement and spent time each afternoon with her, teaching her letters and numbers.

When Beth Anne started kindergarten, it was Morgan that tried desperately to hide her tears as her little daughter marched out with her to the end of the driveway to wait for the school bus.

"See you this afternoon," Beth Anne called as she climbed up the steps of the huge bus.

Morgan knew in her heart that the days of her sweet little baby girl were now over. But, in their place would be good years of learning and growing.

There would be change for Morgan, too. Her days of being a 'stay-at-home mom' were over. Today, she started a part-time job back at the library.

Morgan waited in her car to pick up her daughter after school one Tuesday afternoon in early January. Beth Anne was now in the third grade. She loved school, loved learning, and loved life, just like her mother. Her curiosity was unquenchable. She was about average height for a third grader, had blonde hair, sparkling blue eyes, and a smile that virtually turned on the radiance of the sun. Overall, Beth Anne was a charming little girl, and, she was very polite.

"Mom. Mom." Beth Anne yelled as she ran ahead of the other kids with her coat unzipped and holding a paper tightly clutched in her right hand. "You've got to sign this paper so I can take it back to Mrs. Bennett tomorrow." Mrs. Bennett was Beth Anne's teacher.

"What ... is it, ... honey?"

"Permission."

"Permission ... for ... what?" Morgan asked as she started the motor and put the selector in drive.

"Mrs. Bennett is taking our class ice skating at the park tomorrow."

The city fire department flooded a large circular area each year over one of the ball diamonds in the park. When it froze, it formed a large skating area and was lighted by the huge floodlights that were installed two years ago for night baseball games in the summertime.

Morgan drove home and Beth Anne chattered all the way telling her mother of every interesting and fascinating event of her day.

That night, Beth Anne couldn't wait for her dad to come home from work so she could tell him about her chance to ice skate tomorrow.

"Do you think you can skate?" Ryan asked his bubbling daughter as he hugged her.

"Course, I can. It's almost like walking. See? Like this." Beth Anne imitated skating strokes she'd seen on television.

"But, you don't have any skates."

"Don't worry, Dad. Mrs. Bennett said the park rents them. Oh, I need to take a dollar to school tomorrow."

The skating event was a great success. It turned out that Beth Anne was very coordinated and was able to pick up the basics of ice skating quite quickly. At least the basics of being able to stand up and carefully move around the ice without falling constantly.

For the next week, Beth Anne's constant topic of conversation was ice skating and how great it would be if she had her own skates.

A lady came into the library one morning and asked if it would be alright to post a schedule of ice skating lessons and events being held at the ice arena. Morgan asked for an extra copy and took it home to show Beth Anne.

The ice arena had been built a few years ago as an indoor sports arena that offered a place for their semipro hockey team, called the "Hawks," to play their home games. It also hosted annual curling competition, an occasional Disney show, and lots of other winter sport activities, year around.

"Oh, Mom, do you think I could take some of those lessons?"

"Well, … there's a … beginner's class … starting … tomorrow at … four o'clock. … I could … take you … there right … after school."

The next day, Beth Anne thought the school day would never end. But, much to her surprise, it finally did.

"Hurry up, Mom," Beth Anne shouted as she jumped into the car, slammed the door, and buckled her seatbelt. "We don't want to be late."

Morgan smiled and loved the never-ending enthusiasm of her daughter.

Morgan rented a pair of skates for Beth Anne and they found seats near the ice.

"Hey, Nora," Beth Anne shouted to a girl about her age with her mother. "Down here."

"This is Nora, Mom. She's in my class at school."

"Hello, … Nora."

The little girl smiled warmly. The two girls instantly started talking excitedly as they put on their skates. Soon they were both ready and skated off both wobbling like drunken sailors in the direction of the gathering group of kids near the center of the ice.

"What a challenge," said the woman that Morgan assumed was Nora's mother, as she came and flopped down beside her. "I don't know where those kids get all their energy from."

The two talked for a little while about their kids, school, and ice skating.

"It's all Nora's talked about all last week. Ice skating, ice skating, ice skating. She's even been practicing on the kitchen floor in her stocking feet."

Both women laughed.

The two talked again. This time the woman told Morgan briefly of her life history.

"Got pregnant in my first year of college and dropped out. I've been married three times and divorced three times. Guess I'm terrible at marriage. Got two more girls, too. Diane is twelve and Jessica is thirteen. All three are really good kids, thank God. Good in school, too. Don't take after their mother in that respect, though. Probably a real good thing, too."

"Beth Anne ... talks about ... Nora ...all the time."

The lady suddenly looked up and seemed to study Morgan for a few seconds.

"Do I know you? You look familiar somehow. Have you ever been to Dewey's Bar? I work nights there. It's a terrible job and the pay is crap, but Dewey rents the apartment upstairs to me real cheap. It's small, only four rooms and bath, but we manage."

Morgan smiled and shook her head no that she had never been to Dewey's Bar.

"You probably don't know it, but Nora was born with cerebral palsy. She's not bad. In fact, you would hardly notice it at all, if you didn't look hard.

"The school has been a real blessing for her. They accepted her right from the start, just like any other kid. I'm really thankful for that. It would have certainly been a different story back when I went to school. They would have made Nora go to some special school and learn menial tasks for the retarded.

"The only thing is, she's a little uncoordinated for a girl her age. The doctor told me that swimming or ice skating might help, so that's why we're here."

Morgan noticed that the woman kept glancing at her from time to time. It was like she was wracking her brain trying to dredge up some old acquaintance from a long time ago.

The conversation was interrupted by Beth Anne and Nora skating by.

"Watch me, Mom!" Beth Anne shouted and then tripped and fell.

"Watch me, Mama," Nora yelled out and fell right on top of Beth Anne.

Both girls exploded in laughter.

"By the way, I'm Vicky Salsburg," the woman said and reached out her right hand towards Morgan.

CHAPTER TWENTY TWO
Is This a New Beginning

Morgan didn't recognize the last name, but was pretty sure she knew who this lady was.

"Morgan. Morgan Wakefield," Morgan smiled and shook the woman's hand.

"Wakefield. Wakefield. The name sounds familiar, somehow."

Again, Morgan didn't say anything, but just smiled.

"I dated a guy by the name of Ryan Wakefield back in high school for a while. My maiden name was Hendricks back then. Course, I've been married so many times now, it's almost hard to remember what my last name is anymore. Is he your husband?"

Morgan smiled and shook her head yes.

"So, you married Ryan Wakefield? Wow.

"He certainly was a real heart throb back then. Any girl would have given anything, and I mean anything, to have dated him. He was a football jock, you know. I loved how all the girls turned green when we went to the after-game dances.

"Isn't it funny how life works? Back then, I thought he was sort of a nerd. Oh, I don't mean it in a bad way, but, you know, he was a good student, and all. But, do you know why I really liked him?"

Morgan shook her head no.

"He was such a good dancer. No, not a good dancer, but a really cool dancer. Back then, most boys didn't dance at all or not very well, but Ryan was terrific. I often wondered whatever happened to him.

"Oh, my God. I remember you now. You're the one that stole Ryan away from me. But, that's ancient history now." Vicky smiled and patted Morgan's hand to let her know everything was alright. "Remember that gorgeous green gown you wore to our senior prom? God, it was the most beautiful thing I ever saw, and boy was I jealous."

"I'm ... sorry, Vicky."

"Don't be sorry, Morgan. All's fair in love and war, as the old saying goes. And, I should be the one apologizing to you. I treated you just awful, but I treated everybody terrible back then.

"Oh, Morgan, I'm so sorry. I said some awful things and was just mean. I only thought about myself, and that's all. God, it makes me want to cry. I'm so ashamed."

"Don't ... be sad, ... Vicky. That's ... old history. This ... is today, and ... today is ... good. We both ... have ... great kids."

Morgan put her arms around Vicky and hugged her. Vicky desperately tried to hold back tears.

Ryan was now a full partner in the Albright Investment Corporation. His salary had grown appropriately with his added responsibilities.

One day, on a very hot July afternoon, Sharon knocked on Ryan's door and then came into his office.

Sharon had been assigned as Ryan's secretary when he first joined the firm and was now classified as his administrative assistant. She was in her mid-forties, black, rather tall and very slender. Sharon had a quick smile and a wonderful personality. She was married and had two little kids, a boy three, and a girl that had just turned two. Sharon adored Ryan and loved working for him.

"Mr. Albright wants to meet with you this afternoon, Ryan. His secretary, Alice, said it was important."

Sharon was worried anytime Mr. Albright wanted to talk to Ryan. The firm was opening a new office complex in the La Crosse area and she had a deep, gut feeling that Ryan was going to be picked to manage it. What would she do then? Her husband had a good job right here. They owned their own house. Both of their families lived within ten miles of here. Their kids went to school and had friends here. Their roots were here. Sharon's worry showed in her frown lines. She loved her job and working for Ryan. If Ryan took the new position, she would probably be offered a good promotion to go with him. But, deep in her heart she knew that she couldn't.

"Did she say what he wants?" Ryan asked as he took off his reading glasses and looked into Sharon's worried face.

"Alice didn't say. She just said for me to make sure and clear your calendar for this afternoon."

"Come on, Sharon. Can't be as bad as all that. I've met with Albright lots of times. He's actually a real nice guy, once you get to know him."

While that may be true, Sharon didn't believe it. The rumor mill told otherwise. It told of employees being scolded and even fired for not following the office dress code, or talking around the coffee machine. Most people never saw him. His office was on the top floor of the building and there was a special elevator just for him.

Ryan had heard some of the rumors about Albright, but disregarded them. He had always found Bill Albright to be warm and friendly. He was a 'straight to the point' kind of guy though, and that probably gave birth to the rumor that he was stern, coarse, and unfriendly.

Ryan stepped off the elevator facing the glass doors to Albright's palatial office suite.

"Hi, Alice."

"Hello, Mr. Wakefield," Alice said nervously and picked up the phone and talked in hushed tones. "You may go right in. Mr. Albright is ready for you." Alice held the door open for Ryan.

"Ryan," Bill Albright said as he immediately got up from his desk and quickly walked up to Ryan and shook his hand.

Bill Albright was a short man, probably no taller than five feet six inches. His hair was completely white and immaculately trimmed. He had sharp blue eyes that seemed to peer right through a person. He wore a tailor-made dark blue suit that fit perfectly. Albright was and looked the part of a CEO.

Albright's office was immense. The wall, floor to ceiling, behind his desk was glass windows that looked out towards the countryside. All the furnishings looked incredibly expensive, and probably were. The walls were paneled with deep mahogany and matched the wood of the desk and furniture. The carpet was light tan, deep and luxurious. The office spoke of money and power.

"Come over to the table, Ryan, and sit. Coffee?"

Ryan nodded that coffee would be fine, and it seemed like the next instant, Alice knocked on the door and brought in a silver tray with a coffee pot and two cups.

Albright filled two cups with dark and very aromatic coffee. He made small-talk about the weather and local high school sports teams. He then turned the conversation to politics and even the state of the country. Bill Albright was really a master at making people feel comfortable.

"Ryan, you know I'm not one for beating around the bush. I want to talk to you about the company and your future.

"I believe that hiring you was one of the best decisions I've ever made. When I think about it back then, if you remember, you had two quite lucrative offers, besides the one I gave you. You don't know this, but I was prepared to match or even go higher than either of those offers to get you. What I saw in you was promise and honesty, and you had both. I knew I could teach you the rest.

"You've progressed nicely over the years. You started out as a junior investment assistant and quickly moved up to full investment counselor. I remember the day I had you promoted to senior counselor. You were the youngest counselor on the staff. One of my long-term employees quit because he was passed over that time. But, you made your own way. And, more importantly, your clients loved you and would trust no one else to handle their affairs. You became office supervisor and jelled the counselors into a team. That was something no one else had ever been able to do. It had always been every man for themselves. You convinced me that women were every bit as capable at investment counseling and were successful in hiring and training many. Actually, you were made a partner because of that effort."

Ryan listened carefully, but mentally wondered why Albright was recounting his past history.

"Well, Ryan," Bill Albright said as he opened a folder and took out some papers. "I've kept my eye on you and have been well pleased. I've talked about you at some of our board meetings, and I must say the board is quite pleased with your work, too."

"Thank you, sir, but ..."

"As you well know, the company is building a rather large building complex on the outskirts of La Crosse. We are going to need a highly skilled manager to oversee the complete complex, and Ryan, we feel that the right person for the job is you."

Ryan was dumbfounded. He had heard of the new building. The

rumor-mill was totally alive with partial truths, misconceptions, and outright lies. But, the fact that he would be even considered for such a senior post was beyond his wildest dreams.

"Now, of course your annual compensation will be adjusted accordingly," Albright said and wrote a figure on a blank piece of paper and pushed it toward Ryan.

The shock of such a huge number took a little while to register in Ryan's brain, but when it did, it was so overwhelming that he couldn't find his voice to respond for a few seconds.

"I assume you will want to talk this over with your wife before you make any final decision. Let's meet again next Tuesday afternoon. Alice will set up the time with your secretary."

Ryan was still in shock, but managed to pick up the folder that contained the real facts and figures about the complex. He somehow managed to thank Mr. Albright and quickly left his office.

Ryan raced towards home. Morgan had just picked Beth Anne up from school and was turning into the driveway just before Ryan arrived.

"Morgan, just wait until you see this," Ryan said as they went into the kitchen.

CHAPTER TWENTY THREE
Let No Man Put Asunder

Ryan laid out the whole offer very carefully and then showed Morgan the paper that Mr. Albright had written the annual salary on.

"My ... gracious. Is that real, Ryan?"

"So, what do you think. Should I take the offer?"

"Would ... we have to ... move?"

"I'm afraid so. It's too far to drive every day."

Morgan sat silent for a few seconds.

"I will ... go ... anywhere ... with you, ... Ryan," Morgan said with a noticeable quiver in her voice. "Even ... if ... we have ... to move."

It was at that point when Ryan knew what the right decision was. He put his arms around Morgan and hugged her tightly.

"Together we've moved heaven and earth, Morgan. We started with very little and built a wonderful life together. Our house is small, but you've made it very comfortable. My whole life is you and Beth Anne, Morgan. Not my work. My work is what supports us. You love your job at the library. Beth Anne loves her school and friends. Both of our families live right here. While it was wonderful and considerate for Mr. Albright to even think of me for this new position, what's really important to me is you and Beth Anne. Let's stay right here."

Morgan threw her arms around Ryan. Tears streamed down her face and she made little honking sounds as she tried to get her emotions under control.

"What's wrong with Mom?" Beth Anne asked as she came into the kitchen and opened the refrigerator door. Beth Anne had seen warm emotion between her mother and father all her life, so today was not very much out of the ordinary.

"We were making a very important decision," Ryan said as he came over and put his arms around his daughter. "I was offered another job, but it would mean that we would have to move to La Crosse."

"Can't, Dad."

"Why not?" Ryan played along with his daughter's seriousness.

"Can't miss ice skating with Nora and my friends."
"Oh. Guess that makes sense."

"After a weekend of discussion with my wife and daughter, and hours on end of soul searching," Ryan said with a nervous tone to his voice, "I've decided not to accept the promotion. I know it probably sounds crazy to turn down such a lucrative offer, but I must."

"Well, Ryan," Albright said with a note of surprise. "I must say that I've never had anyone in my whole business career ever turn down a promotion. Would you mind sharing how you arrived at your decision?"

Ryan felt a little more at ease now. In fact, his confidence was rapidly returning now that he had told Albright his decision.

"Well, sir. It's like this. Everyone here knows that there is a rule among the supervisors and above that upper management expects, no, demands, that the first priority is your job and the second is family."

"I don't believe I'm familiar with such a directive, Ryan."

"It's not written anywhere, sir. But, believe me, it's there just the same."

Albright sat and listened. He knew what Ryan was saying was true. He demanded a lot from his people, but they were compensated well. Salaried people were allowed time off for doctor's appointments and other things that hourly people were required to charge off to their vacation time. The problem was, they always made up the time double or even triple. Albright also demanded that all his supervisors and above be involved in community affairs. In fact, the employee handbook didn't say 'demanded' or 'required', but rather it 'suggested' that each person volunteer for community efforts from the 'approved list.'

"Even though I've always volunteered for groups that I had a personal connection to, my family was and will always be, my first priority. I've always given my complete concentration when I'm at work, but honestly, my job is the means to support my family."

"Yes, Ryan, I suppose it is."

"And, Mr. Albright. Our roots are here. Our families live here and my daughter goes to school here. The highest value one can share, in my view, is the love of family."

Albright didn't say anything but leaned back in his chair and watched Ryan.

"My wife and I discussed your offer from every possible direction, but still came up with the same decision.

"I do realize that there is never any turning back and, that you probably have already identified my replacement. Perhaps, he or she has already been told, which is fine with me. I stand ready to resign and only ask for a good recommendation letter from you."

Albright was shocked. First, he never dreamed that Ryan wouldn't take the new position, especially because of the tremendous salary differential. But, what surprised him most was Ryan's understanding how big business actually worked. He had no idea, however, that Ryan was prepared to actually leave the company.

"Ryan, no one has been selected to take your position. It's yours for as long as you want it. Your work has always been exemplary and your management style has your people producing at peak performance. I could never ask for more. That's why I thought this new position would be a good opportunity and reward for all your hard work."

Secretly, Albright really admired Ryan and remembered back to his younger days when he was building his career and how his family suffered because of it. His wife had divorced him years ago. His son struggled to get through high school and then, took six years to finally graduate from college, and only then with thousands of dollars of tutoring. And, for what? He now lives with a friend in Chicago where he works as a tattoo artist. His daughter didn't have much trouble with school and graduated from the University of Southern California with a degree in Russian literature. She'd never come home since her graduation and that was twelve years ago.

Time passed and the years went by. Ryan was never offered another promotion. He also noticed that his annual raises weren't quite as much either. But, he didn't mind. His salary was still considerably above what most people earned and provided a very comfortable living for his family.

Beth Anne was now a freshman in high school. She loved everything about school. She was an excellent student and joined virtually every activity and club available to her. She and Nora were still best friends.

It was early morning on the last Tuesday of July. The temperature was already eighty-three degrees and rapidly climbing towards the forecasted high nineties. Ryan got out of the shower and listened as he heard Morgan going through a fit of coughing in their bedroom.

"You were up most of the night, honey. I think your cough has gotten worse."

"It's ...," Morgan struggled to say and coughed hard. "Just ... a summer cold."

"Don't you think you should take something for it?"

"Took ... two ... aspirins." Morgan had an awful coughing fit that left her exhausted when she finally got her breath.

"Maybe that'll help with a fever," Ryan said as he felt her forehead. "You don't feel warm, but maybe we should take your temperature."

Morgan shook her head that she didn't want her temperature taken, but then started coughing uncontrollably again.

"Cough ... syrup ... in downstairs ... medicine cabinet."

Ryan ran downstairs and found the prescription cough syrup that had been in the medicine cabinet since last March when they got it for Beth Anne.

Morgan gulped down two large swallows and in a little while, her coughing calmed down.

Ryan was worried when he left the house and watched Morgan's car disappear down the street as she drove towards the library.

It was a little after ten when Ryan's phone buzzed.

"Mr. Wakefield," Sharon's voice said. "There's a lady on the phone for you and said it was a matter of some urgency that she talk to you."

"Ryan Wakefield."

"Hi, Ryan. This is Angela Harding at the library. I work with Morgan."

"Hello, Angela," Ryan said and remembered meeting Angela a number of times at library functions and meetings.

"We all think, well …"

"What is it, Angela?"

"Morgan went home sick a little while ago. That's not like her at all. None of us could remember her ever taking sick-time off before. She sounds real bad. It was like she couldn't catch her breath. She coughed almost all the time."

"Thanks for letting me know, Angela. I really appreciate it."

Ryan hung the phone up and ran out to Sharon's desk.

"Sharon, I've got to leave."

"Oh, is something wrong?"

"It's Morgan. She's gone home from work sick and she's never done that before. She has been fighting off a bad cold for a long time, and it seems to have gotten worse lately. I had better make sure I'm there if she needs anything."

Sharon smiled and had always admired Ryan's attention and caring for his wife and wished her husband, Nick, would show her just a little attention sometime.

"The meeting we scheduled at two this afternoon with the three district managers. Would you handle it for me?"

Sharon told him not to worry. She would take care of everything.

Ryan raced home. When he came into the house he found Morgan lying on the couch with a blanket covering her. She was sound asleep. Ryan put the palm of his hand on her forehead and was shocked at how warm she was.

"Morgan," he said gently and touched her shoulder. "Are you okay?"

Morgan slowly opened her eyes. She seemed to have trouble getting them to focus. When she recognized her husband, she smiled lightly and her eyes sunk shut.

"What is it, Morgan? You're burning up. Have you taken any aspirin for your fever?"

Slowly, Morgan opened her eyes and shook her head that she had taken aspirin.

"Call … Doctor … Hendal," Morgan said very slowly, almost as if she had to concentrate on each word. "Need … more … cough … syrup."

Ryan looked at the empty bottle standing on the coffee table.

"My God, Morgan, how much have you taken?"

Morgan didn't answer and drifted back to sleep.

Ryan ran out to the kitchen and picked up the phone. He scanned down the list of 'important numbers' from the sticker on the little plaque on the wall.

Ryan dialed the number for Dr. Jason Hendal's office. Ryan had known Jason all his life. They lived two blocks from each other while they were growing up. They played together and went to school together. Now, Dr. Hendal was a highly respected physician and was Beth Anne and Ryan's doctor, but not Morgan's. Morgan never went to a doctor. She always claimed that she would if she was ever sick enough, but she never was. Never was, until now, Ryan thought.

"Physicians Office," a pleasant female voice said. "This is Amanda. How may I direct your call?"

"Hello, Amanda. This is Ryan Wakefield."

"Yes. Hello, Mr. Wakefield."

"Is there any way I could talk to Dr. Hendal's nurse? We need a prescription renewed, if possible."

"Sure. Just a moment."

Some sort of canned music played a slightly familiar tune in Ryan's ear.

"Dr. Hendal's office, Donna speaking."

Ryan told Donna about Morgan's sickness and wondered if they would renew the cough syrup that had been prescribed to Beth Anne last spring.

"Just a moment, Ryan. I'll check with Dr. Hendal."

Ryan again was put on hold and more elevator music played in his ear.

"Ryan. This is Jason."

"Hi, Jason."

"Now, what's this about Morgan?"

Ryan described her symptoms as best he could.

"First, Ryan. I can't renew a prescription for Beth Anne knowing that it would be for Morgan. But, more importantly, it may be just masking what's really wrong. Is there any way you can get her in here this afternoon? We'll work her right in once you get here."

Ryan told his old friend and very trusted physician that he would get Morgan there just as soon as he could.

"I don't want to alarm you, Ryan, but sooner than later is really important."

It took almost an hour to convince Morgan that she needed to be seen by Dr. Hendal. The decision maker was the fact that she was going to have to be seen before she could get any more cough syrup.

Ryan had to help her get up and when he put his arms around her to help her, he was suddenly alarmed by the sound of her breath making ragged wheezing sounds.

Morgan looked like death warmed over and coughed almost constantly. She and Ryan were put into an exam room right away.

"Hi, Ryan. Hello, Morgan, "Dr. Hendal said as he came into the exam room.

Morgan didn't even look up or acknowledge him. She just sat on the exam table with her head down, wheezing and coughing.

"Ryan, help me get her coat off, will you?"

It took both men to get Morgan's coat off and get her settled back on the exam table.

"Now, Morgan, I want you to breathe normally while I listen to your lungs," Dr. Hendal said as he moved the sender of his stethoscope around her back. "Try taking a deep breath and hold it."

Morgan tried but went into a massive attack of coughing.

Dr. Hendal stepped out for a few minutes and then came back with his nurse. They put a small mask on Morgan that was connected to an oxygen tank with a thin plastic tube.

"This will help you breathe a little better," Dr. Hendal's nurse said as she adjusted the mask.

"Ryan, step out into the hall with me for a few seconds. My nurse will stay with Morgan."

Ryan followed Dr. Hendal out into the hallway.

"We've go a serious problem here, Ryan. Now, I don't want to scare you, but I want you to take Morgan right to the emergency room at the hospital. I'll call over there and they will be ready for her when you get there."

"What's wrong with her, Jason?"

"Sounds like pneumonia in its advanced stage. I'm not painting a very rosy picture, Ryan. Morgan needs help, and right now."

When Ryan drove into the ambulance entrance of the emergency room, there were two people with a gurney waiting. They virtually lifted Morgan out of the car and onto the gurney. They quickly pushed her into the large gallery of the emergency room and into one of the exam suites.

"Mr. Wakefield," the lady behind the large counter said, "Why don't we get the paperwork out of the way. It's going to take a while for the doctors to examine your wife anyway.

"May I have your insurance card?"

Ryan got out his medical insurance membership card and filled out a mountain of papers. He was actually astounded by what all was required and wondered how an older or disabled person would have managed it alone.

"We're almost done. Do you have *medical power of attorney* for Morgan?"

Ryan thought carefully and dug through his wallet for a small card their lawyer had made for both Morgan and him when they had their wills made.

"Yes. Here it is."

"It says, 'Do not resuscitate.' Do you understand what that means, Ryan?"

"Yes. Morgan and I have discussed it at length. She wanted everyone to know that she wanted no miracle, heroic procedures done that would only prolong her biological life with little or no quality. In other words, she absolutely did not want to live in a nursing home as a vegetable."

"Yes, I can certainly understand that."

"Why do you ask? Is that important right now?"

"It's just part of the admissions procedure, Ryan. I just need to stamp your wife's chart with the DNR notification here."

Ryan felt helpless and muddled by all the forms and things that he had to sign.

When it was finally finished, he was told to go into the waiting room and they would let him know what was going on as soon as they knew anything. Ryan had never felt so alone. He was beside himself with worry. He sat and watched what seemed to be an endless stream of broken, sick, and hurt people flow through the various emergency suites.

Finally, the person that had been so helpful in filling out all the forms came over to him.

"Mr. Wakefield, why don't you take this beeper here and go down to the cafeteria. You look like you could use a bowl of soup and a cup of coffee. We'll beep you when we know anything."

Ryan thanked her and stood up just as a young man dressed in scrubs came into the waiting room.

"Ryan Wakefield?"

"Yes."

"I'm Dr. Tanner. I'm an ER doc here. My team and I have been working with your wife."

"How is she?"

"She's a pretty sick lady, Ryan. I've called Dr. Reedy to come in. He's an infectious disease specialist and should be here shortly. We've drawn blood samples and have the lab doing a full workup and are now taking your wife up to have a CAT scan done. It'll be a while before we know much."

Ryan felt nauseous. He felt helpless. He went to the public pay-phone and called Lillian.

"Hi, Lillian. I took Morgan to the doctor this afternoon and he sent her right to the hospital. Could you go over to our house and pick up Beth Anne? She'll probably have to stay the night as it's hard telling when I'll get home."

Lillian asked questions, most of which Ryan couldn't answer.

He then called his mother and told her what was going on.

Suddenly, the beeper went off. Ryan sprinted back to the emergency room.

"Hi, Mr. Wakefield," the lady behind the counter said. "They told me to tell you that your wife got through the CAT scan just fine. They took her to a room in intensive care, so you can go up there now. It's on the fourth floor."

Ryan ran down the long hallway to the bank of elevators and waited for what seemed like a lifetime for one of the doors to open.

When the door opened to the fourth floor, Ryan quickly stepped off and looked around for a sign that would direct him. Then, he saw what almost looked like an office suite in the building where he worked. The large silver sign on the wall said "Intensive Care Unit." Ryan walked in.

"May I help you?" The young woman behind the counter asked.

"My wife is here. Her name is Morgan Wakefield. Could you please direct me to her room?"

"Hello, Ryan," a middle-age woman said as she came out to meet him. It was Mrs. Cole, a friend of his mother's. Her name tag said that she was the nursing supervisor.

"Hi, Mrs. Cole. Do you know what room Morgan is in?"

"She's in Room Six, Ryan and she's resting peacefully. But, I want to warn you a little before you go in. We've got an oxygen mask on to help her breathe, an IV drip going to keep her hydrated and nourished, and a catheter so she doesn't have to get up to use the restroom. We've also got leads connected to a heart monitor. Everything connects electronically to our nursing station so we can tell what's going on all the time. It all looks pretty scary, but it's all there to help her."

The Intensive Care Unit was divided into two sections. Each section had twelve rooms that surrounded the nursing station which made medical help available at a second's notice.

Even though Mrs. Cole had given Ryan a 'heads-up' it did not prepare him for what he saw. This was the first time that he realized how thin Morgan had become. She barely made bumps in the sheet. She was sleeping and breathing easily for the first time in quite a few days. Mrs. Cole was right about the hoses and wires. They seemed to be everywhere. There was a heart monitor by the side of Morgan's bed that showed her heart beat on a tiny television screen and made a soft, but high-pitched, beeping sound with every beat.

"Hello, honey," Ryan said softly as he lovingly touched Morgan's cheek.

Morgan's eyes fluttered and tried to open, but then stopped moving.

"Don't try to open your eyes. I just wanted you to know that I'm here with you."

The high-pitched beeps from the monitor accentuated each passing second and the gurgle of the water-filter on the oxygen flow were the only sounds that Ryan heard.

He pulled the chair up right beside the bed and sat down. Suddenly, Morgan's right arm moved as if she were searching for something. Ryan reached out and she grasped his hand.

"I'm right here, honey," Ryan said but was interrupted by a steady high-pitched sound coming from the heart monitor. Ryan jumped up and started for the nursing station.

A young, blonde nurse met Ryan at the door. Her name-tag said that her name was 'Judy.' She quickly put her stethoscope on Morgan's chest and smiled.

"Here it is. It's just the lead that popped off and set off the monitor. Nothing serious." Judy reconnected the lead and the monitor went back to singing its rhythmic, high-pitched beeps.

Ryan was wet with sweat. He sunk down onto the chair and put his hand on Morgan's arm.

"Must be the sensor pad on her chest that's worn," Judy said. "It's the second time it's happened."

Ryan sat motionless and stared at Morgan lying completely still the rest of the afternoon.

That evening, Harlan and Lillian brought Beth Anne to the hospital and each one, one at a time, came in to see Morgan and talk to Ryan.

It was Harlan that finally convinced Ryan to come down to the cafeteria with them and have supper, but not until Judy gave him a beeper, just in case they needed to call him.

Ryan ate in short bursts and didn't taste anything at all. Then, with their meal finished, he hugged Beth Anne and told Lillian and Harlan how much he appreciated their help.

"Your mom and dad asked to bring Beth Anne over tomorrow night, Ryan," Lillian said as she hugged him.

"Is Mom going to be alright, Dad?" Beth Anne tearfully asked as she held her arms tightly around her father's neck.

"She's going to be fine," Ryan tried his best to reassure his worried daughter. "She's pretty sick now, but the doctors and nurses are great here. It's just going to take time."

Ryan tried his best to sleep in the chair, but kept waking up every time Morgan moved or one of the nurses came in to check her.

Early in the morning, Morgan woke up.

"Where … am … I?"

Ryan leaped to his feet and came close to her.

"You're in the hospital, honey. How are you feeling?"

"So … tired."

Her eyes closed and she drifted off to sleep.

The day shift nurse, Arlene, came in and checked Morgan's vital signs.

"The doctor should be here shortly, Ryan. Then, why don't you go home and rest for a little while. She's scheduled for more tests this morning anyway and we'll call you if there's any change."

"Hello, Ryan," a male voice said. "I'm Dr. Montgomery. I'm one of the pulmonologists on staff here at the hospital. Come out here and meet with Dr. Janikey. He's the cardiologist on your wife's case. Together, we'll show you what we think is going on."

Ryan shook hands with Dr. Ben Janikey.

Dr. Montgomery put a large X-ray on a wall-mounted light box and pointed to two large areas.

"Your wife has very advanced stage pneumonia with extraordinary congestion. These areas here, are our greatest concern."

"That's not the complete picture, Ryan," Dr. Janikey said. "Your wife has a serious heart issue, too. Are you aware of that?"

"I knew that she had cerebral palsy and had scarlet fever when she was a child that caused her to have some kind of minor heart problem, but we were always told it wasn't a real problem. It never seemed to bother her at all."

"Probably true back then, but she's encountering some irregular heartbeats where the heart fibrillates and doesn't pump blood. And, one of her valves isn't working properly."

"Can't that be repaired?" Ryan asked as he remembered reading about some of the new miraculous heart procedures.

"Sure, Ryan. It could be repaired. Especially, if she was otherwise healthy and strong. But, with her pneumonia, she would never survive the surgery. So, our first order of business is to get her heart rhythm under control."

"While that's going on, Ryan, I'm concentrating on getting her lungs cleared up," Dr. Montgomery said in a calm, reassuring voice.

"But, will she be alright?" Ryan somehow managed to choke out.

"I won't mince any words, Ryan. The next few days are critical. She's a very sick woman. But, we're hoping that with oxygen, the right medicine, and lots of time, that just maybe, we can turn the corner here, in a little while."

Ryan heaved a sigh of relief.

"She was pretty dehydrated, Ryan, so with the IV drip running and the oxygen making it easier for her to breath, I suspect she'll be more awake this afternoon."

It was around two o'clock when Morgan opened her eyes. She pulled down her facemask.

"Ryan," she whispered hoarsely.

Ryan jumped up from his chair and put down the magazine he was looking at.

"Hello, sleepy head. How're you feeling?"

"Ryan," she said slowly. "I …. love … you."

"Oh, Morgan. I love you, too."

The middle contact wire to the heart monitor popped off the pad that was glued onto Morgan's chest. Within an instant, a nurse appeared in the doorway.

"Looks like the wire's off, again. But, let me check for heart rate, as long as I'm in here."

Morgan stayed awake most of the afternoon. Occasionally, she would drift off to sleep, but it didn't last long. Ryan was elated.

At five o'clock, a nurse came in to give Morgan an injection, so Ryan stepped out and went over to the nurses station.

"Do you think it would be alright if you turned the volume down on Morgan's heart monitor? It doesn't seem to bother her, but it drives me crazy."

"Sure, Mr. Wakefield. The monitor is connected to our console right here, so we can tell if it goes off. I'll take care of it right away."

That evening Katherine and Benjamin brought Beth Anne to the hospital. Again, Morgan was awake and alert for most of the evening.

"Mom seems a little better," Beth Anne said hopefully to Ryan as he walked them out to the car.

"A little, I think. The doctor told me that it's going to be a long road ahead, but if she can make a little progress each day, maybe she'll be able to come home soon."

"Love you, Dad," Beth Anne said as she hugged her dad.

The next day was a disappointment. Morgan slept almost all the time. She wasn't even awake during her morning bath. Ryan worried.

In the evening, Morgan's mother and father brought Beth Anne to the hospital. Morgan opened her eyes a few times, but other than that, slept the whole time they were there.

The next day was almost a repeat of yesterday. Morgan slept and Ryan paced and worried.

In the middle of the afternoon Ryan turned on the television. Not really to watch, but more for noise.

"Hello, Ryan," a male voice said.

Ryan looked up and saw that it was Reverend John.

"Am I ever glad to see you," Ryan said as he put his arms around the minister and dear friend.

"So, fill me in on what's going on with Morgan."

Ryan spent the next half-hour telling Reverend John what had happened so far.

It was almost five o'clock when Reverend John got up from his chair and told Ryan that he had better get going.

Reverend John came over to Morgan's bedside and placed his hand on Morgan's forehead and prayed. Morgan's eyes slowly opened.

"Reverend… John."

"Hello there young lady. Good to see you."

Reverend John talked to Morgan for a little while. She smiled occasionally and then drifted off to sleep.

"Walk me out to my car, Ryan."

The two men walked out into the corridor and to the elevators.

"How're you doing, Ryan?"

"Me? Oh, I'm okay."

"Beth Anne?"

"She's staying with Morgan's parents. Lillian and Harlan alternate bringing her to the hospital with my mom and dad."

"You know, Ryan, you've got to take care of yourself, too."

"Oh, I know. Every morning, right after I talk to the doctors, I leave for a while. That's when they give Morgan her daily bath and that always leaves her exhausted, so she sleeps for a few hours. I go home, take a shower, and shave. I try to sleep a little while and then be back here by noon."

"Remember, Ryan," Reverend John said as he got into his car. "Call me. Anytime. Hour doesn't matter."

Ryan thanked Reverend John for coming and walked back to the hospital.

The next afternoon, Morgan became very alert. She told Ryan that she didn't want the face mask on, but he tried to convince her that she needed it. Finally, he asked one of the nurses if there might be something else that she could use during the day and they changed the mask for a small pipe that had two nozzles for her nostrils. Morgan seemed to like that much better.

"Ryan."

"Yes, my love."

"Remember … when … you … told … me … that … I … could … make … a … difference?"

"You certainly have, Morgan. Just look at all you've accomplished."

Ryan spent the next hour reminiscing with Morgan as he outlined each of her milestones. She smiled and her eyes even sparkled a little.

"It … was … you, … Ryan."

"Oh, Morgan, it wasn't me. You're the one with the determination and strength to do whatever you wanted to do."

"No, … Ryan. It … was … you. You … were … my … rock. You … were … my … solitude. But, … together, … we … could … do …

anything.

Ryan threw his arms around Morgan and held her. Tears streamed down his face.

Morgan weakly reached up her arms and hugged Ryan back.

"You are my life and my soul, Morgan," Ryan said as he sat back up and eased her back down onto the bed.

Morgan smiled and shut her eyes.

I ... love ... you, Ryan. Now, ... you ... must ... make ... a ... difference."

Just then, Beth Anne came into the room with her grandparents. Morgan opened her eyes and reached out for her daughter. Beth Anne hugged her mom.

"How's she doing, Ryan?" Harlan asked and put his hand on his son-in-law's shoulder.

"Actually, she's been awake most of the afternoon. She's really alert and maybe, even seems a little better."

Ryan watched the evening news on the television that was suspended high on the wall and listened to the sound on the small headphone by the bed. He was just about to change the channel with the remote control when he heard Morgan move.

"Ryan."

Ryan stood up and held her hand.

"I'm right here, my love."

"Cold."

"You're cold? Do you want me to get another blanket?"

"No."

"Want me to call the nurse?"

Morgan shook her head no.

"Want ... you ... to ... keep ... me ... warm."

It took a few minutes for Ryan to figure it out.

"You want me to get in bed with you?"

"Hold ... me."

Ryan kicked off his shoes and carefully lifted the blanket and sheet. He did his best to maneuver around all the plastic pipes, hoses, and wires that were connected to Morgan, but finally, he was lying by her side. He helped her snuggle up and he put his arms around her.

"Love … you."

"I love you, Morgan. I love you so."

"We … will … always … be … together … forever."

"Yes, Morgan, we will always be together, forever and ever."

They both drifted off to sleep.

Susan, one of the night-shift nurses came to the doorway and peeked into the room. She smiled to herself and backed away and walked to the nurses station.

"It's so cute and touching," she said to Mrs. Johnson, the night supervisor.

"What?" Mrs. Johnson asked as she looked over her reading glasses and then put the chart down that she was reviewing.

"Mr. Wakefield."

"Ryan? He's a really nice guy."

"He's in bed with his wife."

"He is? Well, that's something. Those beds are pretty small for one, let alone trying to get two people into one."

Mrs. Johnson got up and walked back to Morgan's room with the nurse. They looked inside and Mrs. Johnson smiled.

"Now, that's real love."

"It's beyond love," Susan said as tears streamed down her face. "Sure wish my husband was that romantic and caring."

It was 1:10 a.m. and Mrs. Johnson was reviewing charts making sure her nurses had made entries and signed each one. Suddenly, the heart monitor light showed up on her console indicating a possible malfunction in Morgan Wakefield's room, again.

"Oh, there goes that darned alarm in Morgan's room," Mrs. Johnson said and immediately stood up.

"I can get it," Susan said.

"That's okay. I need a break, anyway."

Mrs. Johnson grabbed a stethoscope and walked briskly towards Morgan's room.

She went into Morgan's room and smiled to herself as she once again saw the sweet scene of Morgan snuggled up to her husband and he had his arms around her.

She expected to find the troublesome lead unhooked, but couldn't get it because of the position Morgan was in, almost lying on Ryan. She rotated the dial on the heart monitor to select one of the other leads and found the display 'flat-lining' on each one of them. Now, she was really concerned. She grabbed her stethoscope off her shoulders and listened intently to Morgan's chest desperately hoping to hear a heartbeat.

Hearing nothing, Mrs. Johnson pushed the emergency call button on her identification card which activated the 'Code Blue' sequence.

"What's up," the night cardiologist said as he quickly came into the room.

"It's Mrs. Wakefield," Mrs. Johnson said and stepped back so the doctor could check Morgan for vital signs.

"Quick," the doctor commanded. "Get the paddles. We'll see if we can get her heart restarted."

Mrs. Johnson came over and touched the cardiologist on the left arm.

"She's a DNR," she said softly which caused the doctor to instantly display a persona of despair just as Susan rushed in with the defibrillator cart.

Ryan was sleeping through most of the commotion and finally opened his eyes. The cardiologist quickly explained the situation to him.

"We can possibly do a restart. But, we've got to act right now."

Ryan looked up into the specialist's eyes and softly said, "She didn't want anything heroic done. It's even on her chart."

Mrs. Johnson struggled to get Ryan out of bed. His only thought was to hold Morgan.

"She's gone, Mr. Wakefield," Mrs. Johnson said softly and put her hand on Ryan's arm.

After a long pause, Ryan opened his eyes and slowly said, "Yes, I know."

CHAPTER TWENTY FOUR
1:10 In The Morning

Morgan Lynn Wakefield

Morgan Wakefield, age 44, died this morning, August, 2, 1992, at University Hospital in the loving arms of her husband, Ryan. Mrs. Wakefield was the daughter of Harlan and Lillian Carter and was born on May 21, 1949 in Oakwood Heights, Wisconsin. Morgan married Ryan Wakefield on July 29, 1972 at the Little Church in the Country. She was employed at the local library for a number of years and was instrumental in setting up programs to integrate children with special needs into the local public school system.

A memorial service will be held at the Little Church in the Country with Reverend John Bierhoff officiating on Friday at 6:00 p.m. in remembrance of their marriage in the same church. Visitation will be held from 2 to 5 preceding the memorial service. Instead of regular flowers or donations, it is asked that only day-lilies, Morgan's favorite flower, be brought to the church in remembrance of her. Interment will be at the cemetery next to the church followed by a fellowship and supper in the church basement.

CHAPTER TWENTY FIVE
The Memorial Service

The day of Morgan's funeral started out sunny, bright, and hot. But, by late morning the sky clouded over and the temperature cooled considerably making it very pleasant to be outside.

Guests started to arrive a little after one in the afternoon, and by two, when the actual visitation started, the parking lot was jammed full. Cars were being directed to park along the little country road that ran by the church. So many people brought day lilies that they lined the aisles with them and the altar was an explosion of color.

Morgan's casket was placed in front of the alter in the little church. It was the color of white linen. The spray on top was made of day lilies of every color imaginable. The lid was open and on the inside, the words "Always together forever," were embroidered.

The funeral director had worked magic and Morgan looked as beautiful and radiant as she always had. She looked as if she was just asleep and would wake up at any second.

The line into the church extended out across the parking lot as people quietly filed in to express their sympathy to the grieving family members.

At six o'clock, the church bell rang indicating that the service was about to begin. People found seats in the pews and chairs that had been set up in every available space. Chairs had even been set up outside near the entrance with loud speakers put up on tripods so they could hear the service. The pipe organ played softly in the background.

People settled down and the late afternoon sun flooded the sanctuary with deep reds, blues, greens, and purples through every stained-glass window.

The organist began to play very softly. Mrs. Tixlor stood up and slowly walked towards the altar until she was close to Morgan's casket, her white robe reflected the colors of the stained glass as she moved.

Mrs. Tixlor began to sing and the canaries immediately joined in. Suddenly, her voice quivered and she stopped singing. She turned away from the audience and put her hands up to her face. Her body shook as she cried. People in the audience cried with her. Finally, she somehow regained her composure, turned back around, and continued to sing.

Tears still flowed down virtually every face in attendance. Some sobbed. Even though the canaries sang, they somehow sensed something was different from the usual wedding, and were subdued.

"Friends, we are gathered here today," Reverend John's baritone voice said clearly. "Not so much to grieve for our lost loved one, but rather, pay deep respect, love, and homage to her uncountable accomplishments and to her as a wonderful person.

"Morgan," Reverend John's voice cracked and even though he had conducted many funeral services in his life in the clergy, this one touched him deeply. He paused to regain his composure. "Morgan Lynn Wakefield," he started again and read her obituary.

"Morgan started life in this world with what most people would call a handicap. She was diagnosed early on with cerebral palsy and a congenital heart problem. The doctors told her parents to be prepared because most babies born this way didn't live very long. But, Morgan did.

"The doctors told Morgan's parents that she would never walk. But, she did.

"Again, the doctors told her parents that she would never talk. But, Morgan did.

"Then, the doctors told her parents that she would be trainable, but probably never go very far in school. But, Morgan did. She was almost a straight 'A' student all the way through school, even college, and graduated with a bachelor's degree in special education.

"Morgan never asked for any special treatment or accommodations. She never complained about anything or anybody."

Again, Reverend John's voice was quaky and he had a difficult time controlling his personal feelings.

"Morgan was a model child. Even her parents could have never known the unfathomable determination and drive that pushed her forward to achieve and make her way in the world."

Lillian started to sob which was so catching that its effect caused Reverend John to get his handkerchief out and wipe his eyes. Harlan tried to comfort his sobbing wife, but he, too, was crying.

"Then, Morgan and Ryan found each other." Again, Reverend John's voice cracked.

"Right from the beginning they were inseparable. Morgan once told me that their two hearts beat as one and Ryan said in his wedding vow to Morgan that he had loved her forever." Again, Reverend John's voice went shaky and cracked.

"In all my years in the ministry, I've never seen such love and devotion to each other as I saw with Morgan and Ryan."

Beth Anne crumpled in the arms of her father.

"When I went to the hospital to visit Morgan a few days ago, she told me not to be concerned about her at all, but she thought that I looked like I was working too hard." Reverend John suddenly began to cry uncontrollably and turned away from the audience.

Warm deep reds and purples made Morgan's white casket glow and illuminate in an almost spiritual ethereal light.

"If anyone would like to come forward to the microphone and share memories of Morgan, please do."

There was a long moment of silence occasionally accented by the twittering of a few canaries.

Finally, a lone figure stood near the back of the church and slowly walked forward.

"Good afternoon," she said and her voice shook. "My name is Vicky Salisbury and Morgan made her way into my hardened heart and made it melt. She became my very best friend." Vicky lost her composure and began to cry and was accompanied by the whole gathering.

"In high school, I was a senior and thought the world owed me everything. After all, I was the captain of the cheerleading team and even elected prom queen. Morgan was a lowly sophomore and was in one of my classes.

"For some unknown reason, I began to tease her unrelentingly and couldn't seem to stop, but Morgan never seemed to notice at all." Vicky's voice shook and she cried through most of the sentence. "Morgan stole my boyfriend, Ryan. It's funny how God works," Vicky said with a little laugh which was very catching and the congregation shared her own putdown.

People listened. Some shook their heads in agreement.

"I was so mad. After all, I was the queen, you know.

"It was at the senior prom that I first saw her and Ryan together. I was totally humiliated, of course. I was jealous of Morgan's fantastic gown because it looked like it was made in fairyland. But, most of all, I realized right then how wonderful Ryan and Morgan were together.

"My life went onward and so did hers. I, as most everyone knows, have been married three times and divorced three times. So, I guess you might say, I've not lived a very perfect life.

"Then, God gave me my third daughter, Nora. She has cerebral palsy, just like Morgan. Morgan's little girl, Beth Anne, and my Nora met at school and then at skating classes. Unbeknownst to me, they broke the ice. They set the stage for Morgan and me to really get to know each other.

"Morgan reached out to me and taught me what true caring for another person was really all about.

"I desperately tried to apologize to her for my awful behavior when we were in school, but it was as if she had never even been aware of it.

"She became my friend. She became my best friend. My heart was just one of the many that her life touched.

"Thank you."

Vicky walked back to her seat.

Others came forward and talked. Each trying their best to express the way their lives were touched by Morgan. Finally, no one else stood up.

Reverend John stood, but then saw Ryan get up. Reverend John immediately sat back down and watched as Ryan slowly made his way to the microphone.

"Everyone, thank you so very much for coming here today. I don't have to tell you," Ryan's voice went up in pitch and he began to cry. "I don't ... have to ... tell you that ... this is ... the hardest day ... I've ever faced ... in my life."

Now Katherine began to cry uncontrollably for her son's pain. Benjamin pulled her into his arms and tried to console her.

"Morgan wrote me a letter some days before she really got sick. But, somehow, I think she knew the end of her life on earth was coming.

"While I know she meant her letter for me, I would like to share it with all of you, if I may."

Ryan paused and his body shook with grief as he cried. So did everyone in the audience.

"'My dearest Ryan-

I love you so-

You are always in my heart.
You are my hero.
You showed me how good the world can be.
You opened my heart to all the love that surrounds us all.

So, always remember and never forget-

I am the little spring breeze that plays with your hair.

I am the warmth from the sunshine on a hot summer day.

I am the nip at your nose when the air turns cold.

I am the blanket that wraps around you each night and keeps you warm.

I am in your heart so you can feel my never-ending love with each beat of your heart.

I am with you always, every hour, of every day.

I am, and you are, one soul, forever.

Now, you must be both mother and dad to our wonderful daughter, Beth Anne and open the world's goodness to her, just as you did for me.

Remember our wedding vows;

There never was a time that I didn't love you, and there never will be a time that I won't love you.

Our love is forever, dear Ryan.
I'm right here with you, now, and always.

Always together forever.

Forever,
Morgan' "

Ryan collapsed on Morgan's casket and wept.

Reverend John gave the benediction and closed the service. He invited everyone to attend the graveside service just outside in the cemetery behind the church and the evening food in the church basement afterward.
Six pallbearers took their position by Morgan's casket.
"Stay with Beth Anne," Ryan said to his mother, stood and walked to the end of the casket and picked up the handle. "I will be with you always forever, Morgan. Forever."

CHAPTER TWENTY SIX
The Aftermath

As with everything, time marches on. Regardless of the size of the tragedy or devastation, time has a way of healing regardless if in nature or in human terms.

It's often surprising how rapidly new growth appears after even the most devastating forest fire. When a volcano erupts and spews lava for miles, it isn't long before new life can be seen.

The same is true in human events. A wise old man once said, "Regardless how important you think you are, if you're remembered at all, other than your name, twenty years after you've passed on, it's a miracle."

The universe seeks balance. Nature always looks for balance and humans require balance to make any sort of sense about the world in which we all live. Some months after Morgan's passing, life returned to a semblance of normalcy. Even for Ryan.

Pastor Morris was found guilty on all counts and required to pay restitution to the federal government and the State of Wisconsin. He was assessed a punitive fine of $50,000 and sentenced to 12 years in federal prison. His wife filed for immediate divorce. His mistress moved on to greener pastures.

After high school, Brian went to the University of Wisconsin at Madison and then went on to law school. He married a girl he met in college. They now have two children and live in a beautiful lake-front home on Lake Mendota. Brian is an attorney in one of the State of Wisconsin agencies.

Edward started college after high school, but decided after one semester that school wasn't for him. At least, not right then, anyway. He enlisted in the Marines and served four years. While he was in the service he went back to school and completed an associates degree in business.

After being discharged from the Marines, Edward went to work for a small specialty machine shop on the southern edge of Milwaukee that employed nine people. After two years, Edward begged, borrowed, and scraped together enough money to buy the company. Since then, he has increased the business to where he now employs over seventy people and has paid back all the money he borrowed.

He and Sherry, the girl that he took to their high school prom, got married when he was in the Marines. They now have three children and live in a very large home in the country south of Milwaukee.

Vicky went to college after high school, but got pregnant in the second semester of her first year and had to drop out. She has been married and divorced three times and has three children.

Shortly after her third divorce she got a job at Dewey's Bar and rented the little apartment above it where she raised her kids. All three graduated from college.

A year ago, Dewey wanted to retire and sold his business and building to Vicky, so she's now the proprietor. She still lives in the little apartment above the bar.

Nora, Vicky's youngest daughter, graduated from the University of Wisconsin at Milwaukee with a degree in special education. She's not married and owns a house in one of the suburbs and rents rooms to two other teachers. She works for the Milwaukee School System.

Karen, Morgan's older sister, graduated from the University of Colorado and went to work for British Petroleum Corporation. She initially moved to Galveston, Texas. During her career she has lived in California, Wyoming, Alaska, and the state of Washington.

She married a chemical engineer while she was living in Texas, but they filed for divorce after two years. She has no children.

Karen now lives on the outskirts of Seattle, Washington.

Charlie and Stacey dated very frequently all during high school and many people thought it was going to be a repeat of Ryan and Morgan. But, as with many things in life, it was not to be. After they graduated from high school, both went their separate way.

Charlie graduated from The Milwaukee School of Engineering with a degree in electrical engineering.
He accepted a job with General Electric in Syracuse, New York and worked as a large electric generator design engineer.
Charlie dated a girl all through college and they got married right before he graduated. They had no children. Two years ago, they both filed for divorce.

Stacey graduated from the University of Wisconsin at La Crosse with a degree in finance.
Before graduating, she was offered and accepted a position for a large shipping company based in Cleveland, Ohio that owned and operated giant lake freighter ships on the great lakes.
During her third year in Cleveland, she met and married a man named Frank Raddisen. He worked for Coca Cola and traveled for work most of the time. They moved into a large house in Shaker Heights, just outside of Cleveland.
Last fall, Stacey filed for divorce. They had no children.

Both Stacey and Charlie have moved back to Oakwood Heights and have been frequently seen having dinner with each other. Both claim that it's nothing more than just good friends enjoying each other's companionship.

Beth Anne graduated from high school with top honors and was named *Valedictorian*.
She enrolled at University of Michigan in Ann Arbor, Michigan. After graduation she was accepted into the School of Dentistry.
Beth Anne now works as a general pediatric dentist for a large dental practice in Arlington Heights, Illinois.
She is not married and lives in a large condo that she purchased last

year.

After Morgan's passing, Ryan threw himself into being both mother and father to Beth Anne. He went to every event that she was in during her high school years, and she was in most everything the school had to offer.

When Beth Anne went off to college, Ryan suffered the "empty nest syndrome" for a little while. But, instead of wallowing in self-pity, he immediately volunteered in numerous charitable organizations which helped keep his mind off of being alone.

Ryan, over the years, became quite successful, and aged very gracefully. He was considered one of the most eligible and sought after widowers in the area, but he never showed any interest.

One morning, Ryan poured a cup of coffee and opened the morning newspaper. He looked over the national and local news, as his usual habit, saving the comics for last.

As he scanned the local section, an article grabbed his attention. It said that one of his old high school teachers was retiring and that a reception was being held that afternoon at three o'clock. Ryan took a sip of coffee and rubbed his forehead thoughtfully.

Suddenly, he made a decision. He would take off work a little early and attend.

A little before three, Ryan parked his car in the school parking lot and walked to the building. When he pulled the door opened and went inside, he was greeted by the smell of disinfectant and floor wax that reminded him of his old high school days.

Ryan walked briskly down the hall towards the auditorium and let his mind flood back to old memories of his high school days.

Was the hall really this short?, he wondered. *Back then it seemed so long that I hardly had time enough to run from one class to another.*

Lots of people were walking down the hall towards the auditorium now. Some knew Ryan and waved to him.

He walked into the auditorium and looked around. He found a seat and sat down.

"May I have your attention please?" Mr. Brenner, the principal said into the microphone at the podium. "Fellow faculty, students, and friends, welcome. We are here today to honor one of our revered faculty members that has decided to close her career this semester and enjoy a well-deserved retirement."

Polite applause lofted up. Ryan clapped.

"Miss Anderson came to us right out of college in 1961 and has tirelessly taught hundreds of students here ever since. She has served on many faculty committees and has served as the coach for all of the sophomore, junior, and varsity cheerleader squads for over forty years."

More applause. The current cheerleaders went up on stage and went through their latest cheer.

"So, without further ado, please welcome to the podium, Miss Rebecca Anderson."

More applause rose. Ryan stood and clapped which prompted others around him to also stand and applaud.

"Thank you. Thank you, Mr. Brenner for those very kind words. Thank you all for coming today. I'm deeply moved.

"Today, as I look back over the years, it seems like I arrived here only yesterday. But, all I have to do is look into the mirror and I know that's not true."

A trickle of laughter floated across the crowd.

Ryan recognized Miss Anderson, for sure, but remembered her as being considerably taller.

Miss Anderson's speech went on for another twenty minutes as she reminisced and talked about the many changes and various anecdotes of her teaching career.

"So, not to bore you any longer, I thank you for the wonderful opportunity of teaching here."

Everyone leaped to their feet and applauded.

"Thank you, Miss Anderson. Now, if anyone would like to tell their story about our guest, please raise your hand and one of our people will bring a wireless microphone to you."

Hands flew up. Many people spoke about being in Miss Anderson's classes, but most centered around her coaching the cheerleaders.

Finally, Ryan raised his hand. A young boy rushed over with a wireless mike.

"Good afternoon, Miss Anderson.

"My name is Ryan Wakefield and I had the opportunity of being in one of your classes a long time ago."

Everyone craned their necks to get a look at Ryan.

"If I remember correctly, the class was called 'Modern Problems.'"

Miss Anderson nodded that she remembered the class, but Ryan saw in her eyes that she had no idea who he was.

"Miss Anderson, I want to thank you from the bottom of my heart. Because, if it hadn't been for you, I would have never met the girl I would marry. Thank you."

The auditorium erupted in applause and warm sentiment for Ryan as most people there knew that he was talking about Morgan.

Maybe most people knew or remembered Ryan and Morgan, but Miss Anderson was not one of them. She smiled warmly and gave Ryan a little wave of thank you, but not remembrance.

After the program was over many people went up on stage to talk with Miss Anderson, but virtually all the students and faculty made their way to the exits.

Ryan stayed until the crowd around Miss Anderson thinned out before he walked up to her.

"Hello, Miss Anderson," Ryan said and reached out his hand to shake hers.

"Hello, there. Do I know you?"

"I'm Ryan Wakefield. I was in one of your 'Modern Problems' classes a long time ago."

"My, yes. It must have been a long time ago. I've not taught that class in nearly twenty years."

Ryan continued to talk about his class and some of the kids in it that Miss Anderson might remember, but she didn't seem to.

"I'm sorry, Mr. Wakefield, but I don't seem to remember anyone you bring up. So many kids have gone through my classes over the years, I've plainly lost track."

Ryan continued to try and refresh Miss Anderson's memory.

"And, who did you say the girl was?"

"Her name was Morgan Carter. I was a senior and she was a sophomore. Some of the cheerleaders in our class were, Vicky, Patti, and Misty."

That seemed to be the trigger. Suddenly, Miss Anderson remembered. Almost instantly, she frowned.

"Why, Ryan Wakefield. You didn't marry that little retarded girl, did you?"

Before Ryan could answer, Miss Anderson turned away in a huff and marched away.

"It was that attitude that brought Morgan to me, Miss Anderson. And, I thank you from the bottom of my heart for it."

Ryan wrapped the arms of the sweater that Morgan had given him many years ago around his shoulders and smiled.

Somewhere in heaven the angels rejoiced and sang together,

Always together forever